I0673736

Bone Dry

Janet Taylor-Perry

A Laura Beth Copeland Misadventure

Janet Taylor-Perry

Bone Dry

A Laura Beth Copeland Misadventure #2

ISBN: 979-8-9853495-9-7

Dragon Breath Press
Ridgeland, Mississippi

Other Books by Janet Taylor-Perry

The Raiford Chronicles:

1.   *Lucky Thirteen*—Semifinalist, Faulkner Competition
2.   *Heartless*
3.   *Broken*—Short list finalist, Faulkner Competition
4.   *Whatever It Takes*

The Legend of Draconis:

1.   *King Satin's Realm*—Semifinalist, Faulkner Competition
2.   *Spirits' Desire*—Winner Preditor and Editor's Award, "other" category
3.   *Last of an Exceptional Breed*—Semifinalist, Faulkner Competition
4.   *One World*

April Chastain Intrigues:

1.   *Wilted Magnolias*—Finalist, Faulkner Competition

Laura Beth Copeland Misadventures:

1.   *Head Count*—Finalist Faulkner Competition

Hillbilly Hijinks:

1.   *Homegrown Healer*—Semifinalist, Faulkner Competition
2.   *Mountain Moonshine*—Semifinalist, Faulkner Competition
3.   *Gator Aid*
4.   *For Richter or Poorer*

Gods and Children:

1.   *Ain't No Mountain*—Semifinalist, Faulkner Competition

Compiled Anthologies:
1. *Unforgettable Christmases*
2. *Tales from the Dragon's Lair*
3. *Holiday Hearth*

Anthology Short Story Inclusions:
1. *Brick Street Press: 2010 Winners*—"Internot Dating"
2. *Mississippi Profiles*—"Thibodeauxs Do Magnifique!"
3. *What Would Elvis Think?*—"Your Life Is not Over"
4. *Ordinary Miracles*—"Stomach Staples and Cyclones"
5. *Battles: Glimpses of Truth*—"Nothing in Life Is Free"

Bone Dry

By

Janet Taylor-Perry

A Laura Beth Copeland Misadventure

#2

Disclaimer

All entities in this story are purely fictional. Any resemblance to any party, living or dead, is coincidence.

Alert

The subject matter of this story might be disturbing to some. I strongly advise parental guidance for any child under the age of sixteen. Human trafficking and child exploitation/molestation are not laughing matters and not to be taken lightly.

.

Acknowledgments

Thanks to my plethora of author friends who continually encourage me to practice my craft. Great appreciation to my family for putting up with my eccentricities. Bookoos of gratitude to my editor, mentor, and friend, Lottie Brent Boggan for her no-nonsense approach to keeping me on track. Google her and give her books a read. Gratitude goes to my faithful beta reader, Nidia Hernandez, aka Barbra Best, author of *The Rock Star Records*, fun reads to get lost in. I can never tell Aunt Ruth Ishee how much those telephone read-alouds meant to the growth and development of my art. Likewise, my daughter, Mary Catherine Perry (Mcat), will never know how precious it was to me for her to read every word I ever wrote until her untimely passing. And no word can express the debt I owe to my fantastic cover designer, Christopher Chambers. Check out his work at juroddesigns.com.

Bookoos—for those who don't know, this is a southern perversion of the French *beaucoup*, meaning a lot, much, many.

Dedication

For Detective Mitchell Tate with Ridgeland Police Department. You are a fine man who went above and beyond what was required of you at one of the darkest times in my life. Thank you.

Special inspiration came from Tim Tebow and his fight against human trafficking. Having worked with a number of children and teens who were exploited beyond imagination, some by their own parents, this social and spiritual issue has a tender place in my heart. Learn more so you can do more at https://timtebowfoundation.org/stories/anti-human-trafficking.

I am poured out like water, and all my bones are out of joint: my heart is like wax; it is melted in the midst of my bowels.

Psalm 22:14

Table of Contents

1
Got Milk?

Handing each child a list, "Divide and conquer," Tanner McGill said to his two children, Corbin and Roslyn, when they walked through the sliding doors of the Kroger grocery store in Sunrise, Mississippi.

"I thought we were staying the night with Grammy," Roslyn whined, "and eating with Miss Madeleine tomorrow for New Year's."

"We are, but we have to eat next year," her father said. "If we split up, we can get out faster. Remember I have a date with Miss Laura Beth. And"—He tweaked his daughter's nose— "Each of you can pick one treat to add to your lists. Corbin, be sure to get the chocolate milk too. Let's meet at the checkout. Move!"

All three McGills grabbed a shopping cart and went in search of the items on their lists. Fifteen minutes later, they met at the checkout line. Tanner preferred the do-it-yourself lane. The assembly line of passing the groceries to be scanned began. As bags filled, Tanner placed them in a cart.

Teamwork made shopping fast work, and the family headed out the door.

The clerk watching the self-checkout lanes said, "Happy New Year, Detective McGill."

"You too," he replied. *Oh, I hope so.*

Corbin paused to look at the face of a missing child on the bulletin board in the space where the shopping carts were housed. "Dad, I saw this kid once," he said, pointing at the face on the poster.

"You did? When? Where?" Tanner's questions and tone sounded like the cop he was.

"Right here in the parking lot just before Christmas when Grammy brought me with her."

"You're sure? He's from Portland, Oregon, according to the write up."

"Yes, sir. We parked right in front of the truck, way out, because Grammy was afraid someone would hit her new car when opening their doors."

"Did you see anyone with him?"

"There was a man, but he had his head turned away. He was backing up."

"What kind of vehicle?"

"A Chevy Silverado. It looked new. Dark gray, I think. Grammy commented that other folks wanted to protect their cars too. The kid just stared straight ahead. I don't know if he even blinked."

"I need to run to the station and report this."

"Do the kids really get found?" asked Corbin.

"Sometimes."

"Are they dead?"

Tanner hesitated, but he answered honestly. "Sometimes. Remember what I told y'all about Adam Walsh?"

Both children nodded.

"You just practice the things I've taught you. It would kill me to have your faces on a missing-person poster."

Tanner stopped at his office and reported what his son had said to the proper authorities. He was certain he'd have a visit from the FBI again, but he put it from his mind and determined to have a good evening with a lady he was falling in love with.

2

The Thigh Bone Connects to the Hip Bone

Laura Beth Copeland stretched and yawned as a mellow sun filtered through her striped earth-tone drapes. She had not slept so soundly since her husband's violent death seven months before. She pushed the memory of Bruce's exploding car from her mind.

Determined to live again, she focused on the previous night and the New Year's kiss she got from Tanner McGill. Laura Beth reached for him and realized she was alone in bed.

Tanner had slept beside her after their date—just slept, but she felt safe with Tanner around.

Laura Beth sat up as she heard noises toward the front of her house and smelled coffee. She giggled like a schoolgirl. *He's making breakfast.* She lay back, her auburn hair spreading across her pillow. *I wonder if he'll serve me in bed.* She listened as Tanner sang along with the radio.

Tanner sang along with Rascal Flatts and wondered why he and Laura Beth should wait as he mixed pancake batter. Their stars seemed in perfect alignment. He licked the whisk he'd been using. "Yum. Almost as tasty as Laura Beth's lips."

He thought about the kisses the night before.

> *He slowly moved his hand up Laura Beth's thigh to her hip.*
> *She caught his hand. "No. Not yet."*
> *He placed his forehead against hers. "Okay, Sugar. Let's sleep."*

Laura Beth turned her back to Tanner. He spooned against her and pulled her touching his chest.

Tanner shook himself from his reverie as a part of his anatomy stirred of its own accord. "Down, boy," he mumbled. "She's nowhere near ready for sex. She's still mourning Bruce. Give her time."

He got two plates from the cupboard, snagged a flower from the arrangement he'd sent Laura Beth the day before, placed it in a thin vase he'd discovered in her curio, and began to set a breakfast tray for two.

Laura Beth's question was answered a moment later.

Barefoot and shirtless, wearing only his pants from the night before, Tanner used his hip to push open the bedroom door. "Good morning, Sugar. We have Spanish omelets and peanut butter pancakes." He wiggled barely almond-tinted eyebrows over mischievous twinkling sky-blue eyes.

Laura Beth took in his unruly short blond hair and perfectly chiseled body, noting his scar on his side where he had been wounded during his time in the Marines and his tattoo on his left arm denoting his pride in his service.

Scooting up in bed, she patted the mattress. Tanner set the breakfast tray beside her and sat down. He handed her a cup of coffee.

She took the beverage and sipped. "Mm. Vanilla caramel." She closed dark-chocolate eyes and inhaled the steam. "I might have to hold you prisoner, Detective McGill. I like being pampered."

Tanner laughed. "I volunteer to stay." He handed her a fork and picked up his own.

Morning chit-chat took a serious turn when Laura Beth said, "Can you believe Marin's audacity?"

Tanner shook his head. "That man who showed up last night is not Diego Marin. For everyone's sake Marin has to be dead."

"Yeah." She sighed. "For Penny I'll try to pretend that is a different person—not the man who I thought was trying to kill me and who *did* accidentally kill my husband. He might not have lopped off the head of the woman I found, but he has killed a lot of people." She huffed. "Many of them were sanctioned by our government."

"He looks different." He dipped his head from shoulder to shoulder. "He acts different."

"Let's hope his heart is different. When I read my devotional the day after our first date, the Holy Spirit spoke to me and told me that because of Bruce, many would be saved, including the man I want to hate." She shook her head and closed her eyes. "I think he actually loves Penny."

"Love can change a man."

"I suppose." She rubbed his hand. "I found out Bruce had kept secret that he had stage four pancreatic cancer."

"My God!"

"Marin's actions kept him from suffering."

Both were startled from their relaxing morning as they heard a loud thud and whining at the front door.

Tanner chuckled. "That would be Freckles. I hope it's okay that I let him out. I need to install that pet door for you."

"It's fine, but I need to fence the immediate area. No pet should be allowed to roam, but lots of folks are terrified of Pitbulls. I'm glad he's still a baby. I'll get him neutered. That helps with the wandering."

"I'm still training him, but it sounds like he brought you a trophy. Does he do that often?"

"Oh, yes. I've had enough squirrels to feed us for a year. Then, he's brought old shoes, cans, sticks, you name it." She pointed as if showing some place in the distance. "He must go all the way to Penny's and the Purdue property lines. I'm glad I'm treating him with good flea and tick stuff. The other day, he brought up a sneaker that looked new—dirty, but not worn out. I can't imagine where he found it." She shrugged.

"Well, that bump sounded loud enough to be a limb."

"We *have* had strong winds lately."

Tanner stood and held out his hand. "Shall we see what gift he has for his mistress today?"

Laura Beth laughed. "We shall." She slipped out of bed, grabbed her pink velvet bathrobe to cover her pink flannel night shirt, and slid her feet into her fuzzy pink house shoes.

"You are so cute," Tanner said before he kissed her. Releasing her, he said, "Let's see what Freckles dragged up. I still say it sounded heavy enough to be a limb."

Holding hands, they walked to the front door where the puppy still scratched at the door and whimpered. Freckles let out a yip as Laura Beth grasped the doorknob.

She opened the door and shrieked. "A limb, Tanner! Was that supposed to be funny?"

3

Bone Voyage

"Holy shit!" Tanner bellowed.

Freckles yipped and wagged his tail.

Tanner grasped the puppy's collar and dragged him inside. "Sugar, put him in his kennel and keep him there. Stay with him. I'm out of jurisdiction. I'm calling Penny."

Laura Beth took hold of the dog's collar. "Come on, baby."

Freckles whined.

"It's okay," Laura Beth cooed and rubbed his head. "You didn't do anything wrong." She grimaced, looking back at her porch. "I hope."

"He didn't. Now, go!"

Tanner dashed back to Laura Beth's bedroom as she got the puppy to his kennel.

She plopped into a dining chair to wait. "Why me?" she murmured. "First a head. Now—a leg."

Tanner whipped out his phone and, dialing, ran back to Laura Beth.

"I'm okay," she said to his anxious expression.

"Tanner McGill, what do you want?" Sheriff Penny Ulmer growled into her phone as the man beside her caressed her bare bronze breasts. A moan escaped her lips.

"Penny," Tanner snarled, "now is not the time. You need to get to Laura Beth's. Freckles just dragged up a human femur. Still with meat on it. Small enough to be a child."

"What?" Penny yelled, sitting up in bed.

The man with a perfectly sculpted face, black hair and deep brown eyes sat up beside her. "What's happened, Pretty Penny?"

"I'll be there in ten. Call my office and have every deputy on duty meet me."

Penny jumped from bed and snatched a freshly pressed khaki uniform off a hanger in her closet.

"Penny?"

She continued to dress without comment.

"Penelope?"

"Marin, David, Enrique, who the hell are you?"

"David when I'm here. The man who loves you," he replied in a velvety voice. "But I guess Pretty Penny and Ninja Man have to be kept to times alone."

Penny nodded. "Laura Beth's dog found a human bone. I have to go." She finished dressing in seconds.

"I'll come," David said.

"No. Here, you're a civilian, and it would be better for folks not to see you yet. And I pray to God Laura Beth and Tanner are the only two who know your identity."

"Besides my superiors, yes."

"Then stay here. Take care of my dogs. I'll be back as soon as I can." She gave him a quick kiss. "I love you too." She grabbed her Stetson and ran out the door.

As Laura Beth waited, she picked up her phone and dialed Madeleine Blanchard who had her three children so she and Tanner could go out.

Madeleine answered cheerfully.

"Hey," Laura Beth sighed. "There's been an incident. I'm not sure when I'll be able to get the kids."

"Has Marin come back?"

Laura Beth looked toward her living room. "No. One of the bodies on that plane crash in the South American jungle was identified as his. He's no threat to me anymore—never really was. No. Freckles found human remains. Penny and company are about to be all over my property—again."

"You're just a magnet."

"Thanks, Madeleine." She rolled her eyes.

"It's okay, sweetie. The babies are safe with me until you come."

While Laura Beth talked to Madeleine, Tanner called his mother and gave her a skeletal account. "Go ahead and take the kids to Madeleine's. Let's try to keep things normal."

She agreed, and Tanner went to Laura Beth.

"Penny's on her way," he said.

Laura Beth put her face in her hands. "I need to get dressed, and so do you."

"Yeah."

Both dressed quickly, Tanner in his clothes from the previous night and Laura Beth in jade-green warm-ups.

By the time they had changed clothes, they heard Penny barking orders outside. Laura Beth opened her front door to see the sheriff squatting over the leg on the wrap-around porch.

Penny pushed her hat back and looked up. "Not fresh, so Freckles is off the hook. No Pitbull attack," she said with sarcasm. She stood. "My guess is between ten and twelve years old—amount of decay suggests dead about a week."

Tanner clutched Laura Beth's arm. "You said Freckles brought up a sneaker."

"Yes."

"Where is it?"

"Trash."

Penny nodded and sent a deputy to Laura Beth's trash can.

"Oh, God!" Laura Beth cried. "Was a child killed on my property?" She pointed. "Is the rest of him still out there?"

"We're gonna have to find out," Penny said.

The deputy returned with the shoe in an evidence bag and the coroner took possession of the leg after many pictures of Laura Beth's porch.

Tanner put a hand to the back of his head. "Penny, maybe Freckles can show us where to find the body."

"Good idea. I'll deputize you so it's all official." She walked to her SUV and got a badge.

"My own won't do?" Tanner asked.

"Nope. Not County. Raise your hand and take the oath."

Tanner did and put the badge on his belt.

Laura Beth left the room and returned with Freckles on a leash. Tanner squatted and scratched the brindled pup's ears. "Okay, big boy. I need you to show me where you went today."

Freckles whined. "It's okay. I need your help," Tanner coaxed.

One of the deputies chuckled. Penny cut him a scathing look, and Tanner muttered, "He won't do it for you." He stood. "Come on, Freckles, show me."

Freckles yipped and lurched off the porch, jerking Tanner with him. Penny followed and Laura Beth trailed her. The sheriff put a restraining hand on her friend. "No, Laura Beth. You have to stay here."

"Why?"

"Civilian."

"Deputize me too. It's *my* dog." She sounded a bit pouty.

"Fine," Penny huffed. "You're deputized, but don't touch a damned thing."

The humans followed Freckles at a good trot. The dog yipped constantly, now and then finding his big-dog bark, just like a teen with a changing voice.

The group plunged into a heavily wooded area. After a twenty-minute struggle through the undergrowth, the stench of rotting flesh slammed their nostrils.

Catching a glimpse of blue in the winter woods, Penny yelled, "Stop!" She inched forward alone. "Get the forensics team out here. We have a body, partially buried in a shallow grave. Freckles must have smelled it just like a cadaver dog and dug up part of it." She looked around. "I'm not sure whose property this is. It could be mine. Maybe Purdue Plantation."

Penny got closer to Tanner. "I bet there're more. We're gonna have to get x-rays, seismic readings all over Laura Beth's land, Purdue Plantation, and my property. I don't have the resources. It's time for Mississippi Bureau of Investigation.

"Maybe the feds will send Pickering."

Despite the situation, Penny laughed. "I wonder if he'll recognize my fiancé."

"Your what?"

"Fiancé."

4

Purdue Plantation

Tanner clutched Penny's elbow. "You're marrying that…that…"

"Man," she finished for him. "Yes."

A deputy handed Penny a roll of yellow tape. She passed one end to Tanner. "Let's cordon it off."

After they marked off a wide area, they waited. An hour and a half later, a forensics team from Jackson arrived. Penny stayed to work with the team while Tanner and Laura Beth returned to the house with Freckles.

As they walked home, Tanner's phone rang. He answered with a scowl on his face. "McGill."

"Ed Pickering here."

"What can I do for you, Special Agent Pickering?"

Laura Beth raised an eyebrow in question.

"I'm coming for a visit," Pickering said.

"Why?" Tanner asked, not masking his annoyance.

"I got the information about the missing boy."

"Thought you were Organized Crime Bureau."

"I got transferred."

"Great." Tanner groaned. "Penny might be the one you need. We found a body today. Out of city limits. Could be the boy. And Penny's gut says there're more."

"Well, I'm bringing a team. I'll be hooking up with the Jackson gang and then we'll be there."

Tanner disconnected and immediately relayed the information to Penny.

"Great," Penny intoned. "Well, the remains are on the way to Jackson. There's nothing more we can do today. Are y'all going to Madeleine's?"

"Yes. We need to keep things as normal as possible for our kids. You?"

"You think I should?"

Tanner looked down at Laura Beth. "Can you deal with Penny and company at Madeleine's?"

"I'll try for Penny."

"Okay." Penny sighed. "Just remember his name is David Black, my fiancé."

"Okay." Tanner choked on his word.

"Yes. We're getting married as soon as possible before he gets some assignment God-knows-where."

"You'd better tell Laura Beth yourself." He handed off his phone. Taking the dog's leash, he walked on and could hear Laura Beth's shrieks all the way at the house.

Tanner sat on the wrap-around veranda of the ranch-style house and played with Freckles while he waited for Laura Beth. A few minutes later, she stomped up her sidewalk from the circular driveway. She plopped the phone into his hand. "I'm maid of honor day after tomorrow."

"You okay, Sugar?"

"No, Cream, I'm not. That man killed my husband— accident or not—not to mention others." Bruce's words from her dream floated back to her—*Forgive the man.* "I want to believe he's a new person. Penny believes him. She loves him." Laura Beth shook her head. "If he puts his little toe out of line, I still have my .357."

"And you know how to use it. This, I've witnessed." He laughed. "So, has he. You shot him in the ass."

Laura Beth laughed. "Yeah, I did." She sighed. "I'll do this for Penny, but David best know I'm watching him."

"I think he's fully aware. Let's go to Madeleine's."

Tanner and Laura Beth took separate cars to Madeleine's home and arrived at the same time as Penny and David. The four of them stood stock-still for a long moment. "Okay," Laura Beth finally said. "New year—new people." She pointed a sharp finger at David. "I'll be watching you. I know your secret. If you hurt Penny, I'll kill you."

"Yes, ma'am, Little Momma."

"And don't call me that. Nobody but Marin called me that. It's a dead giveaway. I'm Laura Beth, and I just met you."

David held out his hand. "Nice to meet Penny's best friend, Laura Beth. You should know I love her with every fiber of my being, and I'll love her with my dying breath."

She shook his hand. "I actually believe you. Nice to see you wearing something besides black."

"Penny insisted and even forced me to go shopping."

"The burgundy sweater works," Tanner said, offering a handshake.

The two couples walked to the door together. Both parents were met with hugs and questions. Laura Beth took her baby and whispered, "We need to go to Auntie Madeleine's bedroom." She turned to the others. "Excuse Riker and me a few minutes."

Laura Beth escaped to the privacy of her friend's bedroom and nursed her son while Penny introduced David Black to everyone.

When Laura Beth rejoined the other guests, Madeleine called her into the kitchen on the pretext of needing help. Alone, the older woman demanded, "Who is this guy? Where and when did Penny meet him? She's very vague. Said she met him at church."

Thinking about sending the man to midnight Mass, Laura Beth could only grin. "She did meet David at church. She's known him a little while, but they just realized they have feelings for each other."

"I think there's something sneaky going on."

Laura Beth kissed Madeleine's cheek. "You're just protective of us. Trust Penny." *Take your own advice,* her conscience nagged.

Following a hearty traditional New Year's Day meal of black-eyed peas with hog jowl and a penny cooked in for luck, pork loin with rice and gravy, cabbage to be in the money the upcoming year, and Madeleine's addition of chocolate cake frosted with chocolate icing for happiness, all parties returned to their own homes. The day had been long and exhausting.

Sheriff Ulmer was in her office before sunrise. She had barely made coffee before FBI Special Agent Ed Pickering and three officers from the Jackson MBI office arrived with several other people.

"Pickering," she greeted with her bright, slightly gap-toothed smile.

"McGill said you suspect more bodies. Why?"

"Well, cut to the chase. Intuition. I was right about Marin."

"To some extent you were. That's why I have some help—cadaver dogs and forensic archaeologists with sonar equipment. Do you have search warrants?"

"That's why I'm here so early. Laura Beth and I don't care if you search our property. Where we found the body is a bit of a dispute on property line. My dogs never found anything because I have an electric fence a few yards from where the body was found. Old Man Purdue insisted it was his land. He met me with a shotgun when I went down there to get my other dog that's passed on. He didn't mind using racial slurs toward me either."

"So, he'll give us trouble."

"No. He died ten years ago, not long after our run-in. I wasn't sheriff yet, just 'an uppity nigger.'"

"Yikes. So, the family is the problem."

"Nope. Wife is dead, and son lives out West. I just have to get a judge's signature." She hit her print key. "Taking this to Judge Wilson now. Make yourselves at home."

Penny walked down the block to the county courthouse where she caught the judge just coming to work. She thrust the document into his hands.

"You're earlier than I expected," he teased.

"Too late, I'd say," she countered.

"You ready for some excitement?"

"Not really; just a gut feeling."

"Well, Mrs. Copeland is involved again."

"Only because her dog discovered the body. I want to search Purdue Plantation."

"Big place." He signed the warrant with flair and handed it back.

"Agent Pickering is back with dogs and forensic archaeologists."

Judge Wilson chuckled. "He's a bit bumbling."

"Maybe, but he's tenacious, and I trust him."

"Good enough. I've always admired your intuition, Sheriff, but I really hope you're wrong this time."

"Me too." She touched her warrant to her forehead and returned to her office.

Penny spotted a caged vehicle that had parked outside her office. A bloodhound and a large mongrel barked loudly. "Well, you must be the sniffers," she said, stopping. The mutt gave a sharp bark, and the hound bayed. Penny laughed. "Yes, I speak fluent canine."

The sheriff leapt up the two steps to the door of the building that housed her office and the county lock-up. A small, swarthy man with a bald head and a fleshy woman with very short salt-

and-pepper hair had joined Pickering and the agents from Jackson.

Waving the signed warrant, Penny said, "We're good to go."

"Great!" Pickering slapped his thighs. "Sheriff Ulmer, you met these three: Stringer, Potts, and LaDarnier."

"Yeah, but not officially." Penny shook hands with the agents.

Pickering went on. "This is Dr. Basil Daiwa and Dr. Paula Nixley."

"Welcome. I hope I don't need your expertise, but better to have you just in case. Who controls the dogs?"

"Me," said Nixley. "They're my babies—the only babies I want."

"Good deal. I have two Great Danes, but I think I'd like a human baby eventually." Penny smiled and turned to the short man. "You must dig."

"Both of us dig, Sheriff." Dr. Daiwa gave a sincere smile and spoke with a cultured British accent. "I also operate sonar equipment. Shall we get started?"

"Of course. Let me call a couple of deputies." Penny called two real deputies and Tanner McGill to meet at the site where the body was found the day before. She knew Laura Beth would be working at Sun Realty.

Once parties arrived, Penny snapped her hands to her ample hips. "So, what do we do?"

Nixley opened the cage and both dogs jumped to the ground and ran immediately to the place where Freckles had unearthed the body.

"Yeah, yeah, yeah!" Penny hollered. "We know about that one."

Nixley barked a command, and the dogs put noses to ground.

Twenty feet into the thicket, the hound bayed and yelped. Half the law enforcement followed the sound. The dog stood stock-still, staring ahead.

"He's looking toward my property," Penny said.

"How long have you lived here, dear?" asked Daiwa.

"A little over ten years. I bought the house when I left the military but before I was elected sheriff. I was just an older rookie cop. I got it for song—back taxes actually, and it needed lots of work." She pulled out her phone.

At Penny's house, David answered. "News?"

"Turn off the electric fence." She pointed to a thin wire. "Installed a couple of years back when I got two new Danes."

"Ah. That's why Sherlock stopped," Nixley said.

"Sherlock." Penny laughed. "Mine are Leather and Lace."

A low hum ceased.

"Off, Pretty Penny," David informed. "Is there something on your land?"

"Maybe. I'll let you know." She disconnected her phone.

Sherlock stepped forward, nose touching dry grass.

Penny asked with a wry grin, "What's the other one's name—Watson?"

"Nancy Drew."

Penny cracked up laughing.

Suddenly both dogs pawed the ground, but in two separate areas.

Daiwa pulled out a device from a backpack he wore.

"What is it?" Penny asked.

"It sends pings into the ground, and they will bounce off probable bones. We get an x-ray of a sort, and then we dig."

Several hours later, he looked at prints with vague discolorations. Then, he used a spray chalk to mark off two elliptical sections. By this time all available law enforcement had arrived.

"Your office running without you?" Penny whispered to Tanner.

"Officer Montoya is an excellent assistant. I just hope nothing comes up."

Daiwa approached them and thrust shovels into their hands. "Now we dig."

Tanner said, "This January earth is frozen. This could take a long time."

"Yes," agreed Daiwa, "but we dare not risk steam shovels. Besides, I think Sheriff Ulmer would prefer as little damage as possible to her property."

With gloved hands, two teams began to dig. A bit later, their work was interrupted as David arrive carrying a cooler and having two massive Great Danes in tow. "Sit," he commanded Leather, a black male, and Lace, a fawn female. Both whined but obeyed. Passing a root beer to his lady, David said, "I thought you might need food and drink."

Nixley ordered the two cadaver dogs to stay, and they obeyed.

Pickering stared, mouth agape. The FBI agent snagged Penny's elbow. "What the hell?" he growled in her ear.

"Let me introduce you."

"Introduce me? Is that Marin?"

"No." She motioned David over. "David, I'd like you to meet Special Agent Ed Pickering. Pickering, David Black, my spouse come tomorrow."

Pickering glared as David extended a hand. "I don't know what your game is…"

"Game, sir?" David interrupted.

Penny intervened. "David came back into my life recently, Pickering. I'm sure you wish us happiness."

Pickering grunted, snatched a sandwich and drink, and went to stand with the team from Jackson.

Tanner draped an arm over David's shoulder. "That went well," he muttered.

"Even if he suspects, he knows to keep his mouth shut," David said, his lips moving less than a ventriloquist's.

When everyone had food and a soda, David gathered the cooler and whistled for the Danes to follow him.

After a short break, digging resumed. Soon, two skeletons were uncovered.

"Hmm," mused Daiwa. "Early teens or slightly younger. Dead, I'd say two, more likely three years. Before you put up the fence, Sheriff."

"Definitely before I put the electric fence up to keep Leather and Lace on my land."

"I'll need more equipment. I fear your instincts were correct. But the dogs came here because these graves were fresher."

The doctor walked off with his equipment and let the forensics team collect the remains. Several yards closer to Penny's house, he turned back. "Any more bodies will be that way." He pointed toward Purdue Plantation.

When they were back at the original site, Daiwa walked toward Laura Beth's house. "Nothing," he called.

He walked onto Purdue Plantation. Ten feet in, he stopped. "Here." Another few feet and he announced, "Here."

Before nightfall, Daiwa had marked off thirty graves. "It will take several days to excavate. Sheriff, you should go ahead with your wedding tomorrow, but I fear a honeymoon will have to wait."

5

Family Unit

Sheriff Penny Ulmer dragged into her home as darkness and sleet fell. The day that began sunny with a nip was fast becoming frigid. She shook the moisture from her Stetson and hung her waterproof jacket on a coatrack by the front door.

Leather and Lace bounded toward her with happy barks. She scratched each dog behind the ears. David followed the animals with Penny's flowered apron tied around his waist and a pink bandana covering his coal-black hair.

Penny clamped her hand over her mouth to stifle the laughter bubbling from the sight. She felt a twinge of guilt laughing when she knew just a few thousand feet away lay the remains of at least thirty children.

"Compartmentalize, Pretty Penny," David said, slipping his arms around her. "Leave it outside."

She slid her arms up his back and grasped his biceps. "This one's hard," she murmured. "If they're all children"—her voice broke—"How could someone do that?"

"I don't know. I told you in all my assignments I drew the line with kids."

"Yes," she said.

"You asked what my superiors had on me to keep me working. I refused to tell you. I think I have to now."

"Is it bad, I mean, really bad?" She stepped back one step and looked him in the eye.

"Yes. Let's sit." He took her hand and led her to the brown leather sofa.

They sat and David took a deep breath. "Okay. Please remember that I love you."

"You're scaring me."

"Sorry. I guess the best way is to just say it." He sighed. "On one mission, when I worked with a team, when McCormick was with us, a young boy came in behind me. The family was supposed to be gone. I reacted to the sound at my back." Tears welled in David's eyes. "Before I could stop my swing the boy was dead. I came unglued. The team dragged me away. When the report came down, it seemed I deliberately killed the child and three more. I did not!" He shook his head hard.

Penny's mouth dropped open. She covered his shaking hand with hers.

"I'm not done," David barely whispered. "I knew there were five children in that family. Four were dead, along with both parents. That meant one was left—the two-year-old."

"What did you do?"

"I went back—alone. It didn't take much to hear the muffled cries. The child was in a large basket. I just grabbed him and hauled ass, even as authorities descended on the place."

David ran a hand across his head, pulling the bandana off. "I was raised in an orphanage, but those nuns loved me—one in particular, Sister Marta. I didn't want to leave this little boy to the mercy of that government. I couldn't. Pretty Penny, I took him. He's in the very orphanage I grew up in. He's eight now. My current superiors arranged adoption when he was almost four. I'd like to bring him here."

"Oh, my God!" She stood. "Now, you want me to be instant mommy to a kid you kidnapped."

"According to all records he died back then. Abel is my *son*. I've visited him often." He placed his elbows on his knees and put his face in his hands. "Pretty Penny, somebody wanted that entire family dead, not just the man thought to be a terrorist leader. They blamed me. That baby was supposed to die."

He dropped his hands between his knees and looked up with puppy-dog eyes. "I love him, Pretty Penny. Until I met you, he was all I had. I did some things I regret to keep him safe, but I am not sorry I took him."

Penny stood and paced, one hand on her cheek, the other on her hip. "Okay," she mumbled, dropping her hand from her face. "On one condition."

"What's that?"

She pointed a decisive finger. "That you give me a baby of my own."

David laughed and stood. "I'll do my best." He took her face in his hands. "Wanna work on that?"

"Maybe. What do I smell in the kitchen?"

"Mushroom chicken. It needs to roast a bit longer."

"Oh, my! My man cooks too. Yes. Let's practice making a baby."

"As you wish."

Mid-morning the next day, Penny, in a white linen pants suit with a baby-blue blouse, straightened David's periwinkle tie against his white shirt and navy-blue pin-striped suit on the steps of the county courthouse. Both their breaths hung on the frosty air.

Rushing up the steps, Laura Beth Copeland and Tanner McGill left their own trail of frozen vapors. "We're here," Laura Beth panted.

"It's fine." David smiled.

Laura Beth shook her head. "My God! You really do act like a different man."

"I am."

Penny said, "And, um, we'll be a real family unit. David has a son in south Texas."

"Really?" Tanner asked, with arched brows. "How come I didn't find that info?"

"Secret and hidden for safety," David replied.

"Gotcha." Tanner nodded. "Y'all really gonna do this?"

"Yes," Penny said with a wide smile.

"Then, let's go," Laura Beth said. She snagged David's elbow. "Hurt her and you'll wish that shot to your ass had killed you."

"I won't. I love her."

After a simple civil ceremony, David and Penny returned home. She unlocked the door and started inside. He pulled her back and scooped her into his arms. "No, ma'am. We're unconventional enough."

She laughed. And reached out to push the door open.

Leather and Lace greeted them with enthusiastic barking and tail-wagging.

"I can't let you out right now. We'll walk you later," Penny cooed.

The two large dogs loped to the couch, and each claimed an end.

David whispered, "It's a good thing I'm taking you to bed."

He practically ran down the four steps of Penny's split-level home. In the master bedroom, he laid his bride on top of the quilted comforter. He buried his face in the hollow of her throat. "I'm the luckiest man alive. I love you more than I ever thought I could love a woman. I don't deserve you or second chances."

"Stop talking. Make love to me, Diego Marin, Enrique de la Vega, or David Black. And I'll love the boy you've chosen to be your son and any others we might have. We'll be one big happy family."

His mouth claimed hers. No more words were spoken.

6
Lost Child

Before nightfall, Penny and David bundled in warm-ups and heavy jackets to walk two Great Danes since the back of Penny's property was cordoned off as a crime scene, as was part of Laura Beth Copeland's land. Accordingly, they met Tanner McGill trotting along with Freckles leading the way.

Penny laughed. "You sure are spending a lot of time at Laura Beth's."

"Plan to spend more." Tanner grinned. "She has a houseful of kids—hers and mine. David, when yours gets here, he'll have to join the gang."

"Thanks," David said, shocked at the ready invitation.

"When did you have a son?"

"I adopted him. He was an orphan like me." He shrugged. "It just felt right."

Tanner shook his head. "You surprise me more every day. What's his name?"

"Abel. I'll have to get his last name changed to Black."

"Where'd you find him?"

"Can't tell you that, but he'll pass for Hispanic—capisce?"

"Yeah, I get it. You make him an orphan?"

"Enough!" Penny snapped. "Let it go, Tanner."

"Yeah. Sorry."

"No big deal," David said.

"Still, I promise to try and take off my cop hat with you."

"I'd appreciate it."

"Okay. Let me get back to Laura Beth's. She's making pulled pork, potato salad, coleslaw, and baked beans."

David licked his lips. "Sounds good."

"We'll order pizza," Penny said with a grin.

"Later." Tanner tugged Freckles's leash, and they jogged off after the dogs exchanged what could have been interpreted as parting barks.

David sighed and pulled out his cell phone. He dialed a number and when his party answered carried on a lengthy conversation in Spanish.

"Hermana Marta, por favor...Sí."

Penny could hear a woman's frantic voice and wished she could recall more of her high school Spanish.

"Tranquila...estoy bien...sé que ha pasado mucho tiempo...Sí...iré por Abel..." ("Calm down...I'm fine...I know it's been a long time...Sí...I'll be coming for Abel...")

Penny watched David's face take on a look of hostility and his voice rose. Then, he began to speak in English.

"What do you mean it's not that simple?" He clutched the phone, and his knuckles turned white. "I left him with *you*, not the damned Church...No priest needs to get near my son...I have a wife now...Sí...A wonderful woman...I have no secrets from her...No, I haven't...I'll be there in a couple of days...Sí..."

He chuckled. "I love you too."

"Papa!" Penny heard the child's voice through the phone.

David asked, "Ya has crecido seis pies? No? Has crecido tres pulgadas? No te reconoceré... Dos días... Te llevaré conmigo a un nuevo hogar y una nueva madre... Te amo... Sé buena con la Hermana Marta." ("Have you grown six feet tall yet? No? You have grown three inches? I won't recognize you...Two days...I'm bringing you with me to a new home and a mother...I love you...Be good for Sister Marta.")

Penny watched her new husband's face as he talked. *He really loves Marta and Abel, but a priest did something to him.* She clamped a hand over her mouth to keep from exclaiming. *Was he molested? Oh, God! No wonder he's so distrustful.*

David slipped Leather's leash around his wrist and took Penny's hand. He held out his phone. "Say hello to my son. He speaks English."

Penny took the phone. "Hello, Abel. My name is Penny. I can't wait to meet you."

"Penny? I like that name. Do you speak Spanish? Are you Latino?"

"A little bit and no. I'm biracial. My mother was black, and my father was white."

"Grandparents?"

"Oh, no. They've passed on, but when you meet my friend, Madeleine, she'll be like a grandmother."

"Papa says he'll be here for me in two days. Will I have a room at your house?"

"Yes, and you can change it to something you like."

Leather and Lace chose that moment to bark. Penny laughed. "And two dogs."

"Cool. Sister Marta is motioning that it's supper time."

"Here's your dad." Penny handed the phone back.

"I love you. See you soon." David disconnected.

"Were you molested by a priest?" The words left Penny's lips of their own accord.

"Pretty Penny." He sighed. "Yes, and then Sister Marta did something I've helped her hide for over thirty years."

"She killed him."

"Yes. But no more, please."

"But there is more."

"Being an orphan is only a semi-truth. I was brought up in the orphanage." He ran a hand through his hair. "I found all this out when she flew into a rage and killed him with a marble statue of the Virgin Mary, having caught him with me. The priest was my father. Marta is my mother. He raped her when she was a postulate. She was given shelter at the convent, the orphanage. I was raised an orphan, but I found out the truth that day. She asked just now if I had told you. So, now you know.

The Church would kick her out if they knew. Only the nuns who were there at the time know the truth, and most of them have been reassigned. The current priest has no clue."

"She was raped for God's sake! So was I!" She hit herself in the chest with a flat palm. "Then, she killed to protect her son. Justifiable, darling.

"What else did Abel ask you?"

He gave her a lopsided smirk. "If we could bring Marta with us."

"Yes!"

"We'll see, Pretty Penny."

The next morning as David packed a bag for his run to Texas, Penny's phone rang.

"What now?" she barked.

"Nice to hear your voice, too, Sheriff," Ed Pickering said. "I thought you'd like to be kept in the loop."

"Well, yeah. I'll be at Purdue Plantation shortly."

"Me too, but we got an I.D. on the kid from Laura Beth's place."

"And?"

"Dustin Lenox from Oregon. It's the kid Tanner's son saw, the one he reported to the FBI.

"Oh, shit. Maybe we shouldn't tell Corbin."

"That's Tanner's call. I've given him the news."

"Thanks for the update. It's just so sad—a lost child"—She looked toward David as he slung his overnight bag onto his shoulder—"might be more than I could bear. I'm about to meet my stepson. Pickering, we have kids to protect. We have to find an evil, cold-blooded killer."

"I'm with you. See you at the site."

"Yeah."

Penny turned to David. "Abel might not be safe here."

"He will be. What did Pickering say?"

Penny told him.

David scowled. "Nobody lives at that plantation, right? The old man and woman died. The son?"

"Moved away."

"Profession?"

"Truck...Oh, shit!"

"Yeah." He kissed her forehead. "Work with Tanner and Pickering. I need to go."

As he started out the door, his other phone rang. "Oh, no. Not now."

He flipped opened the cheap burner phone. "What do you want?" he snarled.

He was quiet for a long moment before he grumbled, "You're shitting me. I just got married. I'm trying to put my family together...I know, I know...Yeah, I owe you...Send the file to the FTP...I'll get the job done...Send it to the post office box in McAllen. Make sure it's marked 'fragile.'" He closed his work phone, pulled out his laptop, booted it, and plopped onto the sofa.

Mumbling incoherent Spanish oaths, he waited for the file to transfer.

"Should I leave the room?" Penny asked.

"No. This one's not covert. I'll use the name Enrique de la Vega, but mostly it's an extraction. Rich tourists' kid kidnapped. Mexico."

Penny read over his shoulder, leaning on the back of the couch. "Looks easy enough for a man of your talents."

"I guess. I'll be just across the border. I should be back in a week. You okay with this?"

"It's your job. Yeah. I'm okay. I have a doozey here."

He took her hand and kissed it. "Then, I'm off to McAllen."

7

Complications

Sheriff Ulmer and Agent Pickering arrived at the site where the forensic archaeologists continued to unearth bones.

"Update?" Pickering demanded.

Penny looked around. "How many people do you have here?"

"Two dozen," said Daiwa. "This job is huge. Special Agent Pickering, we've uncovered thirty-three bodies. The last is being claimed now. My first appraisal of the situation is that it appears these boys, yes, all male, were killed over a period of about thirty-five years."

"My God!" Penny exclaimed. "I only took one day off to get married. You only had five night before last."

"That's why I called in the extra hands," Daiwa explained.

Pickering cleared his throat. "And we've sent the remains to a federal crime lab. No way could Jackson do this alone."

"I'm sure. Thanks for the help, but the only one killed since I took office was found on Laura Beth's property. And I have a suspect—Dillard Purdue."

"Owner?" asked Pickering.

"Yes."

"But too young for the ones thirty years ago."

"Maybe his old man?"

"Let's see what autopsies tell us."

"Of course," Penny nodded. "It's just there are always complications."

David Black arrived in McAllen, Texas, and went directly to the home for orphaned children. Sister Marta greeted him with a hug. "Diego! You did change your face."

"David. Remember. But Enrique for my mission."

"Sí. You are postponing taking Abel."

"Only a few days. I have to run into Mexico. And I want you to go with Abel and me."

"How can I?"

"We'll talk. Now I want to see Abel."

"Naturally. He'll be in the music room."

"Of course, he will. My little Mozart."

He placed a kiss on Marta's forehead and walked down a hallway. He stopped outside the door of the music room and listened to the melody. *Ah, it's Chopin.* He cracked the door.

The unoiled squeak caused Abel Marin to stop playing. "Papa!" he hollered as he ran toward the man at the door. "Papa?" He stopped, unsure if the man he saw was truly his father.

"Yes, it's me."

"But you look different."

"I had some surgery. And from now on, I'm David Black."

"Why?"

He mussed the boy's hair. "I can't explain it."

"Your work?"

"Yes."

"So, will I still be Abel when I go to live with Penny?"

"Yes. Abel Black."

"And Abuela?"

"We'll see."

"Why is it so complicated, Papa?"

"Soon, it won't be. But I do have a mission here."

"More waiting." Abel plopped onto the piano bench, sulking.

David sat beside him. "Not much more. I promise."

"Papa, don't make promises you can't keep."

"You're too smart to be only eight." He pulled the child into an embrace.

"Don't worry about me. I'll be with Abuela."

"I know you will. I love you, Abel."

"I love you too, Papa."

Face smutted, dressed in black spandex, Diego Marin, aka Enrique de la Vega, aka David Black, used a cyber-jamming device to interrupt the circuitry to an electrified fence. Then he vaulted noiselessly over the barrier.

With the stealth of a panther, he darted from building to building. Children's voices drew his attention to a structure surrounded by barbed wire.

Three armed men exited. Pleas from several voices echoed behind them.

Shit! David thought. *Complications. There are several kids in there. I came for one, but I can't leave the others.*

The three men walked toward David's hiding place, making jokes about sex acts with the merchandise they had secured.

David's mind raced. *Oh God! Not a random kidnapping for money. Human trafficking. Shit! Shit! Shit!*

One of the men stopped and waved the other two on. He turned to urinate against the wall.

Reaching over his shoulder, David slid a long, slender blade from its scabbard. He appeared as a shadow on the wall. Before the man could raise an alarm, his head separated from his body.

Katana wiped on the dead man's trousers and stored safely in its sheath, David stopped long enough to spit on the corpse. He muttered, "Vermin."

David made his way to the barbed wire. He pulled wire cutters from a utility belt and snipped the three strands and then replaced the cutters.

He propelled himself fleetly to the door of what appeared to be a storage shed. A padlock on the door made him grunt in annoyance.

David retrieved a lock pick kit from the same utility belt. After several minutes, the lock popped. *Not as easy as movies and T.V. make it look.* He carefully pushed the door open while at the same time exchanging the lock pick with a shuriken.

The interior of the building was pitch black. He whispered into the darkness, "Annette Sheffield?"

"Yes," came a soft, scared voice.

David closed the door and put the shuriken back. He pulled out a tiny pin light and shined it around quickly. "How many of you are there?"

"Seven," answered a different voice.

"I'm here to help."

David clamped the pin light between his teeth. Cutting the bonds on seven young girls between the ages of ten and fourteen took time. When they were loose, David spoke in a loud whisper. "I need you all to do exactly what I say." He repeated in Spanish and asked if any of them spoke that language.

"Yes and no," said the strong voice that had spoken before. "We all speak English, but I do speak Spanish as well."

"Okay. You have to trust me if you want to get out of here."

He felt a hand in his. "I'm Annette."

"Okay. Be very quiet."

David cracked the door. A voice called, "Rodrigo, where are you?"

Think fast. David yelled, "Getting a little cherry. Then, he whispered to Annette, "Scream."

She did.

"Well, hurry up. This is the last shipment for a little while. You're gonna take the hit in the wallet for it, not me." A man walked away.

"Whew!" David huffed. *He didn't see the body.*

To the girls he said, "Hold hands. Follow me. Stay against the walls."

He led the girls through the barbed wire. Then, they crawled to the fence. He threw a rope ladder with something like a grappling hook at the end to catch on the top of the fence.

"Climb up and sit on the top to wait for me."

The girls made it up, and he followed. The sounds of alarm emanated from the compound. David leapt to the ground.

"Jump! I'll catch you!" He held out his arms.

The eldest girl pushed Annette. David caught her. "Hurry!" he hissed.

The girl who pushed Annette jumped and landed beside David. "I'm okay," she said.

The other girls jumped. Between David and his new helper, they managed to get the girls to the ground.

"Now run!" David commanded.

After nearly half an hour of running, they came to a scraggly wooded area made up of live oaks and mesquite and stopped. All of them breathed in deep gulps.

"Is everybody here?" David panted. He leaned with his hands on his knees, taking air into his lungs.

"Yes. I'm Emma. We have everyone."

"I was sent for one," he mumbled and looked skyward. "What do I do?"

"A few poor complications, huh, Mister?" Emma's sarcasm was not lost on him.

"David." He stood. "Ladies, I have a plan."

8

Pedophilia

David breathed out a nauseous sigh.

"You okay?" Emma asked.

"Yeah. Listen up, girls. I need to ask a couple of questions before we begin a long trek."

"Okay," Emma answered for all of them.

"Did any of those—*men*—touch any of you?" Derision dripped from his tone.

"You mean"—Emma lowered her voice—"sexually?"

"Yes, sweetheart. I heard them saying things."

Emma went to each girl and asked. She came back. "Okay, Mr. David. Shanice says, 'Yes,' and I know one of them made me"—she stopped and huffed a puff of air—"give him a blow job. I think they might have been scared of their boss. I overheard plans to sell us. The man said, 'Virgins are prime pussy.'"

"Jesus, Mary, and Joseph!" He crossed himself. The sky was beginning to lighten. David looked over the group of girls. "I would hope all of you would be virgins."

There were seven girls, only two teens. The assortment was eclectic on race—one black, one Latina, one Asian, four white, with two blondes, one brunette and one redhead. Annette, his target, was ten with blonde hair and blue eyes. Emma said she was fourteen and barely looked it with long dark hair, green eyes, and apricot-size breasts.

David waved his hand. "This way." He pulled back a segment of thatch that looked like tumbleweed. "Inside until dark. It's small. We'll be cramped, but I thought I was coming for one child."

The girls snuggled against one another in the small cave. After a time, David listened to the even breathing. *Oh, the sleep of innocence.*

Emma clutched his arm. She whispered, "Where are you taking us, Mr. David? I don't wanna go home."

He slipped an arm about her slim shoulders. "Why?"

"Um"—she snuggled closer to him—"I'm not prime pussy."

"Don't talk like that!" He felt a tightening in his chest at the child's revelation.

"Do you want me to do something with you?"

"Absolutely not!" His entire body stiffened at the thought. "Who has made you?"

"I can't say. It was my fault. I wore my shorts too short."

"Your dad?"

"No!" She shook her head. "He's dead."

"I can't help you if you don't tell me."

"Can you help?"

"If you're honest."

"I told my mom. She slapped me."

"Stepfather?"

She dropped her head onto his chest. "They aren't married."

"I'll take care of it. Pedophiles are the lowest form of scum."

"What's a pedophile?"

"A grownup that sexually abuses a child."

"So, you don't think it was my fault?"

"No. Now try to rest a little. We have a long walk when it gets dark."

"Can I stay beside you?"

"Sure." A sound outside caught his attention. "Sh."

Outside they heard, "How the hell did they get out? Who killed Rodrigo?"

David pulled his arm back from around the trembling girl. He gently laid a finger against her lips. She popped her hand over her mouth when she saw David pull a katana from a sheath on his back. The men moved away. David breathed a sigh of relief and replaced his sword. *Thank God that child didn't have to see me take a few heads.*

"Did you kill Rodrigo?" Emma whispered.

"I had no choice."

"Will you kill my mom's boyfriend?"

"Don't tempt me." He breathed an anxious sigh. "Please, sleep."

"Okay." She burrowed close to him and finally gave in to exhaustion.

David's mind ran wild. *No way will I let this child go back to an abusive home. I can't believe she referred to herself in such derogatory terms. Shit!* He pulled his own hair. *If I do what I want—I'll find the bastard and take his head with pleasure. Better yet, I'll castrate the son of a bitch, stuff his cock down his throat, and let him choke on it.* He puffed out his cheeks. *The other—Penny will kill me.*

Ed Pickering entered Penny Ulmer's office with Tanner McGill.

"Oh, Lord. The two of you together does not bode well." She leaned back in her chair and waved them to others near her desk.

Pickering began, "I thought you'd want details." Both men sat.

"Of course, I do."

"Cause of death—asphyxiation."

"Why do I think that's not the worst part?" Penny picked up her coffee mug and grimaced when she took a swig. "It's cold. Am I going to need something stronger?"

"Yes," Tanner said.

Pickering nodded. "He had a number of broken bones, and the flesh on his back appeared to have undergone severe

whipping. But the worst is evidence of repeated sexual assault."
He ran a hand across his balding head. "And I get the *privilege*
of telling his parents. They arrived last night."

"I don't envy you, but do you want me with you—I mean a
woman to help?"

"I'd appreciate it, Penny. Yes."

"When do we go?"

"Now, if you will."

"Yeah. Okay." She stood and picked up her Stetson.
Tanner stood with them.

"Strength in numbers?" Penny asked with a wry grin.

"I feel obligated. Freckles found him. Corbin recognized
him." He shrugged. "I told Corbin it was the boy he saw, but I
haven't given him any details. I'm not sure I should."

Pickering rubbed his hands down his face. "I know how it
feels to lose a child."

Penny placed a hand on the agent's arm. "We can do this,
Ed." She gave Tanner a reassuring nod.

The three law enforcement officers sat with the Lenox
family. Ed Pickering gave them the news and cringed as Mrs.
Lenox fell apart, sobbing uncontrollably. Mr. Lenox pressed the
heels of his hands to his eyes, trying to remain strong.

Penny moved from one of the hotel-room chairs to gather
the distraught mother in her arms.

Mr. Lenox finally choked out, "Do you have any suspects?"

Penny said, "I have a lead to follow, but nothing
definitive—yet."

Mr. Lenox nodded as if in a trance. "When can we take our
son home?"

"Tomorrow," Pickering said. "I'll make the arrangements if
you'll give me the address."

"Of course." With mechanical movement, Mr. Lenox retrieved a business card from his wallet. "This is the funeral home. Let me know when you catch the bastard."

"Right away," Pickering said.

Outside, the three officers were quiet for a long moment. Tanner broke the silence. "I need to focus on teaching my kids to fend off a monster like that."

Penny nodded. "I know the perfect person to help."

9

Sanctuary

David jumped awake, and for a moment he wondered who the small person next to him was. "Ah, shit," he groaned. "Wake up, girls."

He scrounged in the pack he had and found several granola bars and beef jerky, which he passed out. The bottles of water he gave out and instructed them to share. He took two long draughts from a bottle and passed it to Emma.

"It's almost dark. Time to move," he said once a meager meal was finished.

For two hours, they trekked through tangled trees and dry grass before coming to a clear spot.

David pulled out a walkie-talkie. "Clandestine Rendezvous, come in. This is Ninja Man. At extraction point. Have extra baggage. Don't give me a hard, effing time."

"Ninja, Clandestine here. What kind of baggage?"

"Young, female, and human."

"Diego, what the hell have you done?"

"The right thing. Pick us up."

Fifteen minutes later, a helicopter came into view.

"Our chariot, ladies."

Once the chopper landed, they all climbed in, only to meet cold, steel-gray eyes glaring at David. The man wearing fatigues growled, "Did you get the right one?"

"Yes," David snapped. "But could there have been a wrong one?"

"All right, all right. Don't get your panties in a wad." The man waved a hand. "Let's get Annette to her folks and then decide what to do with the others."

"What we need to do is stop this shit!" David had to yell over the sound of the roaring engines and thumping of the rotors. "Let me take his head."

"Do you even know whose head it would be?"

"No. But I'm going to find out with or without your blessings. This was not a kidnapping for ransom. That child would never have been seen again if I hadn't got there when I did. This is human trafficking." David bumped his forehead with the heel of his hand. "Damn it, Mosely! I was blamed for some heinous shit, but you know the truth. I never killed anyone without sanction except that one incident."

"Bruce Copeland?" Mosely hooded his eyes. "The whole reason you didn't get to retire."

"Okay. You got me there. I even broke down and went to confession on that one, and I've tried to make amends. But you swept it under the rug, except to hold me to more service time, even giving me two new identities. Don't try to blackmail me with it now. This"—he pointed at the girls—"is just evil."

"Let me see if Enrique needs a new assignment and a new fetish."

David nodded. "I'll be available, but my wife does need me. She's dealing with an evil bastard too. Something like thirty dead little boys, probably molested also. I haven't talked to her in a couple of days."

The helicopter landed in the middle of a football field. "Stay here with the girls," Mosely instructed.

He took Annette by the hand, but the little girl jerked away and shook her head. She pointed. "I want David."

The slightly older man chuckled. "You always did know how to charm the ladies. Take this one to her parents."

A man and woman waited as the rotor whipped the air. David whispered to the child, "Is that your mom and dad?"

Annette nodded, and a big smile lit her face. David jumped from the craft and held out his arms. "Come on."

Annette went to him, and he carried her to the waiting couple. They showered their daughter with hugs and kisses. Then, the mother engulfed David with a hug and poured out profuse thanks.

Back in the whirlybird, his face must have been bright red. Mosely roared with laughter. "Not used to that, huh?"

"No. I'm used to mothers shooting me in the ass."

The girls giggled.

"Sorry," David said with a sheepish grin.

"Okay," Mosely said. "We need to find out where these other little chickadees belong. It could take a little time, especially since nobody knows about your little operation."

David scowled. "I know a place they can stay."

"And where would that be?"

"Santa Madre Santuario."

"Ah. Are you going home?"

"Something like that."

At the undulating roar of the helicopter, Sister Marta rushed through the double oak doors of the old adobe Spanish mission. She shielded her eyes against whirling debris and held her wimple tight, fear rising in her chest as she thought someone could be bringing news of her son's injury or death.

David leapt from the opening of the chopper and gently helped the young girls to the ground. The group clasped hands and ran toward Sister Marta as the craft lifted off.

"He pensado que podría estar muerto. ¿Qué significa este?" the nun asked with wide accusing eyes.

David laughed. "English, Sister." Over the thump-thump of the takeoff he yelled, "I'm very much alive, but they need sanctuary." As the bird gained distance, he spoke normally. "Mosely has to track down their parents, but he has to do it on the sly since nobody knows about our operation. Until they're found, the girls need a place to stay. Once their families are located, they'll come to get them."

Emma clutched David's arm. "No!"

"It's all right, honey," David soothed. "Sister Marta will take good care of you."

"Not her. Please don't make me go back. My mom...she sold me to those men." Tears fell unbidden down her cheeks.

"Jesus!"

"David!" shouted Sister Marta. "The Lord's name!"

"Sorry." He looked beseechingly at the nun. "What do I do?"

Sister Marta reached out and touched her son's cheek. "Follow your heart."

"Madre si seguir mi corazón mi nueva esposa me podría matar."

"I doubt it. You followed your heart with her."

David hugged his mother. "Si. And soon, I want you to join us."

Marta nodded. "As soon as all the children are safe."

Forty-one hours later, David parked his black Chevy Impala in the circular driveway of Penny Ulmer's home. Emma slept with her head against the glass of the passenger-side door, and Abel snored softly in the back seat. "We're here," David said, and rolled his head around to relieve pressure on tired neck muscles.

Both children stirred. Emma yawned. "You didn't tell her about me."

"No. I think seeing you will be the best approach."

"What if she doesn't want me?"

David patted the girl's hand. "You don't know Pretty Penny."

"Pretty Penny?"

David looked toward the house and smiled. "She has beautiful coppery-bronze skin and vibrant green eyes, but she doesn't take crap from anyone. Her short hair has just a bit of kink, but it's soft, not coarse. She's curvy and sexy. Her voice has just a hint of a rasp. I fell in love with her the first time I saw her."

"Wow," murmured Emma. "So, that's what a man who loves a woman is supposed to sound like."

"Sweet girl, someday a man will love you—a real man. But he'll have to get past me. I'm your new papa, and I am not easily fooled."

Abel placed his chin on the seat near David's shoulder. "I'm glad to have a mother."

"Where is your mother?" Emma asked.

David cleared his throat. "She died when Abel was very young. Let's go meet Penny."

The three got out of the car. Even before they reached the porch, deep, excited barking greeted them.

"Leather and Lace," David said when Emma retreated a couple of steps.

The door flew open. Penny, already in uniform, stared briefly before she flung her arms around David. She then, took Abel by the shoulders. "Abel. You are so handsome."

The little boy beamed. He put his arms around Penny, barely above her hips. She laid his head against her abdomen and gulped back tears.

Looking toward Emma, she said, "Who are you?"

David cupped his wife's neck with a large hand and caressed her cheek with his thumb. "Lots to tell, Pretty Penny. This is Emma Gibbons. She's going to be our daughter."

"Inside! Now!" snapped Penny.

Without more words, she set about making breakfast. She set plates in front of the children and dragged David to the master bedroom. "Talk!" she demanded.

David sat on the bed. "Please, join me."

"Don't think you can sweet talk me." She sat beside her husband. He reached for her hand. "Keep your hands to yourself," Penny bit.

David sighed. "Her mother sold her. She was on her way to becoming a sex slave. The mother's boyfriend raped her."

Penny's hand flew to her mouth. David finished Emma's story. "She needs sanctuary. I couldn't leave her, Penny."

"That poor little girl. David, I'm just afraid she's attached to *you*."

"She needs love. That's all."

"Appropriate love."

He widened his eyes.

"Don't give me that wounded look. Let's start as a foster family. See how it works. I will nurture her the best I can. She's a teenager. We'll have to lay some ground rules."

David took Penny's face in his hands and kissed her. "You've already accepted her."

"Oh, shut up. Let me go meet my new family."

10
Mother's Heart

Early the next morning, Penny bustled in the kitchen making waffles and link sausages. She set the food on the table as David and the children came in. He held up two manila envelopes. "School records. We have to get these two in the classroom. Do you know of a good music school?"

"Music?" Penny arched an eyebrow.

Abel nodded. "Yes, ma'am. I play piano."

"I'll talk to Laura Beth, my friend. She'll know."

"Okay." Abel picked up a sausage.

Penny put a glass of orange juice and a glass of milk in front of each child.

Emma asked, "Can I have coffee?"

Penny scowled. "You're fourteen. I guess one cup will be okay. How do you like it?"

"I don't know."

"Okay." Penny smiled. "Milk-coffee." She mixed coffee and milk half-and-half, stirred in a teaspoon of sugar, and handed it to the girl. "Taste it."

Emma sipped. "Yum."

"We'll have to get some gourmet sometime soon. Maybe a trip to Jackson and the mall."

"Yeah. That'd be fun."

"David only brought you three changes of clothes, so it'll be soon." Penny sat down with her own breakfast. "Today, both of you"—She looked from child to child—"get registered for school." She hooded her eyes toward her husband. "Do you have Emma's records?"

"Covered, Pretty Penny."

Abel laughed. "She is pretty, Papa."

"Thank you very much." Penny grinned and dipped her head toward her stepson.

Breakfast done, Penny shooed the children to finish dressing and poured herself another cup of coffee. She sipped. "What was Abel's name?"

"Abdul, so it sounds close to what he'd heard."

"Does he have any memories?"

"Flashes. Nightmares. At first, every night. Not so much now."

"And Emma? Falsified records?"

"No. Mosely, my contact, pulled her real records and got her mother to sign off on adoption."

"Does the mother know who's adopting?"

"No."

"Good. Because if I ever saw that bitch, I'd take a page from Ninja Man, and she'd be headless."

David smiled. "You're going to be a great mother."

"I hope so. Thirty-nine is a little late to be starting."

"You still want one with me?" He wiggled mischievous eyebrows.

"Yes, but at our age, one will be all."

"Not a problem."

"I'll be home for lunch." She set her cup in the sink. "We can practice." She kissed David; called a goodbye to the children, who rushed for a hug, making Penny tear up; grabbed her Stetson; and sashayed out the door.

Mid-morning found Laura Beth typing closing documents for one of her four sales she'd made since coming to work with the real estate office. More often, she produced documents for other agents and manned the phones. Bruce had died with really good life insurance, doubled with accidental death, and Laura

Beth invested wisely, but day-to-day living required her income. She was paid a regular salary as the receptionist, but a fat commission on a house padded her bank account.

As she worked, her boss, Peg Shriver, came in and rushed to her office where she closed the door. A minute after she came in, her husband followed and marched to his wife's office, entering without knocking. Almost immediately, voices reached a crescendo.

The door chimed, causing Laura Beth to lift her head from looking between the computer screen and the door to her boss's office. "Hm. Mid-morning and a visit from the sheriff. What's up?" She pointed. "Did the people next door call you—or I guess that would have been Tanner?"

Penny shook her head. "Does this happen often?"

"Lately, yeah."

Leland Shriver stormed from the office and slammed the entry door behind him.

Peg peeked out of her office. "Laura Beth, I have a showing at one. Will you take it? If they make an offer, I'll split the commission with you. I'm leaving the office for a while." Without waiting for a reply, Peg left.

"I hate to bother you, but help!" Penny said.

Laura Beth slammed her open palms onto her desk. "What's he done? I'll shoot the bastard. I might shoot Leland too."

"It's not my husband. You're the best mother I know. Give me pointers."

"An eight-year-old boy shouldn't be too hard."

"What about a fourteen-year-old girl?"

"What are you talking about?"

Plopping into a chair, Penny rubbed her thighs vigorously as if to restore feeling. "Abel is precious. He's kind of small for his age and apparently a musical prodigy. Do you know a really good piano teacher?"

"The most talented around here is Marge Dixon, I mean, Montoya. She was a Miss Mississippi contestant and played classical piano as her talent."

"How do you know this?"

Laura Beth shrugged. "Tanner told me. Marge hesitates to let the male officers know she was in a pageant or two or three"—She rolled her hand—"You get the picture, and I'm sure you understand."

"Yeah. Do you think she'd teach Abel on the side? David will pay her."

"Ask. Now, what's this about a teenage girl?"

"David's most recent assignment was an extraction. A child was kidnapped. It turned out there were several girls. Some perv trafficking little girls as sex slaves. Most of them are still at the orphanage where David was brought up." She held up a finger. "Remind me to tell you about that. Anyway, this one girl, Emma. She's fourteen, and her own mother sold her to the sex cartel. David brought her home with him and wants to adopt her."

Shaking her head as if she'd heard incorrectly, Laura Beth said, "Is this the same man I shot in the ass?" The still, small voice she'd heard before came back to her. *<Many will be saved...>*

"No and yes. I think we're finally seeing the real man. Laura Beth, he confided that he was molested by a priest. His mother..."

"His what?"

Penny held her hand, palm forward. "A nun who was raped by the same priest who molested my husband, and, yes, the old letch was his sperm donor. She killed the priest and told David the story when she caught the old goat in the act with her son. He helped dispose of the body and has kept her secret since he was eleven."

"Wow!" Laura Beth thudded back in her chair, her mouth agape.

"Yeah." Penny leaned back and stretched her long legs out in front of her. "So, give me pointers, Little Momma." She grinned.

"I don't have teenagers." She held up her hand in a blocking motion. "Hold up. Are you required to report the murder?"

"What murder? Justifiable, and nobody but you knows."

"Oh, just drag me in." She clicked save and print on her computer. She walked down the hall to get the documents.

Upon her return, she said, "I even resented my own mother at that age." Laura Beth sat down and pushed long auburn hair behind her ears. "Okay. First, open the lines of communication. She needs to see you as a real person, not just an authority figure. Let her know you're in charge, but always willing to listen to what she says."

"I can do that. Would it be presumptuous of me to get her to a gynecologist?"

"Is she sexually active?"

"Not by choice."

"Oh my God! Yes! Get her into a doctor. Make sure she doesn't have a disease."

"My thought exactly. I also told her we'd make a shopping trip to Jackson."

"Good idea."

"Could we make it a big thing—like welcoming her to the family? You and your girls. Roslyn. Madeleine. Even Marge and Deannie."

"Good plan. Maybe Bonnie Gustrom would like to go. I know she's a senior, but maybe a big sister influence."

"I like that. Emma is a freshman. Yeah, an upperclassman looking after her would be good. Let's plan it for Saturday."

"Okay. I'll tell everyone else. Let's meet at the Northpark Food Court at eleven. And I'll get Tanner to do something with just the boys."

Penny laughed. "You're putting a lot on him." She wiggled her eyebrows. "He stayed the night New Year's Eve."

Laura Beth held up both hands in a stop motion. "No sex. It's just too soon for me. But I really like Tanner."

"He's a good guy."

"Sounds like David might be a knight in shining armor. Maybe we misjudged him."

Penny's face beamed. "No knight in shining armor. He's been through a lot. A knight in shining armor is just a man who has never had his mettle tested. David's armor is scuffed, dented, and tarnished. But, Laura Beth, I love him."

"I can tell."

Penny rubbed her face with her hands. "You know, he's now determined to pose as a perv looking for some young girls. He's hell-bent on catching this person or group."

"Catch?"

"Well, he'd like a few heads."

"I can't say I blame him this time."

Penny stood. "Duty calls. Thanks, my friend."

"Any time."

While the ladies met in Jackson, Tanner rallied the males to meet at Penny's home. Laura Beth laid a heavy guilt trip on him about an innocent child and then lowered the boom when she revealed it was David's story.

Tanner brought his son, Corbin; Doug Blanchard, Madeleine's husband; Luis Montoya; Clyde Dixon who was still home from college; and Ed Pickering, along with a load of lumber; other building supplies; and a blueprint for a tree house. Tanner also got the privilege of caring for Riker while Laura Beth shopped.

Abel could not contain his excitement. He'd already had a lesson with Marge, and David had bought a piano.

The men set about building a tree house.

In Jackson, the females shopped. By the time they came home, Emma had a full wardrobe, complete with jewelry and makeup. She also had another date with Penny the following Thursday to see a doctor.

The drive home with her new mother brought out the commonality for the two. Both rape survivors, they talked. They bonded.

Approaching the house, Emma said, "Can I call you 'Mom'? I need a mother like you."

Penny's heart almost burst. She took the girl's hand and said, "Yeah, 'Mom' is good."

They arrived home to a party. The driveway was filled with cars, and a pizza delivery stopped right behind them.

"Well," laughed Penny, "a nice welcome home."

"Home," breathed Emma before she unhooked her seatbelt and lunged toward Penny, hugging her in a vice-like grip. "I was so afraid David was wrong, that you wouldn't want me."

Unable to contain her own tears, Penny wept with the child. She loosened her seatbelt and held the girl close, stroking her long dark hair. "You're safe with me. I swear to God, no one will ever hurt you again."

Penny pushed free of Emma and kissed her forehead. "No more tears. Let's go enjoy the party. I guarantee Auntie Laura Beth is behind it. Now, that's one lady with a mother's heart."

"You are too."

"Oh, I hope so, sweet girl. I hope so."

11

A Ghost

Sunday brought church or mass depending on the family. Monday, David took Abel and Emma to school while Penny went to the Archives with a nagging thought on her mind. Entering the old warehouse, she called Tanner.

"McGill."

"You got any pressing city cases?"

"Good morning, Sheriff. Nothing Marge can't handle. You know, I'm making her test so she can get her shield."

"Good move. Now, since you're still deputized, I need you at the Archives."

"What for?"

"Bring your butt over here." She disconnected.

Tanner stood and stretched his full seventy-four inches. "Marge!"

"Yeah, Boss?" Marge Montoya stuck her short blonde-haired head in the door.

"I gotta meet Penny. She's pulling rank as Sheriff and me a lowly deputy." He chuckled. "Hold down the fort."

"Yes, sir."

Tanner arrived at the Archives building where Penny waited. "What's up?" he asked.

"I can check new records on my computer. I recalled something. Clyde Dixon doesn't spook easily. He reported strange movement at Purdue Plantation Christmas a year ago. I checked records. We got an anonymous call this past Christmas—'A ghost,' the caller said. Strange screeching noises.

We did drive-byes both times and saw nothing. This year I was at Laura Beth's. I heard nothing."

She opened the door. "I want to check ghosts of Christmases past."

Tanner followed her inside. "How far back?"

"The place was occupied ten years ago. So, let's look back that far. I've only been sheriff two Christmases. If there were calls, I imagine they were considered pranks."

"You think now it was body disposal." He nodded.

"Murder and then disposal, yep. Let's get busy. I'll take odd years. You take even."

"Sounds like a plan."

Several hours later, Penny walked to the even numbered years, which sat on the opposite side of the warehouse from the odd, with a long walking space between. "Tanner, where are you?" She held up a number of written reports.

"Further down. I found four reports of something on Christmas. I got to thinking—maybe there were reports of some kind long before. We know Daiwa said some of the remains were probably thirty years old."

"Okay. Did you find anything?"

"Yeah. Three reports of noises sounding like someone being hurt. Deputies investigated possible domestic violence as far back as 1981. They never found any evidence. Mrs. Purdue swore nothing happened. One instance in 1989, Mr. Purdue even suggested authorities look for a panther if they heard screaming."

Penny took the report. "Good-old-boy, Sheriff Redd, never dug any deeper." She slapped the file closed. "Figures. They were probably in the same clubs. But now I have to wonder if the old broad was in on something and now their kid is just following in Daddy's footsteps."

"Sick, but you could be right."

"You found these in even years. Let's check odd too. Weathersby took office in '93. What did you find during his time?"

"Two visits to the home."

"Okay. Mind giving me a hand over here?" She jerked her head toward her side of the building.

"No, if you buy lunch. I'm starving."

"You're on. Let's go to Gus's."

"Sounds good."

More searching showed two more domestic violence investigations during Weathersby's tenure as sheriff before Mrs. Purdue died and one afterward. Once Mr. Colvin Purdue died, the son, Dillard, moved out West.

"Has he been back at Christmastime?" Tanner asked.

"I don't know. He's a trucker. That place is huge. If he were to come home, the drive into the property is all the way around the bend from my place. I wouldn't see him. Neither would Laura Beth."

She picked up her Stetson from the top of a box. "Utilities have never been disconnected. Bills are paid by electronic debit."

"That could be a small lead. Check to see if December usage is higher. Even two to three days would make a difference."

"Right after lunch." She put on her hat. "Let's eat before I start paperwork to get warrants for that. It won't be easy." She opened a satchel and placed all the reports inside. They walked out and left for Gus's Goulash.

After a hearty meal, Penny began paperwork to get utility records for Purdue Plantation. Tanner returned to his own office to find a visitor.

12

Kick Ass

"**What** are you doing here?" Tanner demanded. "Get your feet off my desk. Marge!"

Marge Montoya peeked in. "What's wrong, Boss?"

He pointed. She shrugged. "He said it was business. He's Penny's new husband. I didn't think you'd mind."

Tanner rolled his eyes and shooed her away with his hand.

David slowly turned his head and lowered his booted feet. "I need a job, Detective."

"Not hiring." Tanner moved behind his desk. "Listen up. I'm trying like the devil to believe you've reformed. I know you were under some strange circumstances with the Perez mess. I accept you were actually trying to catch a really bad person and keep Laura Beth alive. It's just taking a lot of adjustment for me." He plopped into his chair.

"I have no desire to come on the force, Tanner. Only you and Laura Beth, besides Penny, know my true identity. I actually thought I'd see if Montoya needs help with his security business, and I'd like to start a dojo. I came to see if you'd instruct some of the time."

Tanner steepled his fingers and put them to his lips. "Now, that's not a bad idea. You're a master martial artist. With what we found on our ladies' land, I think our kids need some serious self-defense lessons." He stood. "Very good idea, David. Come on."

David stood. "Where are we going?"

"Luis's office is just down the street."

"The only office near here that isn't government-based is LM Bonds."

"Yep. Luis does do some private security, but he also is a bail bondsman and bounty hunter. I think he prefers alive, though."

"I can do alive." He grinned.

"I bet you can."

Tanner and David walked into a two-room storefront. Luis Montoya sat behind one of two desks playing solitaire on his computer. He looked up. "Well, dang. I thought I had a customer."

"No," said Tanner, "but a proposition."

"Sounds iffy." He pointed to folding chairs against the wall. "Have a seat."

David and Tanner grabbed a couple of chairs and sat.

"Okay, fire!" joked Luis.

Tanner said, "David would like to start a dojo and work with you."

"What qualifications do you have, David?"

"Former military. Black belt in three disciplines. Married to the sheriff."

"Yeah. I don't think I want an answer to the question on my mind."

"Don't ask," Tanner said.

"I think I know the answer. David, do you know martial arts weapons?"

"Very well."

"What does your dojo have to do with me?"

"I'd like you to teach. I think adults, men. Tanner gets ladies, and I'll teach kids. Tanner suggested I work with you here too."

"Hold up!" Tanner objected. "It was your idea."

"I'm not extremely busy," Luis interrupted, "but I am the only bail bondsman in town. You up to tracking bail jumpers?"

"I'd be good at it."

Luis leaned back in his chair. "Tell me more about the dojo."

"Okay. We've been handed a macabre situation. So far, no kids from here, but"—David lifted his hands—"I have a fourteen-year-old daughter and an eight-year-old son. I don't want my kids to be a statistic. Tanner has two children. His girlfriend has three. You, Luis, have a stepdaughter. I don't think either of you wants your kids to be victims. I think teaching them self-defense is one way to help and a great way to protect them and help them learn self-control."

Long black hair fell over his shoulders as Luis nodded. "What monetary investment are you asking?"

"None, except a dojo here."

"I'm game." Luis turned to Tanner. "Are you?"

"Yeah."

David slapped his thighs. "Then we need to find a place. We can be DLT Mixed Martial Arts Academy."

Tanner chuckled. "You know, this is pretty exciting. I really like the idea of a school of martial arts. The three of us are all different styles. We can stretch the DLT to sort of be Delta and use the Greek letter Δ for our log, maybe formed with katanas. D at the top with the L and T at the bottom."

"I like it," Luis concurred. "Maybe put MMAA beneath theDelta." Louis scribbled his idea onto a sticky-note.

D

Δ

L T

MMAA

Tanner nodded. "And I bet Laura Beth could draw it. She did draw a composite of the person she saw when she discover the Perez head."

Luis followed up, "We have a lot to offer, but what style will be our specialty?"

"Shotokan for beginners," David said. "It's practical and strong, not flashy."

The other two nodded. Tanner said, "What kids need. It really teaches great discipline. And I know a place."

"Where?" David stood.

"The old co-op at the end of Main Street. Want to see it? I know it's for sale, and I know a cute redhead that can show it."

A grin on his face, David said, "Call Lit...Laura Beth."

"Hot damn!" Luis brought his hand down on his desk. "I knew it was you."

"You know nothing," Tanner said with authority.

"Right. Nothing." Luis ran his thumb and index fingers pinched together across his lips.

"Good." David made a move toward the exit. "Call your girlfriend, Tanner. I want to get this school going as soon as possible. Luis, I'll be here in the morning."

"Until then."

Tanner called Laura Beth to meet them at the co-op. Then, he turned to David. "You've got to be more careful."

"Yeah, I know." He sighed. "I'd like to be able to relax and just be me." He ran a hand down his side. "Notice. No more black."

"Yeah. You're getting there."

A brisk fifteen-minute walk brought the two men to the co-op where Laura Beth waited.

She unlocked the door. "David, I admit this is a stroke of genius. I'll enroll my girls for opening day."

"Thanks, L.B."

"L.B.?"

He lowered his voice though no one but Tanner was near. "I can't call you Little Momma."

Laura Beth laughed. "Then just call me Laura Beth. Please?"

They walked throughout the building. The large open area was perfect for instruction. Small rooms on one side made for good office space while the larger rooms on the opposite side could be renovated for storage, weight training, and dressing rooms with bathrooms.

"I'll take it," David declared. "What's the asking price? I don't want to rent. I want to buy."

"Commercial property. Prime location—a hundred fifty thousand."

"It's gonna need a lot of updates. A hundred K."

"I'll make the written offer."

"Okay." David turned to Tanner. "Might I suggest backyard instruction beginning today?"

"You could be right. Yeah. Let's get all our kids together."

Laura Beth shook her head. "Guys, my place has the most level yard. And the rye grass is always soft and green."

Tanner locked an arm around her neck. "Is that an offer?"

"Yeah. And don't forget Marge and Luis. We'll barbeque tonight, and I'll have a response for you by then, David."

That evening, as Laura Beth and Tanner cooked, David arranged the children in attendance by age and began basic instruction in self-defense. Laura Beth came up behind him. "Compromise. Are you willing to go one thirty?"

"Hundred twenty-five."

"Okay. I'm authorized to settle for a hundred twenty-five. Come by my office tomorrow. We can get you a structure by next week, but my yard is yours until you have everything ready."

"Really?"

"Yeah. I want my kids safe."

"So, you're past my past?"

"I just met you. Penny loves you. That's a firm foundation."

"Thanks."

"Welcome. Now, teach these little ones to kick ass."

Parents watched as David worked with the children. Most of them laughed as Tonya Copeland and Deannie Dixon tried to imitate stances and moves David tried to teach them. The older children did well. Corbin McGill appeared flawless.

The first lesson complete, David called Corbin to him. He put his hand on the boy's shoulder. "Either you're a natural, or your father's been teaching you."

"Dad's taught Roslyn and me some."

"Good, but you learn fast. You performed every stance from kiba dachi to zenkutsu. I want to show you something. Tell your dad you're going around front with me."

Corbin spoke to Tanner who lifted an eyebrow in question. David lifted both hands, palms up. Tanner gave a nod.

In front of Laura Beth's house, David opened the trunk of his car. "Are you familiar with martial arts weapons?" He opened a hidden compartment. Inside lay a variety of weapons.

Corbin pointed at several. "Bo, nunchucks, katana, kama, shurikens, tonfa, sai."

"Very good. If I train you with some of these, the blades will be wooden." He picked up the tonfa and the nunchucks and handed the tonfa to Corbin. "These first, I think. You can turn broken chair legs into tonfa. They might not be perfectly weighted, but they would work in an emergency. You see the nunchucks. In a bind, you can get some rope or string and tie two similar size sticks together. And look at this one." He lifted out a contraption with two iron weights on a chain. "It's called a meteor hammer. Rope or chain with two similarly weighted balls of some kind one on each end. I made this using two padlocks connected with twine. Broke a couple of guys' cheekbones, but I made my escape. I want to teach you to use these three weapons and how to make your own."

"Just me?"

"No, but only you and your sister and my two kids are old enough to begin weapons, except bo."

"So, do you want Roslyn?"

"Not yet. You get the first lesson. I can work with my two at home, and so can Penny." He chuckled. "And your sister is a little uncoordinated. She'll grow into it, but you need to know how to kick ass. Let's get started."

13

Identification

Sheriff Ulmer raised her head when her office door opened after a soft knock. "You know, you are quickly becoming my least favorite person, Pickering," she said.

"Sorry. I've brought someone to meet you. He's actually the first person to have had doubts about Diego being our hitman."

"Oh, goody. Please." She waved her hand toward the seats in front of her desk.

Pickering and a tall, thin man with long, straw-looking hair in a ponytail sat. Pickering said, "Sheriff Ulmer, this is FBI Profiler Steve Journey."

"Oh. In that case, welcome."

"Nice to meet you, Sheriff," Journey intoned.

"We've also brought in a forensic sculptor," Pickering informed. "She's with Daiwa working to create faces from the skulls. The older remains should still have viable DNA, but without some form of recognition, we won't know who to try to match any good DNA to. It's unlikely these kids ever had their DNA on file. Of course, we'll run it just in case—maybe a paternity test or something could have been done. And needless to say, we're running dental records."

Penny asked, "Weren't they buried too long?"

Journey interjected, "If a body is buried a few feet below the ground, the DNA could last up to ten thousand years. DNA will be useful for testing for only a few weeks, if it's left out in the sun and rain. Your remains were buried in shallow graves and should have some useable DNA. We've managed to identify five boys so far. The nutcase does pick a type."

"And that would be?" Penny prompted.

"Pre-teen, ten to twelve years old. Caucasian. Blond hair and blue eyes. You know that was true of the one still slightly intact. The five we've identified by DNA provided from parents of missing children were all perfect little Aryans, for lack of a better descriptor. And not one thus far has been from the same state."

Penny wrinkled her nose. "How does this help with the older skeletons?"

"Ah." Journey held up a finger. "Assuming they were the same coloring, the sculptor will make a cast from the skulls and then add clay in a flesh color, finally giving each head blond hair and blue eyes. She'll generate possible faces, which we'll broadcast and see if we get calls. We might never identify some of them." His voice hitched. "But we're trying."

"Okay," Penny said. "Interesting stuff. How can I help?"

Journey said, "Pickering tells me that you suspect the owner of Purdue Plantation. Tell me about him."

"Dillard Purdue. I barely know him. He's thirty-fivish. When his father died, Dillard got the hell out of Dodge. Now, Old Man Purdue, that was a piece of work. Racist and misogynistic."

"What about Mrs. Purdue?"

"I never met her."

"Describe the two men."

"They looked nothing alike. The old man might have been blond when he was younger, and he had blue eyes. The son could have been Native American."

"Hm. Can we get pictures of all of them? I especially would like to see Mrs. Purdue."

"I think I know where to find pictures. They weren't in the society pages though they were stinking rich. My friend Madeleine might know what Mrs. Purdue looked like. I think they're about the same age. What are you thinking?" Penny stood. "Gents, would you like to continue this discussion over lunch?"

"At Gus's?" asked Pickering.

Penny laughed. "If you'd like."

"What is Gus's?" asked Journey.

"Some of the best food you'll ever taste," Pickering declared.

"Lead the way," Journey said.

"We can take my car," Penny suggested. "After lunch we can drop in on Madeleine."

"Good plan," Journey agreed.

In her car, Penny picked the conversation back up. "So, Special Agent Journey, what are your thoughts?"

"Obviously, if young Purdue is killing now, he's carrying on his father's work. He's too young to have killed anyone thirty years ago. I'd put money on him having been molested by the old man."

"Strange," Penny mused. "Old Man Purdue really came off as hating women, yet he was married."

"Not so strange," Journey argued. "If he was gay in the '60s and '70s in Mississippi, he would have stayed in the closet. But maybe he really preferred young blond boys."

"Okay. So, assuming we're wrong, what does our killer look like?" Penny asked.

"I'd normally say a white male between twenty-five and forty-five. A victim of molestation. Probably very intelligent, but with feelings of extreme inferiority. He could hate what he's killing—maybe even be killing himself in a sense or someone who hurt him."

Penny parked. "It might just be me, but let's talk about something more pleasant over lunch. I just got married and now have two kids. Do you have family, Special Agent Journey?"

"Steve, please."

The sheriff gave a sharp nod.

After a filling lunch, Penny drove the two agents to Madeleine Blanchard's home. Madeleine let them in and shooed two little girls to the room she had turned into a playroom. Riker Copeland slept in a playpen by the sofa. The law enforcers took seats, and Madeleine sat closest to the baby.

"I didn't know you had started babysitting Deannie Dixon along with Laura Beth's children," said Penny.

"Yes. I keep her after lunch. Pre-school lets out at noon. Tonya and Riker get dropped off at nine and the bus brings Stacey about 2:30. When Luis started working, he couldn't be home with Deannie. He picks her up and brings her here. But you didn't bring these good men here to inquire about my retirement income."

"No. You know about all the bodies, and I haven't made a secret of my suspicions about the Purdues. Special Agent Journey is a profiler." Penny bounced her Stetson on her knee. "He's trying to construct a psychological picture of our killer. We thought maybe you could tell him more about the older man and his wife."

"Well, Colvin Purdue was a horse's ass. We never quite understood why Harriet ever married him." She waved a hand. "Oh, he looked good, but I would have put an ice pick through his temple in his sleep."

"Was he blond?" asked Journey.

"Yes. A head full until his twenties."

"What about the missus?" asked Pickering.

"Was Harriet blonde?" Madeleine asked for clarification.

"Whatever you can tell us."

"Yes, she was tall, shapely, blonde."

"Blue eyes?" asked Journey.

"Yes. She was voted Most Beautiful in high school." Madeleine stood. "I'll be right back."

While she was out of the room, the law officers talked.

"Well, that tells us something," said Journey. "Dillard was not Colvin's son."

"Genetics." Penny puckered her lips.

"Oh, yes," Madeleine said with a nod as she returned with a stack of old high school yearbooks. She laid them on the coffee table and pointed out Colvin, Harriet, and Dillard. "There was a great deal of speculation about the boy's parentage."

"Did you teach him, Madeleine?" Penny asked, tapping Dillard's picture.

"Yes."

"Tell us about him," Journey requested.

"Well behaved. Obedient. Smart as a whip. The girls drooled over him, but he was so shy."

"Were there ever meetings with his parents?"

"Never a disciplinary problem. On the contrary, he was a model student. If the boy had stepped out of line, Colvin would have beaten him to death."

Journey scowled. "Was there ever evidence of abuse?"

"Not that I saw." Madeleine chewed the inside of her mouth. "But I do recall he *always* wore long-sleeved shirts."

"Could have been hiding bruises," Pickering speculated.

"And," Madeleine added, "he had real issues with eye contact. If that poor boy has been molded into a killer by that son of a bitch, I hope he's roasting on a spit in Hell."

Pickering smirked. "Mrs. Blanchard, I do believe you could be violent."

"Threaten the people I love and find out."

Shaking his head hard, Pickering said, "I prefer you as a feisty granny. I see why you and Laura Beth hit it off."

Penny cracked up.

Journey rolled his eyes behind thick, black-rimmed glasses. "I think you've given lots of insight into the family. Thank you."

"I hope it helps. Let me know if you need anything else."

The three law enforcement officers left. Penny glanced in her rear-view mirror at Journey in the backseat. "Did it help?"

"Yeah." He nodded. "I'm pretty sure the father started the killings and now the son is continuing. I just wonder what role the mother played. Let's see how our sculptor is doing."

"You expect me to drive to Jackson?"

"It would be most appreciated."

Penny called David and let him know where she was headed and began the hour-and-a-half drive to the state capital. Once there, the three entered the morgue at the state medical examiner's to find a dozen federal forensics people hard at work. On a good two dozen stands sat approximate facsimiles of faces, long forgotten. Penny's heart lurched within her, and she secretly gave thanks that Abel did not fit the profile of this killer's victims. Then, she sent up a silent prayer for Tanner's son, Corbin, who would be a perfect target—age, gender, and coloring.

Even as she surveyed the approximations, her phone rang. "Sheriff Ulmer," she answered.

"Penny, it's Madeleine."

"Is something wrong?'

"I don't know. I got to thinking and went back through these old annuals. One of Harriet Purdue's, nee Mauldin, goals was to visit every state. Seeing as how these boys seem to be from all over the country, my stomach roiled. What if she helped procure victims?"

"Thanks for the tidbit. I'll share it with the Feds."

Penny told Journey Madeleine's theory.

"She could be right," he said. "Maybe she went along to protect her own child. And maybe she got into her husband's head that he was killing his hidden demon."

"Quite the little family affair."

"But she didn't count on the son picking up where Daddy left off."

As they talked, photographers snapped pictures of the possible faces of lost children. A media blitz began. Every major news network carried the slide show, and Daiwa created a Facebook page just for identification.

Penny stopped in front of one created head. "That is the oldest skull," said a female voice.

Penny turned. A short charcoal-skinned woman extended a hand. "LaQuilla Mix, Forensic Artist."

The sheriff barely felt the handshake since her mind was in sudden turmoil. "This face looks just like the son of my friend, Tanner. It's creepy."

"The person would have been about forty-five today."

"Tanner is thirty-seven. His folks divorced when he was three. Oh my God! He had a brother eight years older. If I recall, Tanner's dad took off, and authorities assumed he took the older son with him. I believe they lived in Tennessee at the time. Is there enough DNA on this one to compare to Tanner?"

"Where's the father now?"

"Deceased and always denied having done anything to the son. He went ballistic according to Tanner. He accused Tanner's mom of neglect and tried to get custody of Tanner and his sister."

"Yes, there's DNA from this skeleton. Can you get DNA from this Tanner?"

"Well, hello, Pretty Penny," Tanner answered his phone.

"Who do you think you are calling me that? Only my husband is allowed that term of endearment—and that in private."

"Sorry. He happens to be only a few feet away working diligently with Corbin on tonfa and meteor hammer. We're all in Laura Beth's backyard. At least he relented and let the kids all wear sweats and keep on their sneakers since it's freezing. But since you're calling me at nearly seven, this must be work. News on the bodies?"

"Maybe. I need you to come to Jackson—now."

"Seriously?"

"Yeah. Listen." She took a deep breath. "The forensic sculptor has been hard at work. She's constructed several faces. The oldest skull...well, it looks just like Corbin. I think it might be your brother."

"Reid?" Tanner's voice sounded an octave higher than normal. "You think it's Reid? He was the first victim? We lived in Memphis when he went missing. How can I help at this late date?"

"DNA. Daiwa says there's well-preserved DNA, enough to get a good comparison to a sibling."

Tanner put his hand on the back of his head. "Oh, God! Should I bring my mother?"

"Wow! That's up to you."

"Okay. We'll be there soon. I can't believe this."

Tanner told Laura Beth and David what was up. Laura Beth volunteered to keep Corbin and Roslyn and get them to school the next day since Tanner would undoubtedly be very late getting home.

Tanner stopped to get his mother. Delta McGill Nolan fell apart. After a long cry, she accompanied her son to Jackson.

Dr. Daiwa waited with Penny after sending everyone else home for the day. Delta stared at the facsimile that was most likely the remains of her long-lost son. Daiwa drew Tanner's blood and began the DNA comparison.

"It'll be a few days, Detective. I'll let you know as soon as I know."

A week later, two-thirds of the victims had been identified—one as Reid McGill.

14

Calm before the Storm

Face resting in his hands, Tanner sat on Laura Beth's sofa. "I can't believe after all these years we finally know what happened to Reid."

She placed her arm around his shoulders. "I'm so sorry, Tanner."

He sat up. "Thing is, I barely remember him. Mom is devastated, but I don't know how to comfort her."

"What are the plans?"

"Mom wants a funeral. Nina will be here tomorrow. She was only five, but she has a few more memories than I do. Mom already has a plot."

"I'll go with you, Tanner."

"Thanks, Sugar. I need your support." He took her hand.

"Not a problem, Cream."

Laughter bubbled out despite Tanner's situation. "Oh, I'm definitely a Cream Puff when it comes to you."

"You've been my pillar this past year. I can't imagine not being here for you." She threaded her fingers through Tanner's short blond hair that had a mind of its own.

He caught her hand and brought it to his lips. "Sugar"—he cleared his throat—"I really need more than caresses and kisses."

"Well, that's really not happening with a house full of kids who are still awake."

"Would it if we were alone?"

She withdrew her hand from his and lowered her eyes. "Do you think I'm using our children as an excuse to avoid sex, Tanner?"

"Not intentionally."

"I'm completely attracted to you, but I'm scared."

"Of me?"

She shook her head hard enough for her auburn hair to fly around her head. "You're amazing. No. I'm afraid of losing you too."

"Sugar, I'm not going anywhere. I think you know I'm head over heels in love with you."

"I know." She stood and walked to the window to check on the children playing with Freckles in the front yard. *I don't want to even think about that awful knock on the door if this becomes a lifetime.*

"I know what you're afraid of. I'm a cop." Tanner followed her to the window and placed his arms around her. "I can wait, Sugar."

"You deserve more than I'm ready to give."

"I only want you."

Pivoting, she turned to face him. She lifted her face to him. His mouth claimed hers.

The front door burst open as four children and one dog ran inside. Fat raindrops fell on their heels.

Laura Beth chuckled into Tanner's chest. "Not today, Detective."

"Oh, but I have hope."

On a dreary late January day, friends and family of Tanner McGill joined to give a memory a final rest. Obligated to help his mother through her grief, Tanner accompanied her home. For most of the afternoon, Delta relived her memories of her son, Reid. At last, she fell asleep and dreamed of what should have been.

As darkness fell, Laura Beth opened her front door. "Tanner?"

"Not sex, Sugar. I just need to feel you next to me."

"Where are your kids?"

"Madeleine's."

"Mine too." She put her arms around his neck and pulled his face to hers.

Across town, Marge Dixon Montoya stared out her window in the old Victorian home Laura Beth had sold her and her husband, Luis. "I've never seen my boss so lost," she murmured.

Luis slipped his arms around her. "Tanner will be fine. The main reason he's at odds right now is because he doesn't know how to react. Yes, his brother is dead, but it's been thirty years. And Tanner has very little memory of Reid. He was only three."

He turned his wife around and put his forehead against hers. "Tanner is strong. He's always been the one to help others. Now, he needs some help. It's hard for him."

"He has me signed up for the detective's exam next week. Where does that fall—Is he trying to push me out of the nest or is he asking for my help?"

"Marge, he thinks you're capable of being his partner, not just his assistant. Your shield will also mean a little more green."

"Yeah." She dipped her head in agreement, her short blonde hair looking more like a man's cut than her spouse's shoulder-length raven locks. "A raise would mean Deannie could take ballet, like she's been begging to do."

Luis wiggled his eyebrows. "It also means soon we can work on a little brother or sister."

Marge laughed. "Well, we could practice that right now since Deannie's spending the night with the Copeland girls."

"Yeah?"

"Yeah. I'll race you." Marge took off with Luis in hot pursuit.

1

In a garden home a few miles away, Doug Blanchard sat beside his wife. Madeleine tipped her gray-haired head to the side at his exaggerated sigh. He intoned, "Tell me again why we're babysitting a houseful of children. Their parents aren't even out of town."

"It just felt right."

"Because they're younger and might want romantic time together?"

"Well, yes."

Doug rolled his eyes.

Madeleine scowled. "Tanner needs some private time with Laura Beth."

"How does that explain the Montoyas and the Blacks?"

"I don't know, Doug. I just felt all these children would be really safe at our house tonight."

He took her hand. "You really feel a connection to all these people."

"I do." She squeezed his hand. "What's that?" she asked, feeling a small knot.

Doug grinned. "Maybe I wanted some romantic time with you." He opened his hand to show a small blue pill.

Madeleine laughed and popped her hand over her mouth. "With a houseful of children?" she squeaked through her fingers.

"They're all asleep."

Madeleine slapped his thigh. "You put that away until tomorrow. I just might have to find something slinky to wear." She winked.

"Oh, temptress!" He pulled her into a passionate kiss, and they went to bed.

Penny flopped onto her bed. David reached for her. "You are becoming a wilted magnolia, Pretty Penny."

"This case is too close to the heart. Tanner was the first friend I made when I moved here and joined the force. Laura Beth came several years later."

"Were you ever involved with McGill?" Every muscle in David's face went taut.

"You're jealous." She started laughing. Her husband's jaw clenched even tighter.

"Chill," she said, still giggling. "I was never involved with Tanner. He was married and very much in love with his wife. She died, and he was grieving. And I was still distrustful of any man. Then, you, probably the most dangerous man I've ever known, came along."

"I confess. I'm jealous. You're mine."

"Possessive?" She cocked an eyebrow and stopped laughing. "I'm Penny Ulmer. A piece of paper says we're married, and it's all legal even with your new name. I don't give a damn about a piece of paper. I love you, but don't try to change me or control me."

"I love it when you get mad. Your eyes snap, and"—He traced a line on her left lip and cheek—"this little muscle twitches." He kissed the jumping culprit. "I would never change a thing about you, but I want to possess every centimeter of you." He trailed kisses down her neck to her shoulder.

"Oh, hell! Why are we fighting?" Penny rolled on top of David.

The sky flashed brilliant white. Boom after boom rattled the entire house. Tanner bolted straight up in bed and clutched his chest.

"What's wrong?" Laura Beth sat up beside him, laced her fingers over his bulging bicep, and planted a kiss on his shoulder.

"He was there with me getting ice cream. Then, he was gone. I started crying because I was all alone and scared. The ice cream man radioed for help. Over and over, the authorities asked me what I saw. Did my dad grab him? I kept thinking my dad didn't want me—only Reid." He shivered. "But it wasn't Dad. They took him, tortured him, sexually violated him. They *killed* him. He was eleven. And I *did* see something—a white Caprice. I didn't know it then, but I remember. A blonde-haired woman. That's it. Nothing more."

Laura Beth ran her fingers through Tanner's hair. "You couldn't have stopped it. What did the ice cream guy see?"

"Nothing. He was busy selling his product to a group of kids, who saw nothing either or, at least, didn't notice or realize anything bad was happening.

Lightning continued to flash, and rain pelted the slate-shingled roof. Freckles whined at the bedroom door.

"He's scared of storms," Laura Beth whispered. She got up and let the puppy in. He burrowed under the bed.

Tanner released a half-laugh. "'If you love children and animals, you're a good person.' Reid said that when we brought up the cat with two broken legs. We kept him, and Mom took him to the vet. He wore two casts for weeks. Even after, he sort of hopped. That's why we called him Hop-Along. I remember that. That and Reid teasing me about a pair of cowboy boots. He called me John Wayne. I wore those boots no matter what else I had on—jeans, shorts, Sunday clothes, even my swimsuit." He lay back and Laura Beth slipped under the covers next to him.

"Am I a good person, Sugar?"

"The best." She kissed his shoulder.

"Then why do I feel so bad?"

"Survivor's guilt, Tanner. You know the answers."

"Yeah."

She rose up on her elbow and propped her head on her open hand. With her other hand, she traced circles with her index finger on the sparse blond hair on Tanner's chest. "You are the best person I know."

Tanner entwined fingers in Laura Beth's long copper tresses. "You are so beautiful, Sugar. Even in just the glow of the lightning flashes, you have the most kissable mouth."

"Then, why are you talking rather than kissing me?"

"Because if I kiss you, I don't want to stop with a kiss."

"Then, don't stop."

Tanner pulled her to him and claimed her mouth with his. He slipped her night shirt over her head. His palm caressed down her side, stopping to encircle her breast and roll her nipple between his thumb and index finger. His other hand kneaded her thigh. Finding the elastic of the silk panties she wore, he slipped his hand inside and rubbed her warm, moist folds.

Laura Beth returned the touches, allowing her hand to find Tanner's full erection. He groaned as she ran her nails the length of it. "Do you have condoms, Sugar?" came out garbled.

"No."

"Well, shit!" He fell back.

"That's not going to stop us from enjoying each other." She straddled him with her back to him and leaned forward kissing and nipping from his navel down his happy trail until her tongue flicked the head of his penis.

"Oh, yeah," breathed Tanner. "I can play this game."

And the game was afoot.

15

Dreams and Visions

*N*ear dawn, Doug Blanchard rocketed from his bed. Not bothering with robe or slippers, he raced as fast as seventy-year-old legs would go to the room where he and Madeleine had arranged for the boys to sleep overnight. Even as the man's hand grasped the doorknob, Corbin McGill awoke screaming.

Doug gathered the boy to him. "It's all right, Corbin. It was a dream—a nightmare."

Corbin sobbed. "He was hurting me, Mr. Doug."

"It wasn't real. The bodies. Your uncle. It all just played on your mind. You're safe here."

He clung to the boy wrestling with his own horror that had awakened him. Doug kept seeing boys, who were his contemporaries, being brutally raped and strangled. *No bodies found were that old. That would have had to have been old man Orin Purdue, and all I remember about him is that he was a World War II hero.* He closed his eyes and saw a young soldier being brutalized by Nazi officers. Though the soldier looked as Germanic as his tormentors, his cries of anguish were in English.

"It was only a dream," Doug whispered as much to himself as to Corbin. His age-spotted hand smoothed the child's hair. "Do you want to go back to sleep or help me make breakfast?"

"I'll help you."

"You sure? It's Saturday. I thought you might want to sleep in."

"I don't want to dream again."

Abel stirred. Doug put a finger to his lips, and the two of them slipped from the room.

Doug could only assume the younger boy didn't wake due to having been in an orphanage and hearing noise often during the night. He was glad not to have to explain the nightmares to an eight-year-old.

As his son awoke from a terrifying nightmare, Tanner started awake, brow beaded with perspiration. His breath came in hitches. "It was just a dream," he mumbled.

He looked toward the sleeping redhead beside him and took a deep steadying breath. *Now, that's the kind of dream I'd rather have.* A smile played around his lips as he recalled the intense intimacy they had shared only a few hours before. *He thought, intercourse couldn't be better than that. Damn! This woman drives me wild.*

Determined to get more sleep, he closed his eyes. Yet, every time he dozed, the shrieks and horrified wails of young boys—all with his dead brother's face—woke him.

Tanner rolled to a sitting position and placed his feet on the floor. He dropped his face into his hands to find it wet with tears. "God! Is that face Reid's or Corbin's?"

Laura Beth sat up behind him and leaned against his bare back, chin on his shoulder. "You okay?"

Feeling her warm breasts against his skin, he sighed. "I will be, Sugar." He reached his hand up and entangled his fingers in her hair. She kissed his shoulder.

"Lady, you are good medicine for me."

"Want to talk about the dream?"

"No, but I guess I'd better. It scared the hell out of me because I couldn't tell if the face of the boy being abused was Reid's or Corbin's. My son, Laura Beth. What if it was my son?"

"You're doing all you can to keep Corbin safe."

"I need to get this monster. How do we get Purdue back here?"

"Hm." Then, she whispered, "David."

"Huh?"

"Enrique de la Vega."

Tanner turned to face her, eyes filled with questions.

David Black tossed and turned and mumbled in his sleep. The sleek black semi with a king scorpion painted on the red trailer rumbled from state to state. The tail of the scorpion reached out and skewered children, both boys and girls, and deposited them in the trailer.

The big rig crossed the border into Mexico. The scene changed as the victims paraded across a stage. Dollar amounts rang into the air. An auction block.

A man with jet-black hair pulled into a ponytail clamped his hand onto the shoulder of a blond-haired boy. The man growled to a Latino with a Poncho Villa mustache, "My bonus. This one's mine. I always get one, and this is the one I want."

Money changed hands and the man jerked the child. The boy turned terrified bright blue eyes toward David. "Help me!"

"Corbin!" David bellowed and bolted from bed.

"What's wrong?" Penny yelled. Leather and Lace bayed.

"I have to stop this. I think Emma and others are tied to your dead boys."

He snatched his cell and dialed a number.

Tanner stared at Laura Beth. "David? As de la Vega?"

Suddenly his cell phone danced on the nightstand. He grabbed it. "McGill."

David's voice was loud enough to be heard beyond the phone. "I have a plan. I think my trafficker and the Purdue killer are linked. Get to Penny's. Call Pickering and bring his ass with you."

He didn't wait for a response.

16
A Shadow

Penny and David with Tanner and Laura Beth sat around Penny's table with coffee and scones.

"You had a dream," Tanner said.

"Yes. How many times do I have to say it?"

"A dream..." Tanner echoed as his own dreams haunted him.

David pointed. "What did you do to him last night, Laura Beth? He's a damned zombie."

"No!" Tanner shook his head. "But to base this on a dream..."

"Don't belittle my dreams. They've been dead on in the past."

"Like some kind of psychic ability?" asked Laura Beth. "I've had a few doozies lately. One was about you."

"Really?" David's eyebrows reached his hairline.

"Not that kind!" she snapped.

"I was teasing." He gave a slight chuckle. "I don't know what to call my ability." David stood to get more coffee as the doorbell chimed. "Pickering."

"Premonition?" Laura Beth grinned.

"No, I called him, Sugar," Tanner informed.

"Is that wise?" Laura Beth asked as Penny went to the door. "I mean, secret identity."

David shrugged. "I just know I have to help catch this nut."

Pickering returned with Penny. "Got enough coffee for me?"

"Sure." Penny poured another cup.

After a large slurp, Pickering got to the point. "Okay. What's this all about?"

"We have a plan to draw out a killer and maybe a human trafficker," Penny said.

Pouring more sugar into his coffee, Pickering said, "What does the trafficker have to do with our serial killer?"

"They could be connected."

"How so?"

David stood rooted in front of the kitchen sink and grunted.

Pickering scowled. "And how does this involve a civilian?"

David whirled around. "I know somebody I've done business with that might have a fetish. He might be partial to little blond-haired boys."

Pickering sipped his overly sweet coffee. "International?"

"Yes," David said.

"Just what do you do?"

"I'm a...negotiator."

Pickering chuckled. "Maybe I can get permission to work with the CIA."

"No CIA here. I work for an international consortium. We work to ensure freedom."

"Yeah. Right. And does your boss give whatever caper you have in mind the green light?"

"I'm waiting for his call."

"Okay." Pickering rotated his mug. "Give me a rundown."

David sat. "You think the Purdue guy might be your culprit. He's a trucker with access all over the country. If he's transporting kids for sale, he might be the guy we're looking for too. Maybe he gets a kid as payment—a bonus of a sort."

"And then he brings them back here for the kill. It's where he learned," Penny added.

David went on, "I can get someone within my organization to pose as a buyer, not only for some pretty boys, but also for the Purdue property. If we can get him back here..."

"How long will it take to set all this up?" Pickering asked.

"A little time, and I don't think it'll be finished overnight."

"McGill, Sheriff, your take," said Pickering.

"We need to get Purdue back here," Penny said. "We need to at least question him."

"And if he brings his rig," Tanner said, "we have a security geek that can get us some surveillance."

"Montoya." Pickering puckered his lips. "Will any of this stand up in court?"

"Do you care?" David gave the FBI agent a cold, hard stare.

"Marin, I'm sure you'll be taking his head anyway."

"Who's Marin?"

"Damn! You're good." Pickering nodded. "Set it up."

"I don't care that the organization doesn't sanction this!" David screamed into his unregistered, untraceable phone. "Mosely, listen up. I *know* they're connected."

"Your intuition?"

"Call it what you like."

"Okay. Get back to the compound. I'll set up a meeting. Maybe you can convince the powers that be."

David returned to Penny's living room where the others waited. "I have to go out of the country."

"Argentina by any chance?" Pickering asked.

"Where is none of your concern. But if you want my group's help, I have to go."

Pickering grunted. "No guarantee *my* group will go for it."

"They want to catch this nut. They'll do it. I believe you can talk a good game."

David walked to the front door and opened it. "Meeting adjourned."

The guests trickled out. David caught Tanner's arm. "Help convince them."

"Why?"

"In my dream, he had Corbin."

They locked eyes. Tanner gave a firm nod.

David closed the door behind the people and leaned his head against the wood. *No way will I ever try to explain that sometimes my visions or dreams or whatever come to me from a black dragon. Nope. They would definitely think I'm nuts.*

Enrique de la Vega arrived at a heavily guarded compound in Argentina. "Home sweet home," he muttered. "God! I can't wait to get back to Penny."

"Sir?" the chauffeur asked in Spanish.

"Nothing. Talking to myself."

"Sí, señor. Welcome home."

"Gracias." He stepped from the sleek black car and entered an opulent villa. Inside, he was greeted by half a dozen high-ranking government representatives from around the world.

The one woman in the ensemble did not wait for pleasantries. She spoke with a crisp British accent. "Mr. Mosely has informed us about what you want to do, Mr. de la Vega. How does this involve our organization?"

Enrique almost came unglued at the coldness of the woman's voice.

"Madame," he said with measured deliberation. "I've never stood in the presence of the rulers of this elite, yet secret, coalition. Do I not even get introductions?"

"No," replied a man with translucent blue eyes. "It's best no names are exchanged."

"But you know mine and Mosely's."

"You're underlings."

The man's clipped, heavy German accent grated Enrique's nerves. *I hope I get the privilege of taking both your heads someday*, jumped into the front of Enrique's mind.

Another man, slight of build with a pencil mustache, asked in clear American English, "What advantage does your request have for us? We're all about thwarting terrorists."

"I recall a recent extraction," Enrique retorted. "How was that thwarting terrorists?"

The man gave a nod. "Go on."

"But it *was*, just terrorism of a different kind—human trafficking. I have good reason to believe that particular trafficker might be using a serial killer to provide his merchandise. This person has killed about ten young boys and is most likely following in his father's path since more than thirty bodies were discovered in a town that means something to me personally. I've done many things for this group, for my country, for freedom's sake. I'm asking that you allow me to use my talents to stop both these madmen. Both these atrocities will continue if you don't help."

An attractive, well-built man wearing fatigues chuckled. In a heavy Middle Eastern accent, he said, "Mr. de la Vega, I feel you would do this thing with or without our support." He stood and approached Enrique. He stood inch for inch, pound for pound the same. He circled Enrique's face with his index finger. "You will need to disguise yourself, Mr. Marin, or should I say Mr. Black?"

Enrique's eyes widened.

"Oh, yes. We know all about you and your wife and children. I understand your need to protect them. You did help tremendously with that nasty Hernandez business. And as you so eloquently spoke on many occasions…"

"Stop!" came a forceful voice from an Asian man in an Armani suit. Not large, he stood and came to stand beside Enrique. "This man has been invaluable to this team over the years. I, for one, stand in support of his request."

"As do I." There was no mistaking the Ugandan accent from the massive ebony-skinned man who had sat silent and rigid for the entire time. His voice rumbled deep in his chest when he spoke with clear, precise English devoid of slang and contractions. "We are two, but each of us has been given proxy vote for several."

"Who?" demanded the woman.

He held up several pieces of paper. The Asian followed suit. The African smiled, flashing brilliant white teeth. "I think Mr. de la Vega has enough votes to proceed."

"Then eet ees decided," a small man with a heavy French accent said. David couldn't help but wonder just how much damage someone of that stature could possibly inflict.

The Middle Eastern man applauded. "Well played." He circled Enrique's face again. "You had my vote. I say again, a disguise is necessary."

An older man with long graying hair who had not spoken but sat in the shadows intoned in almost a whisper that held an Eastern European accent, "How do you plan to lure your killer?"

Enrique shrugged. "I am in the market to buy a plantation. Then, I'll be his shadow, and he'll discover I have a fetish for young blond boys. I think he'll set me up with the trafficker. We'll get both bastards."

"Excellent," said the African, "but this will take some time. May I assist in your initial set up?"

"Why do you want to do that?"

"I had a sister who was taken and sold for God-knows-what. Fear of having children stolen and killed is an old terrorist strategy. My people have known it a long time."

"Do I get a name?"

"Call me Nasser."

17

Bait

Penny snatched her phone. "Hey!"

"It's a go. Not sure how long I'll be here getting things set up."

"Okay. You'll call, right?"

"Every day. I love you, Penny. My Pretty Penny."

"I love you. I'll give Pickering and Tanner the news."

"Okay. I gotta go." He held the disconnected phone to his forehead, took a deep breath, and returned to where the representatives from a secret organization sat. He jerked his head from side to side.

"The rest are gone," Nasser's booming voice informed.

"Mosely too?"

"For the moment. I sent him to procure items to help you transform. I assume you might want to see your family, so you need two looks."

"Nasser? Not your real name, is it?"

"Yes and no." The large man chuckled. "It is sad when you cannot trust your allies."

"Yeah." His thoughts flew to Tanner, Laura Beth, Luis, and Pickering.

Nasser's rumbling throat-clearing got David's attention. "Please, sit with me at this contraption." Nasser indicated a computer.

David pulled up a chair. "What are you doing?"

"I am putting your name out. Take a look."

A gasp escaped David's lips. "Jesus, Mary, and Joseph! How did you do that in such a short time? First, I don't have facial hair. And where did you get the pictures of the young boy?"

"The boy is a South African model. He looks young, but he is an adult, and well-paid for the use of his likeness. Are you familiar with Photoshop?"

"Some."

"I only created two composites. Over the next few weeks, we will leak Enrique de la Vega slowly to the Web. Mosely is procuring the supplies to turn you into this."

"Okay...Why do I feel that has a deeper meaning?"

"Because it does." Nasser pushed the laptop to the side. "Now to get you looking like this picture."

"How? I can't have a beard"—he touched his head—"or graying hair as David Black."

"This, I know. That is why I have a professional makeup artist on the way. We will create a wig and a beard you can wear."

"That'll help, but can you trust this makeup person?"

"She is part of the organization. Most of us have what you call 'day jobs.'

"I also have hired an acting coach, also a part of the consortium." The big man chuckled. "I cannot wait until you meet Mr. Honeycut. You will need his assistance. You do not appear to be a pedophile."

The new Enrique laughed loudly. "Thank God!"

For several hours, Enrique de la Vega met with a makeup artist that Mosely brought, though Nasser summarily dismissed him.

The young woman designed wigs for celebrities and for a great number of chemo patients at no cost, in addition to being paid handsomely by the consortium. She never said a word about the pending job, not even asking her client's real name.

The woman obviously understood what a non-disclosure with the organization meant. Her life mattered to her.

The beard and mustache combo proved a bit harder than the wig. To wear it meant applying adhesive. And taking it off, irritated Enrique's skin. The artist gave him a substantial supply of hydrocortisone cream to use as needed.

Then, she held up a contact lens case.

"I've never needed glasses," Enrique said.

"You do now," Nasser teased. "Did you not notice Enrique de la Vega has green eyes?" He rubbed his chin. "And I think I shall add Buddy Holly glasses. Yes."

Enrique exhaled but nodded.

Nasser assured, "The contacts only change your eye color, and the glasses will be clear glass."

The woman laughed. "Mr. Nasser, do we need a fat suit?"

"No," Enrique asserted. "I'll need to be able to move easily."

"He is correct regarding that issue," Nasser said.

"All right," the woman said. "Let me teach you how to use the contacts."

By the end of the day, Enrique was unrecognizable.

Nasser scowled. "I think you also need a signature wardrobe."

"Fine. Let's go with clothes that scream wealth and power." He grinned. "And I get to keep them after this mission is over."

"You will have earned the clothes and more."

"More? Retirement?"

"That is not my call, but if that is what you want, I shall put in a good word."

"Thanks."

Nasser smirked. "But you would become bored." He held up a camera. "Put on those white linen trousers with a white shirt, unbuttoned. Let us send a picture to your wife."

"Are you gay, Nasser?"

"Why?"

"You're looking at me a little strange. I'm not gay—period—at all."

"Are you homophobic?"

"No, just straight."

"Relax. I am not gay. I am married with five children. I am still unsure you can pull off gay, let alone pedophile."

"Watch me." He jutted his chin out. "Take the picture."

Nasser snapped the picture as soon as Enrique changed clothes. Then, Enrique sent it to Penny's email with a message:

> *I miss you and love you. Hug my kids. Tell Laura Beth to expect a customer in about six weeks.*

He got a reply:

> *I might not recognize you. Please tell me this is only temporary. And other things are unchanged. I love you too.*

Laughter got Nasser's attention. "What is so amusing?" he asked.

"Nothing." He typed another message:

> *Snake remains unchanged. Think of the face as a chameleon with a tongue that is hard for you. Soon, Pretty Penny. Soon.*

He signed out of his email. "What's next?"

Next began the following evening with a Hollywood acting coach—flamboyantly gay.

Mouth agape, Enrique stared at the man. Nasser chuckled. Mosely left the room muttering, "This one might be more than Marin can stand. Good luck, my friend. I can't bear to watch."

"Oh, my!" exclaimed the coach. "Is this the budding star?" He ran a hand up Enrique's arm.

"Yes, this is the man who needs training. You have worked with much less raw talent." Nasser intoned.

"Are you gay, my pretty, or just playacting?"

"This is the role of a lifetime. I need to be very believable," Enrique said. "But a bit more subtle."

"Ah!" The coach touched his chest. "Not a flamer like me. I get it. What do they call you?"

"Enrique de la Vega."

"Ricky."

"Ricky?" *Not another damned name.*

"Less formal." He moved his hand through the air. "Ricky Vega. I can see your name in lights."

"I like formal. I have no desire to see my name appear in Hollywood. I'm too rich with money to burn. I'm looking for a young companion, preferably blond with blue eyes. Now, do you have a name?"

"Alfie. Alfie Honeycut." He scowled, his strawberry-blond brows almost obscuring his honey brown eyes and his freckled nose wrinkling. "How young?"

"Young enough to groom."

"This is just playacting, right? You aren't planning to molest children?"

"Absolutely not. This role is all about stopping a child molester and killer."

"Are you an actor?"

Enrique placed a strong hand on Alfie's shoulder. "A world-class performer, but this is a new role for me. I need your help."

"Fine. You'll need it. You exude testosterone."

Alfie worked day after day with Enrique. "You're impossible!" he shrieked after four weeks.

Enrique flipped his hands up in frustration. "What do you want me to do?" he yelled.

Alfie pranced to Enrique and grabbed his crotch, squeezing. Before he could think, Enrique punched his acting coach.

Alfie fell back onto the floor, holding his bloody nose.

"Shit!" Enrique hollered and grabbed both sides of his head. "I'm sorry." He knelt and helped Alfie up. "Let me get some ice."

Alfie sank onto the sofa as Enrique made an ice pack. He sat beside the wounded man and held the ice to his face. "I'm sorry. Why did you do that?"

With his lip swelling, Alfie muttered, "If you were gay, how would you give pleasure to your partner?"

"I don't know."

"Have you ever given a blow job?"

Enrique placed Alfie's hand on the pack and stood. "I kind of thought I'd be shopping for the pleasure giver."

"Ever performed anal or had it done to you?"

"What does it matter?" He ran his hand across his wigged head. "It's an act."

Alfie felt his nose. "I would say you've probably received head on numerous occasions, all from women; and you've most likely given anal sex, only to women." He laid the ice aside. "But you were molested by a man. Still, you have a gentle side." He stood and went to his pupil, taking his hand. "See how you took care of me after you overreacted?"

"I don't get it. You knew I'd hit you."

"And that you'd feel bad about it. If you want these people to believe you're gay and looking for a young boy, you'll have to be comfortable with being touched in a sexual way by a man." He clapped his hands. "Change clothes. Wear those sexy clinging white slacks and a red button-down. Loafers. Have you considered getting your ears pierced?"

Enrique grabbed an earlobe. "Should I?"

"Yes, but not tonight. Move! You have a test tonight."

Returning as requested, Enrique watched Alfie lick his lips. "Damn! I wish you were gay. You look delicious."

Alfie summoned the limo and ushered his reluctant student into it. He gave the driver an address and sat back to watch Enrique.

"What do I have to do?" asked Enrique.

"Tonight, you will pick up a partner, and you will initiate sexual contact. And you will get this young man to pleasure you."

"Oh, shit."

"If you can't do this, no way will you make the men you're after believe you're looking for a young partner."

"Oh, God!" He buried his face in his hands. After a moment, he sat up straight. "I can do this."

"We'll see."

The limo pulled up to a loud, dimly lit club. Getting out, Alfie looped his arms around Enrique's bicep. "Smile," he murmured.

After a deep breath, Enrique covered Alfie's hand with his. They walked into the club. Same-sex couples filled the place. There were also a number of unattached men and women.

"Work the place," Alfie whispered into Enrique's ear. "If I find someone, don't interrupt."

Enrique grimaced. "Not a face to get a date," Alfie said and slapped Enrique's butt before he moved in to mingle.

Enrique went to the bar and ordered a gin and tonic. Nursing the drink, he looked around the bar. He spotted a blond at the end of the bar. *Is that the South African model? Here goes nothing. I cannot wait to see my Pretty Penny.* He downed his drink and ordered another.

Enrique slipped onto the barstool next to the blond and slid his frosty glass down the younger man's arm. "Buy you a drink?" he asked, using his heavy Spanish accent.

The boy looked his way with translucent blue eyes. "Si."

Enrique addressed the bartender. "Can you make a sex on the beach?"

"Sí, señor."

"Buena. For the man with the captivating eyes."

"Gracias," said the blue-eyed man.

"Where are you from?"

"Sveden."

Not the model. "You're a long way from home. Do you speak Spanish? English?"

"English. Muy poco Español."

The bartender set the drink in front of the Swede.

"I'm Enrique."

"Ivan."

"What brings you to my city?"

"I'm a model. There's a fashion shoot."

"What will you be wearing?" He smiled. "Can I hope for nothing?"

Ivan laughed and sipped his drink. "That could be arranged." He took a long gulp of the sex on the beach. "Lead the way."

Enrique downed his gin and tonic, stood, and took Ivan's hand. He walked them toward a hallway lined with small rooms. The first three stalls were locked; the fourth was vacant, but it reeked of sexual emissions.

"I prefer cleaner," Enrique muttered. He shrugged. "To hell with it." He pulled Ivan into the cubicle and locked the door.

Grabbing his pickup by the lapel, he kissed him hard and thrust his hand into the other's slacks. Ivan's full erection met his hand. Only moments of intense stroking had Ivan ejaculating and screaming with pleasure.

"You like rough," Ivan said with a wide grin. "Me too." He dropped his pants and leaned over a bench in the room. "Do it. Make it hurt."

Enrique jerked him up by the hair and pulled his head back. "I don't do bareback." With his other hand, he unzipped his trousers. "My turn to feel good." He forced Ivan's face toward his crotch.

Ivan clutched Enrique's buttocks and delivered oral sex that had the other man grabbing the walls.

Done, Ivan stood, licking his lips. Enrique placed a quick kiss on him, dressed, and strode from the room. He marched out the door to the waiting limo where he grasped the handle and vomited beside the car. He wrenched the door open and demanded, "Llévame de vuelta ahora. ("Take me back now.")

"Señor Alfie?"

"Vuelve por él. Sácame de aquí." ("Come back for him. Just get me the hell out of here.")

At two A.M. Penny answered her phone to sobs. "Ninja Man? Is that you?"

"Oh, God! Penny! The first time, he beat me with a riding crop before he made me suck his cock. The next time, he forced me over the seat in the confessional and was inside me in two thrusts. I screamed, and he stuffed a handkerchief in my mouth. Next thing I knew, he let go and fell back. Marta had her rosary wrapped around his neck. When he fell back, she lost her grip on it. That's when she picked up the statue and bashed him in the head at least six times." He paused long enough to catch a breath. "She told me that night who she was and what had happened to her. We dragged his body to his car and drove to a bridge. We doused a rope with kerosene and splashed more into the car's interior and on the old perv. We lit the rope on fire and placed it in the gas tank and sent the car careening down the embankment. It burst into flames. We hiked back to the orphanage and scrubbed and scoured the confessional. Authorities ruled it an accident. Said he fell asleep at the wheel. I have to stop these evil men, but I'm losing myself. Please don't stop loving me."

Her own face wet with tears, Penny choked, "Where's my Ninja Man? You can do this. I will *never* stop loving you."

"Swear?"

"What happened?"

"I had to let some guy..." He began gagging. Penny could hear him retching into the toilet.

"David!" she shouted into the phone.

"I'm sorry."

"It's all right. Listen. How much longer until you come to buy my neighbor's place?"

"A month, max."

"Stop thinking about what you had to do in the undercover assignment. It's just like Luis using coke—nothing more. It does not define you. It's a sacrifice for a higher cause. And I'm right here waiting for you."

"I love you, Penny."

"And I love you."

When Enrique came to breakfast the next morning, Alfie flitted around the kitchen preparing a gourmet repast.

"Did you meet Ivan?"

"Why—yes. A beautiful specimen."

"Yes."

"I saw you take him for some fun."

"Fun?" Enrique shivered. "For you, I suppose it is." He gulped coffee. "Let's continue acting lessons. I think I'm ready to set some bait, but I have to be the dominant. End of story."

"Yes, I can see that."

"So? What did Ivan say about me?"

Alfie laughed. "He was so excited he forgot he had condoms in his pocket. He would have taken you bareback."

18

Summer Vacation

On the first Tuesday after school let out for summer, the door of the real estate office chimed as a bearded, slightly graying man wearing a classic gray Christian Dior accentuated by a baby-blue tie entered. Three agents jumped to greet him. Reaching into an inner breast pocket and looking at a card he found there, the man said in a heavy Spanish accent, "I am looking for Laura Beth Copeland."

Her mouth falling open, Laura Beth stood. "I-I-I'm Laura Beth," she stammered.

"Charmed," the man said, and flashed a perfect smile. "I am Enrique de la Vega. A friend of mine, David Black, suggested I consult you about purchasing property adjacent to your own. Can you be of assistance?"

"Of course." She looked furtively at the other three agents whose faces showed envy. Laura Beth waved a hand toward a chair in front of her reception desk. "Please sit down."

"Gracias." He sat and crossed his left ankle on his right knee. He pulled a handkerchief from his inside pocket, took off the heavy black glasses he wore, and wiped the lenses.

Laura Beth gaped at the diamond studs in both ears and his dark-green eyes. She retook her seat. "Yes," she said. "David mentioned a friend of his might be interested in Purdue Plantation before he went out of town on business, but that was over three months ago."

"That is the very property I have in mind. However, it is not listed for sale. I need your assistance in locating the owner so that I might make an offer."

"I'm not exactly sure how to contact him, but I have a couple of friends who might be able to help. As a matter of fact, David's wife is one of them. Have you met her?"

"No, but I would like that. David has been overseas working for me, but he should be back within a few days. Do you think he would mind if you introduced me to his bride? I would really like to locate Señor Purdue as soon as possible."

Laura Beth stood. "I'm certain he would insist. If you would like, I can take you to her now. She and I are meeting at a local establishment, Gus's Goulash, for lunch. I'm sure she would welcome a guest."

Enrique stood. "An excellent suggestion, Señora Copeland."

"Call me Laura Beth."

"Sí, and I am Enrique. Is this Gus's fine dining?"

"Not exactly, but the food is outstanding."

"Then I should anticipate a pleasant meal. I am famished."

"Did you come in a car?"

"I sent my driver back to the hotel."

"Driver?" She shook her head. "Would you be all right riding with me?"

"I see no problem with that."

"Then follow me."

Enrique dipped his head toward the other three agents who began discussing him the moment the door closed behind him and Laura Beth.

Both buckled up in the car before either spoke. Laura Beth put her hand on the ignition. "I wouldn't have recognized you," she said.

"Good. Why don't you call Tanner to meet us? Are you still dating?"

"Yeah." She glanced his way as she cranked. He stared out the window. "He's in court. Come to my house for supper if you want to talk to him."

"As Enrique or David?"

"Not sure I like Enrique. He's brooding. Are you okay?"

He turned toward her. "Do you like David?"

"He was growing on me. How do you plan to be both men?"

He tapped his whiskers. "Adhesive and a wig. Contact lenses. For your information, I don't like this character I'm playing."

"Hey!" she said sharply. "You're *not* a pedophile. Want to talk about it?" She maneuvered onto the county highway.

"No. I just want Penny in my arms, but that will have to be later. I'm Enrique de la Vega right now."

"I'm sorry. I don't know what you've been through, but you're so depressed, I feel it rolling off you."

"Laura Beth, if I have my way, I'll take a few heads. Child molesters don't deserve to live."

"On that, we agree." She parked. "You ready to surprise your wife?"

"Absolutely."

Before they exited Laura Beth's car, Penny burst out the door of Gus's Goulash. "My house! Now!" She screamed.

Laura Beth climbed back into her Jaguar. Out the lowered window she called, "Sheriff, any chance Mr. de la Vega can ride with you?"

"Yes!"

A huge smile spread across the man's face. "I owe you, Mrs. Copeland."

"Go! Y'all come to my house for supper. We'll get to work on Purdue tonight."

"Yes, ma'am." He dashed to the sheriff's SUV.

Penny Ulmer peeled out of the parking lot. Laura Beth sat back in her car and laughed. Then, she went into Gus's to order lunch.

Penny hit the light and siren her vehicle had and gunned the engine.

"Are you crazy?" David yelled.

"Yes. Crazy about you. Why didn't you let me know you were back?"

"Because I'm Enrique right now."

"It's a disguise, and it's coming off."

"Sorry, Pretty Penny. Not right now. It takes a little while to peel this mess off and put it back on."

"So? I get to make love to Enrique de la Vega?"

"He's gay."

She cut him a scathing look, to see a smirk on his face. "I have handcuffs. Maybe I'll just have to detain you."

"Where are Abel and Emma?"

"Madeleine's. Emma wasn't happy about a babysitter, but I wasn't ready to leave her home alone all day."

"Handcuffs?"

"You game?"

"Can you drive faster?"

A couple of hours later, David Black emerged from the master bathroom toweling his short black hair. Penny lay on their bed watching him move. "God! You are so fine." She sat up. "But your face is red."

"The damned adhesive irritates my skin. Do we have hydrocortisone in the first aid kit?"

"Yeah."

"And I need a box to keep my disguise in. I'll have to put it back on."

"Well, the facial hair was interesting, but I prefer my David."

He laughed. "I think you liked me in handcuffs."

"Well"—she grinned and shrugged—"I like being in control."

"Yeah?" He tossed the towel into the bathroom and leapt onto the bed, pinning Penny. "So, do I. Wanna spar?"

"Bring it."

A little later, Penny left the house leaving David with orders to wait on the couch with Leather and Lace who had licked him enough times he felt in need of another shower.

He waited patiently for a short time before he stood and performed a tai chi kata to help with his inner peace. He sat back down with one arm around each dog. "It feels good to be here. I missed you mutts."

Leather barked and placed a paw on David's leg. Lace lay down with her head on his other leg.

A car door slamming caused the two dogs to run to the door. "I really will be fine, Mom, if you let me stay home with Abel." Emma's voice carried through the door.

"Go inside," Penny said.

The door opened and Emma popped in with her back to the inside, tossing a backpack in the corner. Abel came in behind her. "Papa!"

"David?" Emma turned. "Papa?"

Both children ran to him and received tight hugs.

"Are you home?" Abel asked.

"For now. I'll be in and out."

Penny joined the family. "Tonight, we have dinner with Miss Laura Beth."

Tanner opened the door at Laura Beth's when the bell rang. "Ah," he said. "Good to have you home, David. Y'all come in. No fancy meal this evening. Just home cooking."

"Sounds good to me," David said. "What's Laura Beth cooking?"

"Who said she's cooking?"

"You?"

"We're working together."

David wiggled his eyebrows. "Have things progressed?"

"N. O. Y. B."

David laughed and the two men shook hands. "Emma says you've been a slave driver at the martial arts dojo."

"You bet."

"She's complaining about not getting summer vacation from it and that you've even started her on bo."

"Killers don't take vacations."

"True. How's Corbin doing with weapons?"

"Great."

Everyone walked in. Laura Beth and Penny hugged. "Yum," Penny said, peeking into pots. "Fried chicken, mashed potatoes, green beans, corn on the cob. Are you trying to fatten me?"

David slipped his arms around Penny. "I love your curviness."

Laura Beth patted her own behind as she worked at the stove. "I still haven't made it back to the tennis courts and Riker is ten months old."

Penny laughed. "Tanner has you taking self-defense. I've seen how you move." She pointed at her friend as she spoke to her husband. "This chickie can do a full Chinese split, lean all the way over, and touch her nose to the floor."

Tanner laughed and slipped his arms around Laura Beth, kissing her on the neck just below her ear. "My Sugar has many talents." He gave a low growl in her ear, sending shivers all over her.

Laura Beth turned around. "Supper's ready. Gather the kids." She drooped one eye toward Tanner and grinned.

After supper, the adults shooed the children outdoors just as Ed Pickering arrived. "Sorry I couldn't make dinner." He sniffed the air. "Smells like I missed out."

"Another time," Laura Beth assured.

"For sure. So, Mr. Black, what do you have for us?"

"My colleague, Enrique de la Vega, is in town and looking to buy Purdue Plantation. Have you tracked Purdue?"

Penny nodded. "We have to a point. It appears he doesn't come home but once a year."

"Let me guess," David said. "Christmastime."

"Yes." Tanner nodded. "Electric and water bills spike at that time and there are fresh flowers placed on his parents' graves— silk to last a year."

"Where is he now?" asked David.

"God only knows," Penny said. "We know he travels all over the country and into both Canada and Mexico."

"What does he haul?"

"Livestock." Penny wrinkled her nose. "Cows, pigs, chickens, even sheep and goats. If he's grabbing kids, can you imagine the terror from the smell and noise alone?"

Laura Beth shivered. Tanner took her hand. "We haven't been able to coerce information from his lawyer. That's where de la Vega and Laura Beth can help. If they go to Millicent Shapiro, Purdue might bite and come back if de la Vega's offer is magnanimous. At least maybe we can question him."

David nodded with his lips pursed. "Okay then. Enrique will be in your office"—He made eye contact with Laura Beth—"at ten in the morning."

Laura Beth eyed Pickering. He was the only one who did not know David's true identity or that he was also Enrique. "Mr. de la Vega is very rich, I take it."

David leaned his head to the side. "He has unlimited funds."

"Right. Do you have a clue how much he'll offer? I could have documents ready when he gets there."

"What's the value of the property?"

Pickering opened a small notebook he took from his pocket. "Appraised at seven point three million, land and house. Satellite houses not included. Would be more if the fields were cultivated."

David got a gleam in his eyes. "Which Mr. de la Vega might pay me to do eventually."

"Will he actually buy the property?" Pickering slapped the notebook closed.

"Why not?" David looked at Laura Beth. "I'm pretty sure Enrique will offer six million initially. Let's hope Mr. Purdue bites."

19
An Offer He Can't Refuse

David Black walked into a hotel suite near dawn the next morning.

"Where the hell have you been?" rumbled a deep, bass voice.

"Nasser." David shook his head. "With my family." He grinned. "My wife made me an offer I couldn't refuse."

"Did anyone see you come in without your disguise?"

"No. Now"—He held up a bag—"I have to become Enrique again. I could use your help with this shit. And then, you get to be my chauffeur."

Nasser's booming laugh brought a chuckle from David. "When do I get to meet this lovely lady, David?"

"When I don't have to be Enrique."

"Fair enough. And at that time, I shall give you my full name."

"I have a meeting with Laura Beth Copeland, and we're going to Purdue's attorney to make an offer—six mil."

Nasser whistled. "Nice sum. And am I to assume you want to keep the place after all this is over?"

"I think I've earned it as my retirement."

In his best Marlon Brando, Nasser said, "'An offer he can't refuse.'" He stood. "Let us get you looking like Enrique. I think I shall be glad to know David myself."

At exactly ten A.M. Enrique de la Vega came into the real estate office again. Laura Beth was not at her desk. Two agents present pounced on the customer. A bottled-blonde and a young, effeminate, blond-haired, blue-eyed man reached Enrique at the same time. He held up a hand. "Por favor. Señora Copeland."

Laura Beth came down the hallway with documents in her hands. "Señor de la Vega. Susan, Neal, I have this client. Señor de la Vega, meet Susan Lyles and Neal Lister. Susan, Neal, this is Enrique de la Vega. He's making an offer on Purdue Plantation. He works with Penny Ulmer's husband." She turned to the man wearing a suit that would cost her a good two-months' income. "I'm sorry I wasn't here to greet you. Our server was down, and I just got the documents printed. We should go now to Ms. Shapiro's office. I made an appointment for half past ten."

"Good then. My driver awaits." Enrique opened the door.

"Driver?" Laura Beth whispered as she walked past.

David took her arm. "Oh, you have to meet Nasser. Don't let him know you know who I am."

Laura Beth slid into the backseat of the limo. "Nasser," de la Vega said, "meet Laura Beth Copeland."

Looking in the rearview mirror, he rumbled, "Pleasure, ma'am."

"Mr. Nasser." She quirked an eyebrow toward the man beside her.

He just looked out the window. "Sunrise is a quaint town, Señora Copeland."

"I like it."

"Nasser, go to the address Señora Copeland gives you."

"Yes, sir."

"Oh." She fumbled with the folder and handed a card over the back of the seat. "It's just up the road. We could have walked." She eyed the man next to her.

"Señora, perhaps you could arrange a stroll with your colleague, Neal."

Laura Beth's mouth fell open. "I think he has a partner."

"Too bad. He is my favorite type."

"Is this the place?" Nasser asked.

"Yes. Thanks. Will you be waiting?"

He looked in the mirror. "Will I be waiting, sir?"

"Sí."

Laura Beth and Enrique entered the law office of Millicent Shapiro. Just inside the door, Laura Beth said, "You're not actually bisexual, are you?"

"Hell no!"

"Okay. Just your cover. I had to make sure I didn't need to shoot you in the ass again. I almost believed your act."

He chuckled. "Good. Now if only Purdue will."

They approached the receptionist who looked up. "Oh, Laura Beth." She looked at her watch. "Five minutes early."

"We can wait."

The thirty-something woman pointed a light-skinned finger to a short row of chairs. "She's in a meeting with the sheriff."

David twitched. Laura Beth laid her hand on his. "Let's sit."

He whispered when they found their seat, "Penny didn't tell me she was coming today."

"Maybe it just came up."

Millicent Shapiro's office door opened. Penny said, "I'd really like to put up a chain-link fence. Please see if you can get Mr. Purdue to agree to the survey."

"Sheriff, Dillard Purdue is not his father. I don't think he'll quibble over a few feet. Put the fence where you like."

"Fine." Penny turned. "Laura Beth!"

They hugged, and Laura Beth introduced Penny to Enrique. Penny left with a wink.

Millicent Shapiro rolled her eyes. She pointed toward the door. "That is one reason I think I can convince Mr. Purdue to sell, Laura Beth."

"One reason?" asked Enrique, clinching one fist inside his trouser pocket. *Bitch. That's my wife you're talking about, and your client buried bodies on her land.*

Laura Beth felt him tense and looped her arm around his that stuck out of his pocket.

Millicent stuck out her hand and introduced herself. Enrique took it with some reluctance. Millicent said, "Yes. Laura Beth hasn't told you about the discovery?"

"No."

"Laura Beth! Shame!"

"I'll get to it." It was her turn to stiffen.

Enrique looked from woman to woman. "Does this have to do with the bodies that were discovered?"

"You know about it?" Millicent asked.

"Sí. David Black is a good employee. He informed me."

"You know the sheriff's husband?"

"Sí. I believe the news is to my advantage. Señor Purdue might wish to be rid of the property." He nodded toward Laura Beth. "Señora Copeland has prepared a proposal."

Laura Beth handed the documents to Millicent. "Mr. de la Vega is offering six million. I'm sure he's comfortable with you serving as attorney at closing."

Enrique gave a curt nod with a frown on his face. "If she learns discretion and practices business in private. Insulting the wife of one of my best employees is unprofessionable."

Millicent's mouth dropped. She stammered, "My apologies. Please come in and sit while I look this over."

Laura Beth covered her mouth to hide a smile. They followed Millicent into her office and waited in comfortable chairs as the attorney scanned the proposal.

With a nod she said, "Everything seems to be in order."

"Please get with your client and get back to us as soon as possible." Enrique stood.

Laura Beth followed suit. "Gracias, Señorita Shapiro. I have many investments worldwide," de la Vega continued. "I would like to add Purdue Plantation and make it productive again. Please get with Señora Copeland with Señor Purdue's response. Buena dia."

"Of course." Millicent escorted them to the door.

Enrique opened the outer door for Laura Beth, and they waited to speak until entering the limo.

"I hope to hear from her soon," Enrique said. "I shall phone you later. Nasser, take Señora Copeland to her office. I am tired and would like to rest this afternoon."

Laura Beth looked confused and received a wink. She got out and waved as the car pulled away.

In the limo David reverted to his normal speech. "We need to look into Millicent Shapiro. Best case—she's a good lawyer and will represent her client well even in his guilt. She'll push for him to sell. She wants her cut. Worst case—she helps him secure his victims, at least knows more than she's letting on."

"Sixth sense?" Nasser intoned.

"Yeah. Then again, she could just be a gold digger. I just don't like her. She insulted Penny."

A chuckle preceded, "I am still recovering from the fact that little bit being the one who shot you in the ass." He jerked his thumb back toward Laura Beth's office. "Is she aware of who you are?"

"Don't let Little Momma's size fool you. And she's been deputized."

"Ah. Your wife is a beauty also."

"I really am tired. I'd like a nap."

"And you are evasive."

"I had better things to do last night than sleep. Home, James. I'm snoozing."

Laura Beth's phone rang as she prepared dinner for her and Tanner's families, as was becoming a habit. She answered with a cheerful hello.

"Laura Beth, Millicent Shapiro. I reached Mr. Purdue. He's in Mexico at the moment but can be here by this time next week. He'd like to accept Mr. de la Vega's offer. He said to show him the whole property and see if he'd be interested in the farming equipment and home furnishings."

"When can we see the place?"

"I'm free tomorrow afternoon."

"I'll contact Mr. de la Vega and call in the morning."

"Fine. Goodnight."

Laura Beth hung up. "I don't like her."

Tanner laughed. "Why?"

She shrugged. "Gold digger." She dialed David's cell and delivered the news.

Enrique answered and listened carefully. "So, you will call when he arrives, Señora Copeland?"

"Yes. I take it your chauffeur is present."

"Sí."

"Are you afraid of him?"

"Not exactly."

"Are you okay?"

"Sí."

"Do you need a visit from the sheriff?"

"That would be much appreciated."

"Buenas noches."

Laura Beth relayed the cryptic answers to Tanner.

"You met this Nasser?" he asked.

"Yeah. Makes Michael Clark Duncan look small."

"Do you think he'd do something to David?"

"Only if ordered to. I got the feeling he might have a lot of pull on what happens with David's future."

"Ah. Call Penny."

Laura Beth relayed the information to her friend.

Penny laid her phone on the kitchen counter.

"Is everything all right, Mom?" Emma asked.

Looking at two children, Penny said, "I need to go out as sheriff."

"Is it about Papa?" Abel asked with fear edging his voice. "Is he okay?"

"That's what I intend to find out. Emma, I'm leaving you in charge. This is your chance to show me you can be responsible. I know school's out for the summer, but Abel's bedtime is still ten and yours is midnight. I need you to walk the dogs."

"What time should I expect you?" Emma stretched her eyes wide.

"I don't know."

Still in uniform, Penny retrieved her sidearm and prepared to leave. She kissed both children on the cheek. "I love you. I'm going to help Papa."

In the lobby of the fanciest hotel in Sunrise, Penny showed her credentials and demanded to see Enrique de la Vega.

"No problem, Sheriff," the clerk said. "Mr. de la Vega said to expect you. He's in suite five-oh-one."

Penny took the elevator and knocked on the door.

Nasser answered. "She is a beauty, my friend," he intoned over his shoulder. "Nasser." He extended his hand.

Penny shook it. She looked up as her spouse in full Enrique garb, including the white linen slacks and open white shirt, vaulted the sofa. He pulled Penny into the suite. "Don't you have someplace to go?" He lifted one eyebrow toward Nasser.

The big man roared with laughter. "I have been dying to try Gus's Goulash. I eat fast." He paused at the door. "Isooba. It means 'walk stealthily.'"

"What?" David said.

"My last name. I told you I would tell you when I met your wife. My first name is Nasser." Nodding to Penny, he left and could be heard laughing all the way to the elevator.

"A ploy?" Penny nearly screamed. "Just to get me here?"

"I can't really leave and be David right now."

"Is this a booty call?"

"You are never a booty call." He chuckled. "I confess to putting a bug in Laura Beth's ear. Nice to see she cares. "

"Oh! You!" Penny punched him in the chest.

He grabbed his solar plexus. "Damn, woman! You enjoy inflicting pain on me."

"That's not even where I hit you." She pushed him over the couch. "I'll show you pain."

Sometime later, Nasser entered the suite. "Are you decent?" he called.

"No!" David laughed. Penny bit him. "I'll be bruised," he grumbled.

"You love me though."

"Oh, I do." He kissed her. "I had to see you tonight. I won't be able to come home until I get Purdue to sell and can leave my best person"—He touched his own chest—"in charge."

"You could have called."

"Nope. I want Millicent to think you're suspicious of me."

"Gotcha." She rolled out of bed and began to dress. He caught her around the waist. Prying his hands loose, she said, "I have two kids at home."

"You left Emma babysitting?"

"Yes."

"Good call, Pretty Penny."

She leaned forward and kissed him. "I need to go."

He fell back. "I hope this case works itself out fast."

"Me too. I love you."

Penny walked into the sitting area of the suite. "You're a teddy bear, aren't you?" she said to Nasser.

"Unless I need to be a grizzly."

"I bet you can be." She pointed to where her husband was. "Take care of him."

"That is my intent. He is a much better man than he believes. I shall be glad to call him 'friend.'"

Penny nodded and left. When she got home, she found both children and both dogs asleep on her bed. "They feel safe here," she murmured. "Good thing it's king size." She slipped into her room, kicked off her shoes, nudged Emma with, "Move over," and lay beside her daughter to sleep.

The next afternoon, Enrique and Laura Beth met Millicent. They took the limo to the plantation and drove around the property. Without making any comment until the car took Millicent back to her office, the potential buyer merely said, "I shall consider the other properties and equipment once I have spoken with Señor Purdue."

A week later, Laura Beth looked up to see Millicent Shapiro and a man that looked Native American. She appraised him: Shorter and stockier than Tanner. A bit fidgety. A few strands of gray in black hair in a ponytail.

"Laura Beth," Millicent said, "this is Dillard Purdue. Dill, Laura Beth Copeland."

Purdue held out a limp hand. Laura Beth shook it. *Dill?* She felt a gag coming on and forced a smile. "So glad to finally meet you."

"Will you call Mr. de la Vega?" Millicent twittered. "Dill would like to walk around the property with him and, perhaps, convince him to purchase equipment and furnishings."

"Of course." Laura Beth took out her cell and dialed.

"De la Vega," came an answer after two rings.

"Mr. de la Vega, Laura Beth Copeland. Mr. Purdue is in my office and would like to tour the property with you."

"I'll be there shortly after I call Penny. Half an hour?"

"Half an hour is good. Will you bring your driver?"

"Absolutely. We'll take the limo. Relax, Little Momma." He chuckled. "Nasser has my back."

"We'll see you soon." She said to Purdue and his attorney, "He would like to take his limo. Can I get you some coffee or something while we wait?"

"I'd like water, please." Purdue smiled.

God! He's beautiful. Laura Beth could not help noticing. She walked to the break area and returned with a bottled water. Purdue took it and sat in an armchair to wait. Millicent flitted to sit near him. *Maybe Millicent is just man hunting. Sorry to tell her, but she's the wrong gender.*

Laura Beth discreetly texted Tanner of the latest development.

Exactly half an hour later, Enrique de la Vega entered the real estate office. He looked as if he'd stepped from the pages of a travel guide as he wore the white linen slacks that draped to show his package and a white linen shirt with sleeves rolled to the elbow and unbuttoned to reveal the thick patch of hair on his chest. With the tan deck shoes, he looked as if he might be about to set sail.

"Señora Copeland, I came as soon as I could."

Laura Beth stood and shook his hand. "Mr. de la Vega, you remember Ms. Shapiro, and this is Mr. Dillard Purdue."

"Of course." He shook the lawyer's hand and then Purdue's. He let his hand linger on the latter.

Purdue smiled. "My friends call me Dill."

"Am I your friend?"

"I hope so."

"Perhaps. You may call me Enrique. Still, I am most anxious to complete this transaction and return to my villa."

"Where is that?"

"Argentina."

"I've only been as far south as Mexico."

"In Argentina, I have a home and special friends. I make much money and want to have diverse investments: petrol, technology, agriculture, entertainment. I hear from David about your plantation, that it sits fallow. I wish to make it productive."

Purdue nodded. "Then let's visit the place. I hate it, but the land is rich, and I have equipment, and the house is fully furnished."

Laura Beth interjected, "Is that why you only come home once a year?"

Purdue laughed. "Guilt, Mrs. Copeland. I stay long enough to put flowers on my mother's and her husband's graves."

Her husband? Not my father? "You could make arrangements with a florist and not have to come back."

"I'll keep that in mind."

Enrique said. "Shall we go? My driver awaits."

"Let's go," said Purdue. He opened the door for the others to leave. They piled into the limo.

"Nasser, to Purdue Plantation," Enrique instructed.

They drove out of city limits and around a long curve. Laura Beth glanced up to see the road sign that read, "Elm Street."

"Are there any elms, Dill?" she asked as they turned down a long drive with several unoccupied houses before they saw the mansion at the end.

Purdue nodded. "Interspersed with lots of other trees native to Mississippi."

Enrique asked, "Are the servants' homes part of the plantation?"

"Yes, if you add a hundred thousand for each."

"Another million?"

Purdue smirked.

Enrique laughed. "It is about money. Señora Copeland, what would a house like that go for here in this lovely town?"

"How big are they, Dill?" she asked.

"Fifteen to eighteen hundred square feet. All three bedrooms and two baths. They are all the original houses that have been remodeled."

"In this market?" She puckered her lips. "Clapboard siding?"

Purdue nodded. "Original hardwood floors. No carpet. Just like the house itself."

"The smaller ones if kept up would run seventy-five thousand. The larger ones might go for a hundred."

"Hm." Enrique scratched his beard. "I would need workers to live there, I assume as part of their compensation. I will go fifty thousand. They look in need of repair."

"Eighty thousand," Purdue dickered.

"Sixty-five. Final offer."

"You drive a hard bargain. Done."

They stopped in front of a massive antebellum home with flaking paint. Enrique grunted, "Needs work."

Purdue countered, "I think you already came out here."

"Sí, but today we walk."

Laura Beth almost had to run to keep up with her client as he looked carefully at every room in the house, touching and knocking on walls, even in the attic. Then, he began a circular, spiraling trek of the land until they reached the cordoned area.

Purdue panted behind them, "Does he ever get winded? He hasn't even broken a sweat." Then he called, "Enrique, do you run marathons?"

"No, but I stay in shape."

Purdue muttered, "That I can see. I'm dying."

Finally, they returned to the car where Nasser leaned, smoking a Black and Mild. Enrique waved a hand. "Stop at each house."

With precision, Enrique examined each residence with Laura Beth on his heels. Purdue refused to get out of the air-conditioned limousine, and Millicent stayed with him. In a long building much like a chicken house behind the largest outer home, David gripped Laura Beth's hand. Seeing they were alone, he whispered, "It's the truck I dreamed about."

"This was your dream?"

He told her about his nightmare.

"Oh, my, God!" she exclaimed as he tried to open the trailer.

"Locked. Let's get back. I want to get in."

"You think he kills the boys in the truck?"

"I don't know. I didn't see any evidence of murder in any of the dwellings."

Back in the limo, Enrique said, "Impressive rig. Why is it hidden?"

"It's not," said Purdue. "When I have it here, I park it in there to keep it safe. Would you like to see it?"

"Sí."

"How about dinner with me? I have read you right, haven't I?"

"Sí. I would like that."

Laura Beth felt another gag constricting her throat. She touched David's hand. "Are you still buying?"

"Sí. Complete the sale and add another two hundred thousand for the machinery and furnishings."

Nasser coughed.

"Are you all right, Nasser?" Enrique asked.

"Yes, sir."

"Then return us to the real estate office."

When they arrived back at Laura Beth's place of business, Enrique said, "Nasser, return Dill and Señorita Shapiro to their respective locations. Dill, where shall I meet you?"

"If you'd like to see the truck, at the plantation. I actually stay in that smaller house by my makeshift garage."

"Seven?"

"Seven is good."

Enrique entered the office with Laura Beth. "You aren't actually going to do something with him, are you?" she hissed under her breath.

"Only if I have to. I didn't see a damned thing that would prove he's a killer or trafficker."

"Except your nightmare."

"Don't worry about me. I plan to ply him with expensive cognac before anything can happen. I'd like to spend summer vacation with my family. Call Tanner. Tell him about the truck."

"Okay. What about Penny?"

He shuddered.

"I'll call her for you."

"Thanks."

Dressed to seduce and bearing a bottle of Remy Martin Louis XIII cognac, Enrique arrived at the home Purdue used when he came to Sunrise. "I shall be right here if you need back up," Nasser said from his position as chauffeur.

"Thanks."

Enrique took a deep breath and went to the door.

Purdue answered, and his guest entered. An Italian feast waited on the dining table, complete with wine and candlelight.

"Muy bonito," Enrique commented and presented his gift.

"Gracias."

They dined and chatted. Purdue revealed nothing that would paint him a killer.

At last, after two glasses of cognac following the wine with the meal, Purdue put a move on his dinner guest. Enrique pushed away. "I do not do submissive."

"Ah." Purdue sat back. "I will never be a submissive again."

"It seems we are at an impasse."

"Too bad."

"Sí, but I confess, I like my lovers younger, and I prefer blond."

Purdue shivered. "Leaves me out." He stood. "You wanted to see my rig."

"Sí."

Purdue waved a hand toward the back door. Enrique followed him to the truck.

At the chicken house turned garage, Purdue unlocked the trailer and climbed inside. He offered Enrique a hand and helped him in.

"This is very clean," Enrique said. He walked to the walls that were like a cage, allowing air in. "I would have thought livestock would leave a mess."

"So, Millie told you I haul animals?"

"She mentioned it, sí."

"After deliveries, I have the thing scrubbed. I couldn't stand the smell." He pointed out grooves in the floor. "Depending on the animals, different partitions are slid in here."

"Interesting." Enrique walked the length of the vehicle. He scowled, and then turned to his host and placed a subtle kiss on him. "Too bad we do not fit, but I have specific tastes. Still, perhaps, we will be friends."

"Do you ever share?"

Enrique arched an eyebrow as Purdue's voice sounded a bit different.

"I might be able to get you what you want," Purdue explained.

"A threesome?"

Purdue shrugged. "I have connections, and that would be a new experience."

"Hm. Perhaps. How long?"

"I don't know."

Enrique jumped out of the rig. "You have my number. Call when you have news."

20

Questions

Enrique slid into the backseat of the limo. "Home, and I don't mean the hotel."

"What did you discover?"

"There's something off about his rig. He offered to find me a partner."

"You want your wife to bring him in."

"You bet."

"You cannot go home looking as you do."

"Damn it, Nasser." He rubbed both hands down the sides of his face. "You're right. Take me to the hotel." He rubbed his forehead. "May I ask a question about one of the consortium members?"

"I will answer if I can."

"The little Frenchman…"

Nasser's laugh reverberated. "You are wondering how dangerous he can be. Looks are deceptive. Remy Bardin is known for stealth. His code name is Ferret."

"That's Ferret?"

"Yes. You know of his reputation, I see."

"In and out of anywhere undetected. Connoisseur of poisons."

"Oui." Nasser laughed again. "Would you like a rundown on the others?"

"Sure. Entertain me on the drive back. Start with the woman."

"Trojan."

"Computer whiz. Does she have a real name?"

"Tamar Stewart. She is from old money, British aristocracy that married into Indian aristocracy."

"That explains the rudeness. The German."

"Klaus Stein, a master of interrogation. Do not ask more."

"Nazi background?"

"Perhaps. At least his parents could have been. He and I will *not* be having afternoon tea. The Asian is your expert forger. Fu Shin. I do not trust him. The Israeli is Moshe Arnow. He is former Mossad and a sniper of unequaled ability. He and Remy I would trust with my life. I have on a number of occasions. The American is Chameleon. I do not know his name, and I am certain that the face we saw was not his."

"I've heard of him. Master of disguise. And the man with the long gray hair who never spoke until the end?"

"Varujan Daesque. Right now, he is our leader."

"Why are you telling me all this now?"

Nasser glanced over his shoulder. "You and Mosely have earned it."

David chuckled. "And Alfie?"

"Alfred Honeycutt would die rather than betray a one of us."

"Code name?"

David did not think Nasser could possibly laugh louder, but he was sure the passing traffic heard the big man's guffaw. "You will love this, my friend. Drama Queen."

David's chortle rivaled Nasser's.

With the chuckles still spasmodic, David said, "And your code name?"

Immediate seriousness took over when Nasser answered solemnly, "Reverend."

"That one's strange."

"No. I am an ordained minister. Even with my size, many will trust me simply due to that fact."

"Maybe that's why I feel fairly comfortable with you. I trust you."

"And I you."

Back in his suite, David called his wife. "Bring him in." He relayed his thoughts.

Early the next morning, deputies detained Dillard Purdue and brought him to the sheriff for questioning. The first words from his lips were, "I want my lawyer."

When Millicent Shapiro arrived, Penny began her questions.

"Mr. Purdue, I know you must have heard about the bodies found on your property."

"It was all over CNN."

"Why didn't you contact my office when you knew we were looking for you?"

"I had every intention of visiting your office on my annual pilgrimage."

"Dead boys didn't compel you to come for an extra visit?" She glared across the table.

"I called my attorney. She advised against it."

Penny shot Millicent a look. "Counselor, perhaps, I should charge you with obstruction of justice."

Purdue said, "What would you like to know, Sheriff?"

"Why are you following in your father's footsteps?"

"If by *father* you mean Colvin Purdue, I think I'm not following him at all. I'm not a farmer, and I'm even selling the place. If he killed anyone, I know nothing about it."

"Did you?"

"No."

On the table between them, Penny placed photos of the most recent victim. "So, you have no knowledge of this?"

Purdue's eye twitched and he turned his head away.

Shapiro intervened. "I believe those remains were found on property belonging to Laura Beth Copeland."

"True, but several more bodies were unearthed on Mr. Purdue's property."

"I don't even live here anymore!" he blurted.

"No, but you do visit, and this child was killed about the time you would have been home. He came up missing last August. Where were you in August?"

"Vancouver, if I recall."

"Dill, be quiet," snapped Shapiro.

Penny nodded. "Not too far from Portland, Oregon."

"If you have a charge for my client, do it." Shapiro stood. "Otherwise, we're gone."

Penny sighed. "Child molesters are scum."

Purdue rolled his eyes. "Because I'm gay, I'm now a child molester?"

"You're gay?" Millicent squeaked.

Purdue chuckled. "Why do you think I've never paid any attention to your advances? You can hang up flirting with Enrique too." The timber of his voice changed. "I've had one woman in all my years, and she vanished without any explanation from my life."

"Who?" Penny asked from sheer curiosity.

Dill gave her a truly beautiful, but sad, smile.

"A gentleman does not kiss and tell."

Millicent almost whispered, "Oh, my God! How can two such gorgeous men be gay?"

"Maybe they were molested." Penny looked sternly at Purdue.

"Is that a question, Sheriff?" He cocked an eyebrow.

"Could be."

Purdue laughed. "Colvin Purdue was a bastard. Former sheriffs called knocking on our door investigating domestic violence. 'Oh, no officer.' That's all it took for them to turn a blind eye. And when we did fight back, we paid dearly." He hiked a sleeve to show a long scar.

"I'm sorry. *I* would have investigated."

"Yeah. Sure. Probably like you've looked for Lynn."

"Lynn?"

"I've said enough about her. Now, if there's nothing more…"

"I guess we won't see you again, huh?"

"Not once I have Enrique's money."

"And if more bodies turn up, I guess Mr. de la Vega did it."

"Only in Argentina."

After Purdue left, Tanner escorted Enrique de la Vega into the interrogation room. Ed Pickering had joined the sheriff.

A smirk played around Enrique's lips. "All that is missing is bamboo shoots for my fingernails."

"What can you tell us?" Pickering demanded.

"I am trained in investigation. I saw no evidence of anything out of place as I toured the property. Remember I am doing this for a friend, although I have secured an excellent investment."

"Okay."

"Agent Pickering, patience is a virtue."

"That would be Special Agent."

"My apologies. I also was privileged to inspect his truck and trailer. Nothing obvious catches the eye. However, I think the dimensions are off."

"You're an expert on big rigs?"

"No."

Pickering shook his head. "We have nothing. There's not enough evidence to tear that truck apart. We'll have to get a warrant."

Enrique cleared his throat. "He did offer to get me a partner—young and blond."

"No crime if he finds you an eighteen-year-old blond boy."

"Then I have done all I can do. I am returning to my villa until the sale is complete. I will leave all my contact information." He stood.

Pickering stood. "Thanks for trying."

Enrique walked out.

Pickering pointed. "We haven't seen the last of him." He grinned at Penny. "Have we, Sheriff?"

Enrique climbed into his limo. "Get to Purdue before he takes off."

As the limo approached Elm Street, Purdue's rig waited to enter the road.

Nasser blocked it in.

Enrique climbed out of the backseat, and Purdue descended from the cab. "Are you leaving?" Enrique asked.

"I have a job and an assignment to find something for a friend."

"I would like to dine with you again. Can work not wait one more day? Then, I, too, shall leave until all legalities are done."

Purdue twirled his ponytail around his finger. "There's nothing between us. Why?"

"We are kindred spirits." Enrique waved a hand. "Leave the truck where it is. Come. You must eat at this Gus's Goulash with me." He knitted his brow. "Do you have nothing smaller to drive?"

"No." Purdue huffed. "Fine." He climbed back into his truck and cut the engine.

Enrique returned to his car texting Tanner. "Get Luis to the rig now. He's leaving town."

21

On the Road Again

While Enrique de la Vega dined with Dillard Purdue, Luis Montoya and Tanner McGill installed a tracking device and video surveillance in Purdue's semi. Luis explored the interior of the trailer. "I think that David's right. The dimensions are off."

"A tad wider, maybe."

"I don't think so. It appears standard, eight feet, six inches by a hundred two inches. It's these strange grooves that got my attention."

"How so?"

"He hauls different livestock, so, of course the partitions would need to be adjustable." Luis walked to the center of the trailer. "Here in the middle, though, it looks like you could add a special carrier smack dab in the middle and still surround it by animals. And an eighty- to a hundred-pound child would not tip the weigh station scales. "

"Even half a dozen kids wouldn't." Tanner pointed toward the equipment. "The video is just like Skype, right?"

"Same principle, but he won't know it's there."

"But the GPS tracking, it doesn't have that long a range."

"I'm certain David and his bodyguard plan to follow Purdue."

"Ah, of course. Presto-change-o."

"You know, I've known David is Marin who is also de la Vega, even before he started the dojo. That man has some stones. I did undercover druggie, and it was hard as hell. Not sure I could do pedophile. Don't worry. His secret is safe."

"Good. Now let's get out of here."

Near midnight, Enrique delivered a somewhat inebriated Dillard Purdue to his final night to sleep on Purdue Plantation. Enrique caressed the other man's arm. "Promise me again that you will wait until morning to drive that monstrosity. I do not want to be responsible for your driving under the influence and having an accident."

"I promise." He sighed. "I wish I could convince you to stay the night."

"No. We are too much the same." Enrique laughed. "Perhaps we were brothers in a past life."

Purdue scowled. "One totally screwed-up brother is enough."

"Pardon?"

"Nothing. Perhaps one day you can show me your country. I'll see if I can find you that companion."

"I look forward to hearing from you." Enrique leaned in and kissed Purdue before Purdue exited the limo.

Nasser eased away. "My hat is off to you, David. That was a flawless performance. Did he mention a brother?"

"Yes. There is no record of a sibling."

"Strange."

"Yes. Now, to the hotel and get Luis Montoya there. I'm hiring him to accompany David."

"It sounds as if I am being dismissed."

"Nasser, you stand out far too much."

"I suppose I do, and Purdue has not seen Mr. Montoya."

"Or David Black."

"What will I do?" The big man glance over his shoulder.

"Keep the suite and be ready to respond. If anyone asks about me, I went overseas."

It was hard to tell which spouse screamed louder—Penny Ulmer or Marge Montoya—before their husbands packed into David's Impala ready to follow Dillard Purdue, surveillance equipment and all.

Luis took Marge by the arms at the shoulders. "I'm being paid extremely well for this job."

She tried to shake loose, but he tightened his grip. She pouted, "So, you're just taking off with someone you barely know."

"No, baby. I'm helping someone catch a killer."

She glared at her husband and hissed, "He's Marin, isn't he?"

"No clue."

"Liar. He's going to kill Purdue, probably without due process—judge, jury, and executioner."

"No, but if Purdue proves to be our boy, I won't stop him. And he's determined to get the trafficker." He let go. "Damn it! The man adopted Emma."

"And married Penny." She scowled. "Am I the only one in the dark?"

"Don't know what you're talking about, sweetie."

"Okay. Fine. But if you die, I'll hate you forever."

"I promise not to die."

Penny was just as angry. "I thought this was going to be long-distance surveillance."

"Penny!" Exasperation gushed in that one word. "How can I take down this trafficker here?" He jabbed a finger downward into thin air. "Think like a cop, not a woman."

She arched one eyebrow. "I *am* a woman who just happens to be a cop." She walked away, one hand on her hip and one on her head. "I just have to live with the fact that you're on the road again. How are we supposed to have a marriage, a family?"

"Pretty Penny." He held out his arms. "Please?"

She huffed but slid into his embrace. He kissed the top of her head. "Nasser has promised to push for my retirement after this. I'll get to keep all of Enrique's assets. I guess, I'll be a farmer."

"Can you really let it go?"

"For you, anything."

"No." She pushed back. "I would never want you to resent me."

"This mission is of my own choosing, but it needs to be my last. Something changed when I came here. I'm not that hard-ass I used to be. You, the Laura Beth incident, made me realize I'm not a heartless bastard."

"Sh." She laid a finger on his lips. "Go get these jerks. Be careful. Stay safe. Come back and be my husband, Abel and Emma's papa, and a farmer." She kissed him. "If you need action, teach martial arts and help Luis. Does he know who you really are?"

"Yeah. He figured it out."

"I know you won't be able to resist if the right situation presents itself. Do me one favor."

"Name it."

"If you *must* take an assignment, always tell me you're going even if you can't tell me where you're going."

"I promise."

"Okay. Go before I change my mind and cuff you."

He held her close a moment longer. "I love you." He was out the door.

Luis yawned and took a long slurp from the coffee he held. He glanced at the console. "He must still be asleep."

David drummed his fingers on the steering wheel. "He's a lightweight with booze. I bet he has one hell of a hangover."

Luis sat up. "He's moving. He'll pass us in about fifteen minutes. Remember to stay back to avoid detection." He tapped his tracker. "This baby will keep up with him even if we lose sight." He booted up one of several laptops. "Empty trailer." He tapped a different button, and a split screen appeared.

David laughed as he watched Purdue down a B.C. Powder with a long swig of coffee. "Told you he'd have a hangover."

"Yeah. He's alone."

About fifteen minutes passed before the scorpion truck rumbled by. David waited until Purdue turned the bend to pull onto the county highway. He stayed a healthy distance behind the truck as Purdue followed the Mississippi River south on Highway 61 toward Vicksburg and the bridge across the river on Interstate 20 into Louisiana.

A short distance into Louisiana, Purdue pulled into a truck stop. He ran into the restroom and then sat at the bar to order breakfast.

David and Luis slipped in and took a booth. As long as they had to wait, they decided to grab a bite as well.

Purdue took his time eating, but the other two ate quickly and made a pit stop in the toilet. They returned to the car to wait.

Seeming to be in no big hurry, Purdue paid his tab and sauntered back to his rig.

The drive continued on I-20, bypassing Dallas and turning south onto I-35 with a couple of weigh station stops. After six hours, Purdue pulled into another truck stop. He went in, showered, and ordered more food.

David and Luis waited. "We can't be seen again," David muttered.

Purdue came out and crawled into the cab and the sleeper compartment.

"He's going to sleep," David said in disbelief.

"Good. It gives us a chance to eat and bathe."

"You go first."

"Diego…"

"Excuse me?"

"Sorry. David, he's sleeping. We can take a short break."

"You're right."

"Yes, I am. However, we will take turns showering. Then, we'll eat and get some sleep ourselves."

"In shifts."

"Of course. It's going to be a bitch sleeping in this heat in a black car."

David pointed. "Sleeping bag on the grass under the trees."

Luis pointed across the parking area. "Cheap-ass motel. One room. You get four hours. Then I'll take four. Now, I'm showering, and not in the truck stop." He walked to the motel and got a room.

The night passed without incident. The sleuths grabbed a quick breakfast before Purdue ever woke.

Near eight, Purdue ate a large breakfast and got on the road again. A black Impala followed.

The cab cam picked up a phone ringing. Purdue answered and spoke in halting Spanish, but with a higher pitched voice. "Buenas dias, Ortega...Shipment to Baja? Fillies? Sí....I'm in Texas. Need to stop at home...A week...Do you have any blond colts? No, for a friend this time...What do you care? I'll call." The phone conversation ended.

David and Luis eyed each other. "Real horses?" Luis asked, wide-eyed.

"Or is it code for young girls and boys?"

Mozart's *Requiem* suddenly blared.

David shook his head. "Never figured him for classical."

They continued their trailing to the outskirts of Tucson, Arizona, and a small peach-colored adobe house set out from town.

Purdue unlocked the rust-colored door and went inside just as darkness fell.

22
Trip down Memory Lane

David wiped sweat from his brow with the back of his hand.

Luis eyed him. "At least it's not as humid here, and once the sun goes down, the temp will drop dramatically."

"I recall desert weather."

Luis unbuckled his seatbelt and retrieved a case. He lowered his window before he opened the case and took out a couple of metal tubes and something that resembled a steamer basket when popped open.

David watched his friend's nimble fingers. Along the bottom of the case, Luis clicked open a ridge and inserted the connected tubes with the basket attached to the top. Then, he manipulated a dial on the ridge. Before long, Dillard Purdue's voice came through a small speaker in the corner of the case.

"I love parabolic surveillance." Luis grinned.

"Pretty cool, but who the hell is he talking to?"

"Let's listen and find out."

David lowered his window and cut the engine. The desert air at night cooled fast, and soon both men donned light jackets. They sat back and listened.

"Well, well, well," said a voice that was higher pitched than Dillard's. "You finally admit what you are."

"If I had met Enrique long ago, I would never have needed you."

David elbowed Luis. "I've heard that voice. The night Dillard and I had dinner, but only for a moment."

"Sh." Luis scowled. "Same one as on the phone."

The voice said, "From what I heard, your Enrique would like me better."

"He prefers blonds, not assholes."

A cackling laugh preceded, "I think he loves assholes."

Dillard snorted. "Oh, you and your warped humor."

"Just not yours, big brother."

"Shut up, Phil. You know, I hate you."

"But you can't survive without me. Not after what Daddy did."

Dill growled like a rabid dog.

"And gave you experience with a woman. No reason not to have the best of both worlds." Sarcasm filled Phil's laugh.

In the car, David phoned Penny. When she answered, he said, "There is no record of Dillard Purdue having a brother, right?"

"None."

He cut his eyes toward Luis as he spoke to his wife. "Then I think we have a seriously mentally disturbed man on our hands. Luis and I are listening to two distinct voices carrying on a conversation—well, arguing. The new voice referred to Dillard as 'big brother.'"

Penny asked, "Are you recording this?"

"Yes, we're recording." He lifted an eyebrow toward Luis for confirmation and received a nod.

"Get everything you can," Penny said. They closed by exchanging, "Love you."

David looked toward his surveillance genius. "You got any infrared?"

Luis grinned and wiggled his eyebrows. "I have it all." From the backseat, he pulled a camera that plugged into his laptop. The palm-sized recording device buzzed softly as it booted up.

"You think the man's dissociative. There'll be only one warm body inside."

"You bet."

Luis hung his arm out his window and aimed the camera toward the living room where a light had come on. They continued to monitor and record.

Dillard went on with his conversation. "Colvin was *not* my father! I hate him more than I hate you. And you know I don't like to talk about him, and you can leave Lynn out of anything you have to say."

"Only one image," Luis confirmed.

Dillard changed ends of the sofa in the house. Phil spoke. "But you don't see Enrique as just like him? I mean, he asked for a young blond companion—just like the ones Daddy always had."

"Stop it!" Dillard's infrared hands reached out hands as if to strangle something in front of him. Then, it seemed as if his hand was slapped away.

Phil laughed. "You haven't got the balls to hurt me—or anyone."

"If you so much as mention Enrique being remotely like *your* father, I'll kill you."

"Right!" Phil laughed again. "Your mommy had to get Daddy his little toys just to keep you safe."

"Enrique would never hurt anyone like your father did." Dillard stood and paced. He stopped and pointed to an empty space. "And you! You're just like him. I told you to stay here, but you tried to talk to Enrique."

"He would have wanted me. I'm his preference."

"I went back to get rid of your playhouse. If I can't get rid of you, I can at least do away with that evil place."

"Dillard Purdue! That place is where I thrive."

"I know, Phillip Purdue. I don't want you to thrive. As soon as I get Enrique his gift, I'll never go back to Sunrise again."

"But I will. I have to."

"Over my dead body."

"That can be arranged."

It appeared someone punched Dillard, and he fell back.

"Get off me!" he screeched. "You can't live without me either."

"I hate you. You're a sniveling weakling."

"I hate you more."

Dillard grabbed both sides of his head and began to sob. He fell onto the sofa. Soon all became silent.

"He's asleep," said Luis barely above a whisper.

"I'll be damned," David murmured. "No doubt he was abused and molested. In order to keep her son safe, Harriet *did* help get Colvin victims. At some point, another personality manifested in order to help Dillard cope."

Luis nodded. "Phillip, and Phillip is our current killer. But that's still strange. Dissociative personalities aren't usually violent."

"Usually." David nodded. "Dillard wants Phillip dead. He doesn't want this nightmare to continue." David rubbed his temples. "But the only way to get rid of Phillip is to get rid of Dillard. Phillip will fight to stay alive."

"I'd say that neither can survive without the other." Luis looked at David. "Enrique really made an impression on Dillard, and it sounds as if Phillip might actually be bi-sexual."

"Unfortunately." He gusted a breath. "But there was a woman, at least one. It sounds as if Dill might actually love the woman, but he couldn't perform sexually with a woman. Thus, another reason to have Phil around. Damn!" David rubbed his temples. "This is giving me a headache. And I'd really hate to hurt a person who has already been hurt beyond repair."

Luis took a deep breath and plunged into his next question. "David, do you have something in common with Dillard?"

"Yeah. Too much."

"Care to elaborate?"

"No."

"Okey-dokey." He reclined the seat and prepared to sleep.

"It's not you, Luis. Suffice to say we were both molested by our fathers."

"I thought you were an orphan."

"It's a trip down memory lane I don't want to take."

"I can respect that. Let's get some rest. You take first watch."

"Yeah. Sleep tight."

Soon Luis snored.

David gripped the steering wheel. *I'm not gay or bi, and I'm not a pedophile. I've never had an issue performing when it came to straight sex. Still, I've only ever loved one woman—my Pretty Penny. But, my God! I have killed a lot of people. God, forgive me. I don't want to kill Dillard, but I will if all else fails. And I have every intention of killing this trafficker. After that— no more. I swear it.*

23

Across the Border

Early the next morning, Purdue roared his rig to life. Luis nudged David. "He's leaving."

David rubbed his eyes. "I have to piss."

"Make it quick."

David took care of his personal needs behind a pile of sage brush. Purdue's rig rumbled by the barely hidden black car. David waited three minutes and pulled onto the road.

"Where's he headed?" asked Luis.

"Mexico."

"That Baja delivery?"

"Yep."

"Do you think he's picking up girls?"

"Yeah, I do. And I think there's an auction in Baja."

Luis chuckled. "Dillard or Phillip?"

"God! I know he's totally screwed up in the head, but this has to stop." David ran his hand across his head. "I'll think twice about taking his head, but not the lowlifes he works for."

"What if we find he's not the mule?"

"I'll cross that bridge then."

They followed Purdue due south from Tucson, toward Nogales, Mexico. Traffic backed up for miles as Border Patrol on both sides checked vehicles.

A good three cars behind their quarry, David observed, "Nogales. Not a big place."

"Good plan. Hide in plain sight."

"Chances are the general population might be terrified of the cartel."

"That too." Luis pointed. "He's been cleared to cross."

David jabbed a finger toward the laptop. "You need to hide that."

Luis chuckled and pulled up a mahjong game on the screen.

Twenty minutes later, they crossed the border. Luis brought up the surveillance screen. "He's still on the move."

"He must have a bladder the size of Texas."

About fifty miles farther south, before Magdalena, in the middle of nowhere, Purdue turned onto a dirt road. David passed the turn-off and pulled onto the miniscule shoulder.

"We can't really follow down the goat path," he muttered.

"Are we on foot then?" Luis asked.

"Looks like it." He pointed "Let's stash the car in that clump of tumbleweed. Can you carry that stuff?"

"That's what the backpack is for."

Luis stowed his equipment and shouldered the pack. David stuffed another pack with water, granola, and jerky. Then, he pulled his cased katana from inside a hidden compartment beneath the backseat.

"You think you'll need that?" Luis asked, his brow etched in worry.

"Don't know, but I won't leave it here. Too valuable."

"More than the car?"

"To me." David caressed the case. "This blade has saved my ass many a time."

"Gotcha." Luis added a shoulder holster and a nine-millimeter. Both men relieved themselves and began a hike.

A mile up the road, they came to a mesh fence interlaced with barbed wire and topped with razor wire. They crept along the perimeter. Ducking behind a saguaro cactus, David pointed out three guard towers and the iron gate guarded by two armed men.

"Have any doubts now?" he asked.

"No, except which personality." Luis went about setting up parabolic and infrared surveillance. He opened multiple laptops onto a tarp.

"It'll take you a year to pack that shit," David grumbled.

"Trust me." He pointed. "See. Our boy—boys—have stopped. Now listen."

David cringed listening to Purdue speak badly accented Spanish.

Luis typed a sequence, and the cab camera moved, catching Purdue and a Latino man with a beard.

"Well, shit!" exclaimed Luis. "Definitely can't be seen. That's Jorge Ortega."

"The only one of Perez's men to get away?"

"The one."

"So, he's stopped drug trafficking and gone to humans?"

Luis shrugged. "Who said he stopped?"

"Good point. Double trouble."

They listened for a while before the men moved away. Luis angled his parabolic equipment.

"How many are you shipping?" asked Purdue.

They heard sheep bleating, and the conversation was garbled.

Purdue's voice came through. "So, Antonia has secured my gift?"

Luis punched David's arm. "Phillip's voice."

"Yeah."

Ortega said, "Sí. You can get it when you make this delivery."

David pointed to the laptop. "Check to see what's happening in the trailer."

That camera showed workers sliding in metal partitions. "They seem to be leaving a center section open," Luis said.

"Looks like it."

Leaving the video feed going, they turned back to the conversation between Purdue and Ortega to hear the latter invite the former to dinner.

David's stomach grumbled at the mention of food. Luis laughed. "Open your pack. I think we'll be here a while."

David passed out food and water, and they relaxed as much as possible. They heard any number of conversations as Luis had to continually adjust the parabolic microphone before they eavesdropped on dinner and talk that could have taken place at any meal.

The laptop stream caught their attention as bleating grew louder. "There!" shouted David.

"I see—six girls."

David's hand went to his katana. Luis's hand caught it. "No. We have to get both sources. We know where this is. Time for your friend to help."

"Damn it! I know."

"Hey, you have my permission to take Ortega's head, but later."

"Yeah, yeah."

"Time for us to get back to the car."

24

Special Delivery

Purdue's truck bumped by the dark car camouflaged against the desert night and behind a think batch of tumbleweed. Luis feverishly worked to get the tracking equipment operational again as David muttered against the bleating, "'Baa, baa, black sheep, have you any wool'?"

"What?"

"One of the sheep is black. Even in this low light the face stood out with all the white ones around it."

"I'm giving myself a nervous breakdown getting this equipment up and running"—He shook his head—"And you're quoting nursery rhymes. I can't believe you actually noticed the sheep."

David shrugged. As the rig's taillights left view, he pulled the car onto the road.

"Bingo!" Luis's shout sounded triumphant. He reached into the knapsack between the seats and handed David water and granola. "Relax. It's a long ride to Baja."

"My ass hurts. I need a good workout."

Luis laughed out loud. "Worse than when Laura Beth shot you in it?"

"Ha, ha." David flipped his partner the bird.

"Sorry."

"No sweat." He released a long sigh. "You know, I'm taking Ortega's head eventually."

"I'll watch and applaud."

"I wonder who's on the other end of this jaunt."

"We'll find out in about fourteen hours."

"I don't believe this," David muttered.

"Me either." Luis puffed out his cheeks. "He's actually going back across the border."

"The roads are almost nonexistent between Magdalena and Mexicali."

"Yeah, and maybe he's going to California, rather than Mexico. Could the place be in San Diego?"

"Could be. It's a nice little resort area at Rosarito Beach. And he does have to do something with the sheep. But you would think that it would be safer to stay in Tijuana."

They watched intently as the drug dogs circled the rig. "He's not smuggling drugs, morons," David grumbled.

"Or illegals, but he does have people. Come on. Find the girls."

David growled, "But if they do, our mission goes bust."

"Shit. Well, they didn't find anything. He's going through."

"And so are we."

After a thorough inspection of their vehicle by Border Patrol, they continued on the tail of Purdue.

Purdue made several stops en route to his destination. David and Luis noted that he entered the trailer at each stop.

"Humph!" David grunted. "Presumably to care for the livestock."

"Yeah," agreed Luis. "He has some precious cargo."

"At least his stops give us a chance to find a restroom and grab a bite to eat."

"And gas up." Luis chuckled. "Penny's rubbing off on you. You're finding something positive in our situation."

"Penny's the best thing that ever happened to me. She is my special delivery straight from Above." He let out a long breath. "I love her and can't wait to get home."

"I know what you mean. I feel the same about Marge. And Tanner? Oh, yeah. He feels the same about Laura Beth."

"He's one patient man with her for sure."

"Heads up." Luis tapped the computer screen. "He's turning onto a county road."

"Outside city limits." They remained a discreet distance behind, finally stopping outside a gate with a sign that read, "Baa-Ram-Ewe Shearers."

Luis quickly set up the parabolic equipment.

"How many?" a distinctive female voice asked.

"Three dozen sheep. Six fillies."

"The wool will be harvested tonight. I have buyers lined up for the other merchandise."

"Ortega said you have what I want?"

"I do. Let's get everything unloaded. Then you'll get your bonus."

The woman began to bark orders. Purdue mumbled something about not being the hired help, and Luis began a voice-recognition trace on the woman.

Sometime later, Luis shouted, "Antonia Herro!" A few more keystrokes yielded, "A rap sheet going back to her teens. Drugs, prostitution, check fraud. Originally from San Diego." He turned the screen so David could see the photo.

"Shit! That's Tia Rojas, Perez's mistress."

"Well, well. Seems she and Ortega went into their own business when Perez went to the big house. Good thing they kept quiet, or their heads would have been served up with all those you tried to keep alive."

"I had enough on my hands trying to keep Laura Beth alive after she discovered Mrs. Perez's head."

Luis stared at the screen. "I never once saw this chick with Perez while I was undercover." He grunted. "Of course, he used women. She was probably one of many. But why use an alias?"

David scowled. "Any chance she was undercover? Maybe a snitch?"

"Not FBI."

"DEA? They get info; she goes her merry way to do something worse."

"Could be."

"Can you compile a file fast? I want to send it to Mosely. I can't be everywhere at once."

"Sure."

Within an hour, Luis said, "Got a special delivery for your boss if you get me somewhere with Wi-Fi."

Just as he spoke, David's "Enrique" phone rang. He put a finger to his lips. "Ola. Enrique de la Vega...Buenos dias, Dill...You found what I want, but you need a little time to get it to me. How long?...I see...No, Señora Copeland has not called...I await your next call."

Luis held up a hand when the call ended. "Listen. It's Phil again. And look." He turned the computer screen again.

A blond teenage boy got into the cab with Purdue. "Have you hurt him?" the man demanded of Antonia.

"No. He's a little older than your usual."

"Not for me. For a friend. Is he old enough to consent?"

A slap made both men listening jump. "Answer the man," Antonia screeched.

"Hey!" Dillard's voice took over. "Don't hit the kid."

"I'm sixteen," another voice said.

"Okay," Dillard said. "Old enough to consent in Mississippi. What's your name?"

"Aaron."

"Aaron?"

"What the hell difference does it make," grunted Antonia.

"It matters to me," Dillard asserted.

"Gunn," the boy said. "Aaron Gunn."

Dillard said. "Okay. How'd you hook up with this bitch?"

"If you want, I'll show you bitch," Antonia hissed. "He was turning tricks on the street."

"Runaway?" Dillard asked.

No answer came. "Why?" Dillard's voice continued.

"I got tired of the beatings."

"Who beat you?"

"My dad when he was drunk."

"Siblings?"

"No."

"You okay going with me? I promise my friend won't beat you."

"He just wants sex?"

"A companion. He's filthy rich and lives in South America."

"Cool. Yeah. I'm okay."

"Good. Antonia, you can leave us."

A woman's voice uttering obscenities and profanities could be heard fading away.

Dillard said, "Aaron, in a couple of weeks, I'll take you to him."

Sudden bleating drowned out more conversation.

"Time to move," Luis said. "He's taking the naked sheep home. Hopefully, one of the truck stops will have Wi-Fi, and I can send this file to your contact."

"Yeah." David pulled onto the road ahead of the truck and waited for Purdue to eventually pass.

Luis kept up the conversation. "Whatcha gonna do when you get the kid?"

"Hell if I know."

Luis began to chuckle as David drove onto the main road. "What's funny?" David demanded.

"Aaron Black. You'll adopt him—give Penny another special delivery son." He laughed harder. "All this time, I thought you were this super badass. No! You're a big soft marshmallow."

"I guess I am with kids. I'm not ashamed to admit it."

"Good enough. It's not a bad thing." He looked over his shoulder. "Our boys are behind us now. What state tag do you have on this baby?"

"Texas. Don't worry. He won't associate it with Mississippi."

As he spoke, the "Enrique" phone rang.

"Ola, Dill," David answered.

"I'll have your delivery ready by the end of July."

"That suits me well. I must go to Spain for a while to visit with my entertainment company. Is there a chance you can procure new talent for me? I shall pay handsomely."

"New talent? What kind of entertainment do you produce?"

"Americans would call it adult, but the branch caters to those with unusual tastes."

"Unusual?"

"BDSM, for one."

"Uh-huh. Kiddy porn?" The voice changed.

"On occasion."

"Well, shit!"

"Not for me personally. Young, yes, but old enough to make the decision."

"Male or female?"

"I have clients who go both ways."

"I might know someone."

David nodded at Luis. Luis pointed to an ear bud and the computer screen to indicate he was recording the conversation on that end.

David said, "Let me place a call to Señora Copeland about our transaction. When we meet, you can make a delivery and, perhaps, we can arrange more business."

"I'd like that. Until then."

The call ended. Luis chortled. "Phil is pursuing you."

"I get that. Dill won't be happy about it." David grimaced. "I'm afraid for Dill to survive at all, Phil has to die. How do I kill a personality?"

"I don't know. Let's get past this. I think we can go home. Let your Mosely see about the girls in Cali. Spend the next month with your family. Get ready to close on a couple of deals at the end of the month."

"Okay. The cameras will still give us feed, right?"

"Yeah."

"Okay. Let's go home."

25

Off the Streets

Stopping briefly for Luis to upload files to Mosely so Mosely could pose as a buyer and rescue the victims and again to get gifts for their families, David and Luis took turns driving to arrive in Sunrise at sunrise on The Fourth of July. Luis whooped, "Get me home so I can make some fireworks."

David laughed and stopped to let Luis out of the car. Luis said, "See y'all tonight at the balloon glow and fireworks display." He grabbed all his equipment.

"Yeah. Go surprise Marge."

"You go find your Lucky Penny."

"Pretty Penny, but I can only call her that in private."

Luis waved as he opened the door to his home.

David sped to his house. He let himself in and could hear Penny singing in the kitchen. Surprised Leather and Lace were not barking, he surmised Penny had installed the chain link fence she wanted, and the two dogs were romping across the back of the property.

He peeked around the kitchen door and watched his wife still in her pajamas, wearing headphones, and making coffee. He sneaked up behind her and engulfed her. Instantly, he found himself flipped over her hip and on the floor, Penny's hand poised to strike.

"Are you crazy?" she shrieked.

"Yes. About you." He pulled her face down and kissed her.

As the sun climbed higher in the sky, David and Penny returned to the kitchen after passionate lovemaking. David handed her a small box from his bag he had dropped on the floor by the door. "I love you."

She opened the gift to find a silver and turquoise bracelet. "It's beautiful."

Before she could show proper appreciation, they heard squeals of, "Papa!"

Both Emma and Abel barreled in. After prolonged hugs, David reached into his bag, pulled out a box, and handed each child a dream catcher with turquoise and silver woven in. Penny caught sight of another one but did not ask questions.

David said, "Hang them above your beds to keep nightmares away."

Barking at the back door made him laugh. "Open the door."

Two dogs loped in as Penny opened the door. David gave both of them loving and produced silver and turquoise collars.

"You went on a shopping spree," Penny said.

He shrugged. Penny scowled because she knew something was brewing in her husband's mind.

Later in the day, David asked, "Are we going to the Independence Day celebration?"

"Yep," Penny answered. "I was to meet Laura Beth and Tanner."

"Works for me. Luis and Marge?"

"Marge, yeah, so, I guess Luis now as well." Penny set her mouth. "You aren't going to tell me anything, are you?"

"I've told all I have. I sent you daily updates."

She sat on his lap. "You're keeping something quiet."

"Nope. I just want some time with my family before Purdue comes and I have to become Enrique again."

Penny started to speak. He put a finger to her lips. "Please. Leave it alone. I promise I'll talk to you about it later, just not today."

The families met at the annual celebration where bands played; vendors set up with food, drink, and souvenirs; dozens of hot air balloons put on a show; carnival-like games awarded prizes; and the night ended with a fireworks display.

As the children played and the mothers visited, David dragged Tanner to the side. "I need you to look into someone."

"Who?"

"A teen named Aaron Gunn."

"Your toy?"

"Yeah. He told Purdue he ran away because his father drank and beat him."

Tanner rubbed his head. "Oh, boy. Do I see another adoption in your future?"

David shrugged. He whispered, "I still have to talk to Penny."

"Okay. I'll need Pickering's help on this."

"Fine."

Tanner pointed. "Speak of the devil."

"He's still here?"

"Won't leave until the case is solved."

"I guess that's good."

Pickering arrived and made pleasantries just as the first band took the stage.

A few days later, Tanner entered LM Bail Bonds where Luis and David sat. He handed a file to David.

David opened it. "Jesus, Mary, and Joseph!" he shouted.

"What?" asked Luis.

"This child is angelic. Come look."

Luis peered over David's shoulder. "Pretty enough to be a girl." He flipped the original picture. "Oh, God!"

Subsequent photos showed golden curls matted with blood, arm casts, a battered face, royal-blue eyes with stitches above the left and across the left cheekbone.

"And he was never taken from that home?" David mumbled.

"On two occasions," Tanner said. "Kansas must have a broken system too."

As they spoke, David's phone rang. "Hey, Little Momma," he answered.

Tanner rolled his eyes and Luis chuckled.

"Hey," Laura Beth said. "I have closing documents."

"Oh."

"You don't sound too excited."

"I just dread the transformation. Call Shapiro and set it up. Make it far enough out that Enrique has time to get back from Spain."

"You got it."

He disconnected. "Well, the shit is about to hit the fan."

His phone rang again. "What?" he snapped.

Mosely said, "I thought you'd like to know, I just got six little girls. All are en route to being reunited with family."

"Sorry. That's good news. Tell Nasser it's time to come back. The suite is still ours. Why'd he leave?"

"Family. He has one too."

"Okay. I understand that."

"Listen. When you get a buy set, we'll go in. The big man will be back in two days."

David hit end call.

Tanner raised an eyebrow. "We still can't connect Purdue to the bodies here."

"Yet." David stood. "I guess I need to get into Enrique mode."

Ten days later, Enrique de la Vega, along with Laura Beth Copeland, emerged from a limousine and entered Millicent Shapiro's office to find Dillard Purdue kicked back. He stood. "Enrique!"

The two men clasped hands. Enrique said, "The technicality should not take long, but I must leave tomorrow. May we have dinner in my hotel suite?"

"I would like that. Perhaps you can visit Tucson."

"Sí."

"I do have a housewarming gift for you."

"Bring it to my suite."

"Excellent."

Shapiro cleared her throat. "I have more appointments today."

Laura Beth scowled. *Yep. She was hunting a man and struck out with both.*

Shapiro placed documents on her desk and explained the property transfer, the fees, and a few more legal items. Enrique handed her a check for her services, Laura Beth a check for her commission and the real estate agency's cut, and Purdue a check for all properties. The payments were drawn on the same account David had used to set up college trusts for Laura Beth's children—part of he penance for accidentally killing Bruce Copeland he had called it—the least he could do for the man's family.

Both men signed forms, and the transaction finalized.

"I shall see you for a late dinner—nine." Enrique smiled. "Just come to suite five-oh-one."

"I'll see you this evening."

Promptly at nine, Purdue knocked on the door to the suite Enrique de la Vega had kept. Nasser opened the door. The young blond boy with Purdue flinched and stepped back when he saw the behemoth black man.

In his rumbling voice, Nasser said, "Mr. Purdue." He waved his hand to indicate entrance. "Please, come in. Señor de la Vega is waiting."

Purdue prodded Aaron ahead, and Enrique rounded the corner from the bedroom. "Buenos noches, my friend." He eyed Aaron and rubbed his hands together. "Perfect." He turned to his help. "Nasser, give us two hours."

"Yes, sir. I shall be at the hotel bar if you need me." He discreetly tapped his ear bud and left.

Enrique approached Aaron. The boy trembled. "You have no need to fear. Dill called me. You are Aaron."

"I'm not afraid. Just hungry."

Scared shitless ran though his mind, but Enrique chuckled. "I have lobster, shrimp fettuccine Alfredo, and Caesar salad waiting. Come." He held out a hand. Aaron took it.

Enrique slipped an arm around Purdue. "You too, my friend."

The three sat down to a delicious meal. Aaron watched the two older men. When Enrique poured wine, he asked, "Do I get some?"

"No." Enrique smiled. "You are not old enough to drink."

"Do you get drunk?"

"No." Enrique walked by and stroked Aaron's hair. "And I do not beat my lovers. I do expect submission. You will do exactly as I say without question or argument. Has Dillard not explained this?"

"Yes. Sort of." He looked down at his plate.

Enrique knelt beside him and lifted his chin. "Explain."

Aaron cut his eyes toward Purdue. He whispered, "He's two people. Dillard is nice. Phillip, not so."

Purdue began to fidget. In a higher voice, he said, "You promised me a threesome." He stood.

"Who are you?" Enrique asked, standing.

"Phil. You'll like me better than my brother. I'm what you prefer."

"How so?"

He ran his hands down his sides. "Look at me."

"What am I seeing?"

"What you like."

Enrique furrowed his brow. "I have decided not to share my special delivery. I do not need two blonds at once, and I shall take Aaron with me." He turned to the boy. "Aaron, go to the bar and find Nasser. Stay with him. He will not hurt you."

"Yes, sir." The boy ran from the room.

Enrique turned to Purdue. "Talk to me."

"I don't want to talk." He sprang forward and planted a kiss on Enrique.

Enrique pushed back and stroked the other man's cheek. A sad smile flickered across his face. "You are too special for this."

Purdue shook his head. "What are you doing?" Dillard's voice asked. "Oh, God! Phil was here."

"He has left, as should you."

"You'll take Aaron?"

"Yes. And expect a visit in Tucson. Friend to friend. I shall call about my entertainment business."

Purdue nodded and left.

David counted to a hundred and then said, "Nasser, you can come back."

A couple of minutes later, Nasser and Aaron returned.

David sat on the sofa. "Aaron, come and sit down."

The boy did as requested. "Your accent is gone."

David pointed to his face. "Nasser, get this shit off me."

In short time, Enrique became David as Aaron watched, mouth agape.

David leaned toward the shocked boy. "My name is David Black. I'm law enforcement. Chances are Purdue is a serial killer. Now, I have a few questions. Are you gay?"

"I-I-I don't know. You don't want me now." He dropped his face in his hands.

"Do you want a safe home?"

Aaron jerked his head up. "More than anything, but I have nowhere to go."

"You might."

A knock on the door made the boy jump. "Open the door, Nasser," David requested.

Nasser opened the door, and Penny entered. She looked at her husband and the young man with him. "So, this is your special delivery."

"Yes. Penny, meet Aaron Gunn. Aaron, this is Sheriff Penny Ulmer, my wife."

"Am I going to jail? I didn't do anything."

"No." Penny squatted beside the boy. "David told me about you. How would you like to come home with us?"

A nervous laugh escaped Aaron's lips. "Are you serious?"

"Yes. We already have two children, both adopted. We have room for another."

"What's the catch?"

Penny shook her head. "Too young to be cynical." She looked Aaron in the eye. "You follow our rules, go to school, see a counselor, become family."

"But you're black and he's Hispanic. Why would you want me?"

"I'm half white." Penny grinned. "And children are gifts from God. We know all about your dad. We're offering you an alternative to abuse and the streets. You make the call."

"I don't think I'm gay. I just did what I had to do to survive. That doesn't bother you?"

"We all do things we regret." Penny pushed his long hair from his face. "It's still your call. At sixteen, you can be emancipated, but how will you take care of yourself? We have signed documents from your father allowing us to take custody of you, but you have final say."

"How did you get my dad to agree?" He glanced up at David and then at Nasser.

The big man chuckled. "He wanted to avoid prison," he replied with a voice softer than anyone expected.

"What if you change your mind?" He looked at Penny with eyes that brimmed tears.

"We won't."

Aaron turned his gaze to David.

"We won't," David reiterated.

"What about Dillard?"

Nasser intoned, "He is already on his way back to Arizona."

The boy looked from one adult to another. "No tricks? No beating? Good food? A bed? Siblings?"

"All those things," David assured.

"What about your other kids? How will they react?"

"We already talked to them," Penny continued in a soothing voice.

"But," David added. "You can't tell them about Enrique."

Aaron arched an eyebrow.

David explained. "That is an undercover disguise that my kids don't know about. It could get me killed if you tell anyone."

Aaron knitted his brow into a frown. "Okay," he barely whispered. "I can keep your secret." He looked David squarely in the eye. "Are the other kids unwanted street urchins too?"

"Yes and no," David said. "Abel was orphaned at age two. I adopted him before I met Penny. He's almost eight. Emma came to us just a few months ago. You and she have a lot in common. She'll be fifteen next week."

Aaron looked from David to Penny. "What if I am gay?"

"Your choice." Penny patted his leg. "And still your call." She stood.

Aaron still hesitated.

Penny said, "There's always DHS."

Aaron's head snapped up. "Is that like CPS?"

"Yeah, in Mississippi."

"You're willing to take me off the streets now, but will you kick me out at eighteen or if I have problems?"

"Nope. Family sticks together and helps one another."

Aaron nodded. "Okay."

David stood.

Penny held out a hand to Aaron. "Let's go home."

Aaron leapt to his feet.

26
Back to School

Just over a week went by before school started back in the Deep South. The first problem with a sixteen-year-old boy flared.

Penny's four-bedroom house on the second floor allowed each child a private room. The ground floor had all the living area and the master bedroom, and there was an entire unused third floor. Abel and Emma stumbled to the breakfast table. "Wake up, sleepy heads," Penny teased. "Where's Aaron?"

"Still asleep." Abel yawned.

Penny looked toward David. "On it, Pretty Penny."

David knocked on the bedroom door and stepped in. Aaron snored.

"Aaron." David cleared his throat to no reaction. He walked to the bed and shook the boy.

"What?" Aaron whined.

"Time to get up. First day of school."

"I don't wanna go."

"Too bad. That's one of the rules."

Aaron slowly sat up and glared at David. "Shit. You're gonna force this."

"You bet."

"I can survive on my own."

"You know where the door is." David pointed. "And I guess you know about safe sex and disease and nut jobs that kill pretty little boys."

"That's why I don't want to go to school." He scowled. "I don't wanna be a pretty boy. Jocks will be mean to me."

"Hm." David scratched his chin. "Back to school for you will definitely include martial arts."

"Fighting?"

"Self-defense. Beginning this evening. And this weekend I open my dojo with a big party." He went to the door. "Now move."

1

Because work had become hectic all around with the various parts of investigation, the children in each family had to ride the school bus. The elementary children arrived without incident. The middle school commute was a little harder when three different girls wanted to sit with Corbin McGill. But the high school ride became a roller coaster.

A dark-skinned boy whistled at Aaron. "I heard the sheriff brought home a new stray."

"A pretty one," another boy laughed.

Aaron clenched his fists. "Sit down," Emma hissed. They took a seat together with Emma on the aisle.

"Hey!" the boy who laughed called. "You bangin' your, um, sister, or you wanna share?"

"That's it!" Emma bounded over seats and put a palm-heal strike to the boy's nose.

Aaron slid to the floor, wanting to hide and feeling phantom blows to his body.

The bus driver pulled to the shoulder of the road, put on the emergency flashers, and cut the engine. Doug Blanchard, who had gotten his license to drive a school bus, stood and turned around. "Emma Black!"

"Did you hear what he said, Mr. Doug?"

"Every word." He opened his cell and made three calls before he hauled Emma to the seat right behind him. "Omar Dinks, I do *not* tolerate bullies. Your momma will meet us at school. You don't want to cost her job. Todd Gustrom, you have never insulted a young lady like that. Your dad is on his way." He glanced at Emma.

She shook her head. "I know. You called Mom."

"Nope. Your papa."

"No! Not David."

"You'd rather the sheriff come?"

"He'll be disappointed in me."

"He taught you the karate move."

Doug retook his seat and gazed in his review mirror to see a cute Asian, Suzy Quantrill, who was known as Suzy Q, slide into the seat with Aaron. He cranked the bus and drove toward the school as a satisfied smile crossed his lips. *Sweet girl.*

"You can get up," Suzy said without looking down. "I think Mr. Blanchard has this under control."

Aaron eased back onto the seat. "I feel so stupid."

"Not. I'm Suzy."

"Aaron Gunn, soon-to-be Black."

"Nice to meet you. Don't sweat Omar. He used to call me Gook and Chink because my grandmother was Vietnamese. Todd is easily led. He'll apologize before the day is over." She giggled. "Your sister humiliated him. He's kinda nice actually." She leaned close. "He's crushing on Emma."

Aaron laughed. "Still?"

"Yeah. His sister was her mentor last year. Sheriff Ulmer won't let Emma date 'til she's sixteen. Do you date?"

"Haven't. But I might if you go to a movie with me."

"Yeah. You drive?"

"Not yet. David says I have to take driver's ed first."

"Me too. I signed up for it this semester."

"So, did I."

"Hey! Maybe we'll have some classes together. I'm a sophomore."

"Me too," he huffed. "I sort of skipped a year of school."

"Why?"

"I ran away from home."

"Wanna talk about it?"

"No."

She blinked her almond-shaped eyes at the curt answer. "Okay. But if you ever do, I'll listen."

Parents of the children involved in the bus incident met at the high school. David stared at Aaron who shrugged. Suzy dragged him away.

David grinned as Aaron looked back. He mouthed to the boy. "Girlfriend already?"

Aaron responded with a huge smile.

David turned to Emma. "Explain."

She pointed at Todd. "Ask him what he said."

Gus Gustrom, owner of Gus's Goulash, put a hand on his son's shoulder. Todd blurted, "I'm sorry. I just like you. I didn't mean it."

"Funny way to show me," Emma snapped. "And you!" she pointed at Omar.

Omar's mother, Sadie, a single mother who worked in the elementary school cafeteria cuffed her son. "I won't have you pickin' on nobody. That boy's had a hard life—worse than yours. We ain't rich, but you been loved. Mr. Black is trying to give that boy a life."

"I'm sorry, Momma." He rubbed his cheek.

"Don't tell me. Tell that boy."

"I will."

The principal shook her head and let out a long sigh. "Not the way I wanted to start the first day of school." She looked each child in the eye. "I have an idea so that we don't start with a suspension. Parents, I want these three to work together every afternoon for a week at the homeless shelter."

"Great idea," said David. "If that doesn't work, my wife can let them spend a night in jail."

"I like that idea," Gustrom grunted.

"How about I pick y'all up when school is out?" David lifted an eyebrow.

The adults agreed with the plan.

Not only did Emma and Aaron Black seem to have love interests, but Corbin came home boasting about his harem. Laura Beth laughed at the look of consternation on Tanner's face. She put her arms around him. "You have had the *talk* with him, haven't you?"

"He's not even thirteen yet."

"Tanner, talk!" she huffed and shook her head.

"Stop fretting. Yeah, I've had the birds-and-bees talk with both of them."

"Good."

Corbin came back into the room with a glass of chocolate milk. "Oh, and I'm seventh-grade quarterback. Games start in September on Tuesdays. Miss Laura Beth, will you come?"

"Of course, I will. Are any of these girls cheerleaders?"

"Yes, ma'am. Two. And one's on the dance team."

She put her arm around his shoulders. "Goodness! You're as tall as me. Now, listen. Girls come third. Football, second. First is keeping grades up. Just because you can play sports with a C average doesn't make mediocre acceptable."

"I hear you. I made honor roll every nine weeks last year."

"Keep on doing that. Homework?"

"Not yet. First few days, we just cover the handbook. We even have to take a test!"

"Then learn the rules!" Tanner laughed.

Corbin wrinkled his nose. "They never change, but some are stupid."

Laura Beth said, "Then go into student government and make changes."

"You think?" The boy tilted his head.

"Absolutely." She nodded. "What rules do you think are stupid?"

"Like guys can't wear earrings"—He spread his hands out—"I mean, it's the twenty-first century. I can see no dangling earrings for anybody, but it's kind of sexist to target guys these days. It's socially accepted."

"A good point." Laura Beth nodded. "And well spoken."

Corbin laughed. "Dad, maybe I'll be President someday."

Tanner mussed his son's hair. "If that's what you want, work toward it."

He punched his father's arm. "Of course, I have to be old like you to be President."

"What!"

Corbin ran off laughing.

Laura Beth laughed too. "I love the relationship you have with your kids."

Chuckling, Tanner said, "Me too. I'm proud of them. Now, time for me to round up all our imps and get to karate class." He planted a sound kiss on her.

She waved him out. "Supper will be ready when y'all get back."

Martial arts class having swelled among children in the wake of the bodies that had been discovered, Tanner had taken over instruction of the boys. Mondays and Wednesdays from seven until nine was devoted to children. Tuesdays and Thursdays were adult nights.

On one end of the dojo, David called the girls to attention. "*Yoi!*"

The girls responded with, "*Oss!*"

On the other end of the wide-open space, Tanner barked stance and exercise commands. "*Kiba dachi...Kokutsu dachi...Zenkutsu dachi!*" Starched gis snapped.

The oldest, but lowest ranked, Aaron appeared uncoordinated and lost. Once initial warm-ups were complete, Tanner pulled him to the side for one-on-one lessons. He paired the other boys to work through katas. Sparring took place on Wednesdays.

After a time, Tanner called Corbin to them. "Work on *taikyoku shodan* with Aaron while I check on everyone else. Remember we're having a rank test as part of the grand opening Saturday."

"Yes, sir." Corbin turned to Aaron who rolled his eyes.

"Hey," Corbin said. "Just because I'm younger than you, don't diss on me. My dad has been teaching me almost since I started walking. When David set up the academy, the training just got formal."

"Sorry. I just feel so stupid when I look at seven-year-olds doing this stuff, and I trip over my own two feet."

"It's new to you. You'll catch on."

Aaron pointed. "Your belt is brown. Mine's white."

"White is for beginners. Miss Laura Beth just has yellow."

"Which means?"

"Two steps up—white, white with a stripe, yellow. But she's going for orange Saturday. Dad won't judge her because she's his girlfriend. We'll have a couple of guest judges from Jackson.

"Too soon for me."

"Yeah, but real soon. And be sure to go to tournaments. I have three trophies since the school officially opened—well, not the building, but the name, DLT Mixed Martial Arts Academy."

"You ranking up?"

"Going for black. You bet. I'll be thirteen in October. I hope they'll rank me at twelve. Now watch."

Corbin performed the beginning kata. "It's almost like a dance. Just memorize the steps. Walk through with me."

Aaron followed Corbin's steps. The younger boy nodded. "Not bad. We'll work in thirds. Get your feet first. Add punches, then blocks. It'll all come together. And remember, 'Ki ai!' at the end of each punch." He grabbed a towel and wiped his sweaty face. "Next rank test, you'll move up. And at sixteen, you'll be able to rank fast if you apply yourself."

"Thanks."

Corbin jutted his chin toward David. "Get him to work with you in private. He's a master in three disciplines. He started me on weapons right off and pushed me through ranks. He said my dad did a good job with me. Now, Roslyn, my sister, is getting more coordinated. She'll go for orange Saturday. Follow me."

Aaron trailed his mentor. They entered a smaller room that contained weights and punching bags. Corbin said, "Work out in here and build some muscle. Get David to set you up a routine. He says I'm too young for real weight training because I'm growing too fast, and it could actually strain my muscles. He has me on minimum weight."

The boys felt a clamp on their shoulders. Tanner growled, "You're supposed to be working on kata."

"Sorry, Dad." Corbin grinned.

Tanner jerked his head back to the open room. "Class is almost over. Line up."

The boys found their places in the entire group arranged by rank. David called, "*Yoi!*"

The students responded, "*Oss!*" And popping gis echoed as they took the *kiba dachi* stance. Aaron cut his eyes left and right to make sure he was in the attention stance. He smiled. He had done it right.

David then gave a few commands in Japanese to which the children replied before he dismissed the class.

Aaron stood beside Tanner and watched the children bow out of the dojo and put shoes on just outside in the lobby. "Respect for the art," Tanner whispered to the boy's confused look. "No shoes allowed, and you bow in and out. Corbin will be about another half hour. Weapons with David."

"You think he'll train me?"

"Yep, if you ask."

"Cool."

Tanner pointed to a padded bench. "Let's watch. The girls will all shower and change. So, will Abel. You can too if you'd rather."

"I'd like to watch. I can shower later."

They sat and watched as Corbin performed several routines with tonfa and meteor hammer.

The other Black, McGill, and Copeland children came and sat on the floor as Luis picked up Deannie and waved a goodnight.

"It takes dedication," Tanner said as Corbin put his weapons away. He looked down at Aaron. "And discipline."

Aaron nodded. Corbin pointed to the showers.

"Be back in ten," Tanner said to the girls and Abel.

Two fathers and two sons showered, glad to be back to school, each for a different reason.

26

Late for Class

On Labor Day, David was jarred from a sound sleep to his "Enrique" phone ringing.

"Shit!" he moaned and then answered groggily, "Ola, Dill."

"I have a shipment for you, and you still haven't visited me."

"I have only just returned from Spain, as I told you when we discussed talent recruits."

"Well, if you want this delivery, you need to get to southern California by Friday." He gave David the address that David and Luis had gone to previously."

"Do you have the merchandise as we speak?"

"No, I'm on my way to pick it up."

"Gracias. I shall fly out as soon as possible."

First, David called Nasser who was still in the hotel suite. "We have to get to Magdalena, Mexico tonight."

"I shall make the arrangements."

"Include Luis. We might need the backup."

"Understood."

Then, David called Luis followed by Mosely to meet in California.

Finally, he called Tanner as Penny tapped her impatient foot.

Tanner answered, "This had better be good. It's a holiday and I'm off work."

"Dill called. I think it was Phil though. I have to get to Mexico and California. Luis is going with me. You have the school to yourself." He grinned at his wife. "Get Penny to help."

She dropped her crossed arms in exasperation and defeat. Shaking a finger at David when all calls were done, she griped, "This on top of the fact I'm no closer to finding a killer. Great."

"Sorry, darling. Maybe at least one criminal ring will be taken care of this week."

"Right. Okay, I'll give you that, but you better not get killed."

He held up a hand. "I swear."

Within two hours, David as de la Vega, Nasser, and Luis were on a private jet.

Wednesday, Tanner went about his normal day. Sunrise had very little crime. A malicious mischief call, a missing skateboard or scooter from a carport, an occasional domestic violence call, and the rare drug bust made up most of his investigations.

The murder of Consuela Perez a year and half before had been the biggest case he'd worked. The now unearthed dark secret so near the woman he'd fallen in love with still had his head spinning.

At three on this quiet day, he called, "Marge!"

Marge Montoya, Tanner's assistant and new detective, stuck her head in her boss's office. "Yeah, Boss?"

"Not boss anymore, partner."

"Trying to break the habit."

"Take off. I'll be here until four-thirty when I have to pick up Corbin from football practice. First game is next week."

Laughing, she replied, "I'm glad they don't pay us by the case."

"Me too." He waved a shooing hand. "Now go!"

"You got it. See ya tomorrow."

An hour later, Tanner's phone rang. "What's up, Sheriff?" he answered.

"Something. I need you to get to Gus's. It's barely in city limits. I just pulled into the parking lot to get dinner since I have to help with karate class. I see Gus with his hands raised. Something's going down. I'm going in."

"Penny, stay put until I get there." He jumped to his feet. "I'm out the door."

He heard a gunshot. "Penny!"

"Inside." She disconnected.

"Shit!" Tanner dialed Laura Beth as he ran to his car.

She answered, and before any greeting, he shouted. "I need you to pick up Corbin for me. Gunshots at Gus's." He did not wait for a reply. He hung up and called for backup at the local eatery.

Penny got to the restaurant entrance with her weapon drawn. She cracked the door and heard shouting.

"Give me the money, old man! Next time, I'll shoot you or your faggot son."

She spied Todd Gustrom cowering at the end of the lunch counter. Several bottles of liquor behind Gus had shattered from the shot.

"Okay, okay," Gus said as he opened the cash register.

Penny popped through the door. "Drop the weapon, Omar, you little thug."

Omar Dinks whirled and fired.

Penny flew back into the glass door, splintering it into shards.

Omar snatched the cash Gus had and dashed out the door, leaping over Penny. He jumped into an older, rusting

Oldsmobile Alero and peeled out of the parking lot just as Tanner squealed in.

Instinctively, Tanner radioed the car's description before he bolted from his vehicle, taking in Gus holding a towel to Penny's chest.

On his shoulder radio, Tanner bellowed, "Officer down! Gus's Goulash!"

Tanner dropped to his knees. "It's my shoulder," Penny growled. "Not fatal, but it hurts like a bitch. Omar Dinks. Good thing the little prick didn't have hollow points. Tanner, he's higher than the rings around Saturn. His poor mother."

"Hush. I hear the ambulance. You're about to be higher than a space rocket yourself. I need to call David."

"No. Let him finish this case."

"He's going to go ballistic."

"I can handle David. Go get Omar before he kills someone or gets killed. I think he can still be saved."

"Okay. I'll get by the hospital later."

She gave him a push.

Laura Beth went to her Jaguar. "Damn it!" She muttered, looking at a flat tire. She went to her trunk, got her jack and tire iron and spare tire, and began the process of changing the driver's side front tire.

"What are you doing?" asked Millicent Shapiro, pulling in beside the Jaguar.

"I have a flat and need to go get Corbin McGill. Tanner suddenly got called out. Shots at Gus's."

"I'll give you a lift to the school. Call roadside assistance."

"I know how to change a tire."

"But can you get the lugs off?"

"They *are* tight." She looked at her watch. "And I'm already late. Okay. Thanks."

Tanner received notification from a patrolman. "Detective McGill, we have the kid. He's strung out."

"Take him to the hospital. I'll get by there in a bit. I have a karate class to teach, and I'm late. I've ignored several calls, so I didn't have to tell my girlfriend her best friend was shot. She's going to brain me."

He wheeled into the parking lot of the martial arts school to a crowd. A quick scan of the group sent his stomach into a tight clench.

Laura Beth marched to him as he got out of his car and delivered a right hook that rocked his head. "I called you twenty times!" she shrieked. "Marge has issued an Amber Alert! Corbin is missing!"

Tears streamed down her face.

28

Missing

"**What** the hell do you mean?" Tanner bellowed. "He was at football practice like every day."

"When I went to leave to get him, I had a flat. Millicent gave me a ride. Nobody was on the field. I went into the field house. The coach said he'd run back to the school because he left a book he needed for homework, but he was gone."

"No!" Tanner screamed. "Not my son!"

He whipped out his phone and dialed.

"David Black."

"Corbin is missing, and Penny's been shot."

"What?" Laura Beth screeched.

"Shot?" David's frantic voice resounded through the phone.

Marge grabbed Tanner's phone. "David, Marge. Penny is fine."

Tanner crumpled to the ground. Laura Beth wrapped her arms around him.

Marge continued, "She was hit in the shoulder. She wants you to stay on the case."

"What's this about Corbin?"

"Missing. Amber Alert issued."

"Purdue already picked up the shipment. He's missing too."

"What about surveillance?"

"We lost the feed in the trailer. Just gray. Nobody in the cab. We're nowhere close enough to pick up movement."

"Stay on it. I'm running the show here, and I have Pickering. He's got this national."

"Tanner?"

"Laura Beth has him."

"He's in good hands."

"True, but she just socked Tanner in the jaw. She's frantic too."

"Well, they both have you." David disconnected. *Oh, God! Please don't let my dream come true. Please.*

Pickering approached Marge. "Am I working with you?"

"Yes, sir. Tanner can't do this one."

"I've broadcast this nationwide, and I have state police helping stakeout Purdue Plantation."

"What if they aren't connected?"

He placed his hand on the back of his neck. "Kid fits the victim profile. I don't believe in coincidence."

"You think Purdue set this whole day in motion? Gus? Laura Beth's flat?"

"Could be. Maybe the alter ego, but he's the one that would want the young blond boy."

"Aaron was too old?"

"Right. I need to talk to that lad."

"Neither parent is available."

"I don't care." He stomped toward Aaron Black.

Emma stood between them. "You're not gonna talk to him without Mom. He's a minor."

"Bossy Britches." Pickering shouted over his shoulder, "Ms. Shapiro!"

The lawyer raced over. "Yes?"

"This boy needs representation. That's you. We don't have time for formalities. A child's life is at stake. And I don't want to hear a word about conflict of interests involving your demented client, Dillard Purdue."

"I didn't do anything," Aaron said as his lip trembled.

"I believe that," Pickering said, softening his tone. "I just want to pick your brain about Purdue."

"I told David he's like two people. He even uses two names. Dillard is nice. Phillip—evil. He thinks he's blond like me."

Pickering led his witness to the grassy curb and sat down. Aaron sat beside him with Millicent on the other side of the boy. Pickering said, "David shared that information. Tell me about Phillip."

"He's mean."

"Did he hurt you?"

Aaron shook his head. "He was afraid of Enrique. And every time he tried to have sex with me, Dillard came out. They literally fought."

Pickering rubbed his hand across his bald head. "You were in his house."

"Yes, sir."

"Tell me about it."

"Small. Not much furniture. But one night he tied me up and blindfolded me. He forced me into a car or truck, not the rig, and took me somewhere else."

"You didn't see anything?"

"No."

"But you're sure he had a different vehicle?"

"Yeah. It was easy to get in the seat."

"That helps. Corbin McGill saw the first victim we found in a dark gray Silverado."

"And now *he's* missing." Aaron breathed heavily, as if he might be sick.

"I refuse to let him die." Pickering put a hand on Aaron's head. "You just helped—a lot."

"Call Purdue," Luis told David. "Enrique just got to the States."

"Yeah." David dialed Purdue's cell from his alternate number. It went to voicemail.

"No answer." David disconnected with force.

"We need to get into this compound and take care of business here," Nasser intoned.

"We already know the girls are missing," David thought aloud.

Luis snorted. "Ortega still needs to go, and there could be more."

"Good point," David said. "We're almost to Magdalena. Might as well take Ortega's ass out."

From the backseat of the rental car, Nasser rumbled, "I am in."

David gave a nod. "Let's do this."

Outside the desert compound, three men donned spandex in military tan-and-black camouflage. David slung his katana over his shoulder. Luis holstered two nine millimeters with a bandolier filled with clips while Nasser sheathed a short sword and buckled a belt of shuriken.

David touched the guns. "Stealth," he whispered.

Luis produced a garrote. David nodded.

They crept close to the fence and stopped. "It is too quiet," Nasser breathed.

"Agreed," David said. "Something's not right."

"Stay alert," Luis continued. "I think they've been tipped off."

David collared Nasser. "Who in the consortium is dirty?"

"I do not know."

"Guess."

"Tamar has always been on my radar."

"Tamar?"

"The British bitch. Technology geek like Luis. Code name Trojan, but she is also deadly with a gun and in hand-to-hand combat."

"Oh yeah. I hope it's her."

Luis put a hand on David's arm. "Let's check the place out."

"Yeah. Okay." David patted the big man's shoulder. "Sorry."

"I am with you. I am not the enemy," Nasser assured.

"I know." David jerked his head toward the compound. The three men moved in.

They searched building after building. "Nothing!" David yelled. "Missing."

They entered a large metal building. "Empty," David echoed, heaving a sigh of despair.

"Not a total loss," Luis said, picking up a few strips of film negative. He held them up to the light. "Evidence. Child pornography." He passed a strip to both David and Nasser.

"Bag it," David said. "Let's move on to California."

"The jet is waiting at the airfield," Nasser said. "Perhaps we can get lucky and find them all under one roof."

"Let's move fast," David went on. "My wife and my friend need me."

Ed Pickering issued a BOLO for Dillard Purdue with a description of him as well as his rig and any and all gray Chevy Silverados.

Next, he arranged constant surveillance on Purdue Plantation—FBI, state police, Sunrise PD, and county deputies.

Finally, he made a pilgrimage to the home of Laura Beth Copeland where he found, not only Tanner McGill's family, but also David Black's and Luis Montoya's, along with the Blanchards.

"Was I the only one missing?" he asked with a frown when Laura Beth answered the door. "I see even our wounded sheriff is here."

"We all sort of stick together."

"I notice Shapiro is missing."

"Her choice. She said she hopes Dill will call her."

He looked toward her living room and saw Tanner slumped over, head resting in his hands. Laura Beth followed the agent's gaze. "We have to find Corbin," she whispered. "Tanner's the strongest person I know, and he's falling apart."

"I have all available manpower at work."

She rubbed her arms as a chill shook her. "I can't believe I wish Diego Marin was here."

"So, when does David Black get back? Or should I expect Enrique de la Vega?"

29
Not for Sale

As soon as the wheels of the small jet touched the tarmac at the private airfield between Chula Vista and San Diego, three men, ready for battle, crowded the door to exit as fast as possible. Before the hatch opened completely, they bailed, already dressed to invade another facility in the dark and armed as they had been at the desert compound.

Waiting for the three at the entrance to the hangar where the aircraft would wait sat a black SUV with dark-tinted windows. A man's silhouette could be seen through the smoky glass. He cranked the vehicle the minute he saw the other three men.

David, Luis, and Nasser piled in. "Nice to see you came dressed to be part of the team, Mosely," David said. "You know there's a rat in the organization."

"You've known me long enough to know it's not me. I'm not for sale."

"Fully aware."

"For your information, full sanction to terminate when we discover who."

"Works for me."

The SUV stopped outside the shearer. "Looks legit," Luis mumbled. "But our evidence shows more."

"Yeah." Mosely nodded. "I bought kids here."

Under a velvety, starless, obsidian night, the men exited the vehicle and maneuvered with great stealth to the entrance. "I'll be damned!" David muttered "Purdue's rig."

The red-and-black scorpion tractor-trailer was parked inside the fenced area.

Loud laughing and the sound of bells and gongs got the quartet's attention. "They're about to have an auction," Mosely informed the others. "That's the call to order."

"I say we crash the party," David snarled.

Luis passed out mini-mikes and ear buds. "Not without communication and care."

"Okay," David agreed. "Let's split up and come from four directions.

They checked their communication devices and spread out.

A crackle preceded David's question. "Does anybody see Purdue?"

"Not me," Luis replied, and two more negatives followed.

"I do see Ortega and Antonia," Luis said.

"And Tamar," Nasser rumbled. "That bitch is mine."

"I kind of want her head," David countered.

"Boys, boys," Mosely chided, "there are enough riffraff to go around. I don't think she was in on this before. She took advantage of your request, David. It's all about making a buck. Listen up. Luis and I are going for the kids. We need to get them out of here before you two blood-thirsty crazies begin a headcount. They don't need to see that."

"Get them to the rig," David said. "It's the safest place for them right now, believe it or not."

"Copy that," Mosely said. "As soon as we get them secure, we'll be back to help the two of you."

David barked, "Okay! Go!"

Just as an auctioneer paraded a dozen young girls onto a makeshift stage, Luis and Mosely raced from opposite sides of the room and leapt onto the raised platform. Mosely sprayed the ceiling with automatic weapons fire.

Ortega clutched Antonia's arm. "Luis Gonzales."

"He was with Perez. The other man bought a shipment a few months back."

"Cops. Luis must have been the undercover FBI."

Screams from employees and potential buyers drowned out the rest of their exchange. Mosely snatched the auctioneer's microphone. "Shut up!" He fired into the ceiling again.

"Hear this!" Mosely thundered. High-pitched feedback caused a number of people to slap their hands over their ears. Mosely went on. "These children are not for sale. We are taking them. Don't try to stop us."

As he spoke, movement behind the stage caught Luis's eye. Without hesitation, he fired a nine-millimeter. One of Ortega's guards dropped dead.

"Go!" Luis yelled.

"Girls, come on!" Mosely urged.

Older girls pulled younger ones off the dais. The whole group ran toward the scorpion truck.

Arriving, the girls hesitated. "That's how we got here," one said.

"Where's the man who drove it?" asked Luis.

Nobody knew.

"Well, just wait here," Mosely said. "We have friends back there." He pointed.

"Are you cops?" a girl asked.

"Yes."

"Are you gonna kill those people?" another wanted to know.

"Only if necessary."

Luis and Mosely helped the girls into the empty trailer. The last one in turned to Luis. "You killed that man."

"I had no choice. He would have killed us."

"I'm glad."

"Did he hurt you?"

The girl nodded.

"You'll be safe now." He turned away but left the doors open.

1

As Luis and Mosely ran with the children, David and Nasser stormed into the crowd, swords swinging. The first traffickers to fall were two armed guards.

David and Nasser went straight for the three most wanted— Ortega, Antonia, and Tamar.

Several buyers went down with slashes to hamstrings or Achilles tendons. Hobbled, they tried to crawl away.

Out of nowhere, both men saw Tamar moving faster than either thought possible. Using zip ties, person after person found themselves fettered to chairs by her swift hands.

Screaming, Nasser charged toward her. She lifted a chair to block his blade swing.

"Nasser, stop!" she barked "Do you truly think I'm one of them? I came on pretending to look for young girls for the film industry. Marin got to me. I'm not a cold bitch." She pointed. "Get those two!"

"Go!" David yelled.

Nasser grunted. An instant later, a throwing star caught Ortega in the left butt cheek. He dropped to a knee with a shriek.

Antonia paused long enough for Nasser to catch up and yank her by her long black ponytail. Before either of the two traffickers could react, Nasser had used a set of nunchucks to bind their wrists together. He put a back fist to Ortega's nose, and Antonia crumpled to the floor.

She reached into her boot and retrieved a switchblade, plunging it into Nasser's calf. The big man bellowed. A flash of red and black hurtling through the air stopped his cry of pain. David stood beside him, katana raised. Antonia's head lay a few feet away.

Ortega screamed and cowered by the dead woman's body. "I am not armed."

Tamar was beside David a few seconds later. A moment after that, she heard a click at the back of her head.

Mosely growled, "I have full sanction to kill a rat."

Tamar raised her hands. "No rat here. Did Daesque tell you to kill me?"

"Told me to eliminate the rat."

"Then a trip to Romania is called for. Five thousand dollars says he's gone."

"Are you saying the head of our organization is the rat?"

David and Nasser exchanged glances. David gave a half-shrug.

Nasser's ebony face creased with a scowl.

"Fu Shin and Remy sent me," Tamar continued. "They thought de la Vega was walking into a trap." She looked toward David. "But then you were late. Why?"

"Purdue said he was on his way to get a shipment. It appears he informed me late."

Tamar showed no sign of nervousness. "Kill me if you want, but you'll still have to get Daesque."

"Call Remy," Nasser said.

Tamar reached for her pocket. Mosely pushed his gun harder against her head. "Phone, Mosely."

She pulled out a cell phone and dialed. "Putting you on speaker," she said when the party answered.

"Who is speaking?" Nasser asked.

"Remy. Ees that Nasser? What has occurred?"

Nasser gave a nutshell story. "So? Whose head does David get?"

"Tamar has told zee truth. Even as we speak, I am dispersing operatives to the home of our traitor. Tamar, Mosely, remain with zee prisoners. FBI and local police are on zeir way. Tamar has identification and documentation for zis 'steeng.' Ees zat zee correct word, David?"

"Yeah."

"Bon. Zhou, Nasser, and zhour friend need to leave. The girls will be safe with zee authorities."

David scowled.

Mosely jerked his head toward the exit. "We'll be good," he assured his companions.

"One question for Ortega." David grabbed his shirt at the throat. "Where's Purdue?"

"I don't know."

"You know, I'm going to ensure all your prison mates know you're a pedophile. You won't last a day."

David turned to Nasser and Luis. "Let's go." He gave a half-smile. "I got one head. I think I like the idea of you being somebody's bitch, Ortega."

With one arm on David's shoulder and one arm on Luis's shoulder, Nasser and the other two left. Looking down at a trail of blood, David said, "You need a doctor."

"Yes, I do, but let us stop at the rig where the girls were left."

"Of course," said Luis. "We need to let them know the authorities are on the way."

"And check the rig for evidence," David said. "Will you be okay for a few minutes, Nasser?"

"I have endured worse."

Once they arrived at the tractor-trailer, the girls bombarded them with questions. Nasser sat just inside the open trailer door and answered as best as possible, all the while wrapping his injured leg with an ace bandage from a first aid kit found in the sleeper compartment.

David and Luis climbed into the cab after snatching the first aid and tossing it to Nasser. "Oh, shit," David groaned, finding shorn black hair and a ponytail intact, along with a box of blond hair dye on the floor.

Luis snapped pictures with is phone and relayed them to Pickering.

They examined his surveillance equipment.

"Not sabotage or detected. A simple matter of circuitry coming loose." Luis puffed out his cheeks in frustration.

A beep indicated a reply to Luis's texted photos. "We're needed at home. Tanner's not functioning. They found something more bizarre on your new land."

Distant sirens triggered the need to move fast.

"Good luck, girls," Nasser called as the three men moved into the dark and a black SUV.

30

Storm Cellar

The first stop for David and friends was an urgent care facility. The doctor at the small clinic near the Mexican border scowled. "How did this happen?" he asked.

"My ex-wife," Nasser said with a lopsided grin.

"I think you're lying."

"Just treat the wound and give me a tetanus shot."

Nasser returned to his waiting friends with a fresh bandage, instructions for care, crutches, and rubbing his arm. His face looked like a pouting little boy. "That shot hurt."

David and Luis snickered. David jabbed, "You just got stabbed in the leg, but the shot hurt?"

Nasser lifted one crutch. "The doctor says to stay off my foot for at least a week. This will make a good club, and I am in a testy mood. Let us go." He held up a prescription. "Pain medicine and antibiotics."

David and Luis walked at a clip with Nasser swinging his large body behind them.

In the SUV, David said, "I'm making a detour by Purdue's place just in case, after we get Nasser fixed up." He glanced right. "What did they find on my property?"

"Pickering just said we'd have to see it to believe it." Luis shrugged.

"I went over that place." David released an exasperated sigh. "Spiral navigation. No more than three feet away. I walked it for hours. Laura Beth got blisters on her feet trying to keep up with me." He paused as a snore reverberated from the backseat. "Purdue walked with us and collapsed in the limo." Another snore made both men up front chuckle.

Nasser, with his wounded leg propped across the top of the backseat, leaned against the door, sound asleep.

Luis said, "Doc must've given him a stout shot." He pointed. "Walgreen's—twenty-four-hour service." He poked the sleeping man. "Wake up. Pharmacy."

Nasser hobbled into the drugstore and filled his prescriptions for penicillin and oxycodone. He returned to the car and tossed sandwiches, chips, and sodas from a vending machine to Luis. "We need food," he rumbled. "Be careful opening the cans. They might spew from being shaken." He tore into a ham and cheese combo before he swallowed his medication. "Wake me when we get to our destination."

The only sound for a long time was soft chewing, crackling bags, and gentle roaring of tires on pavement.

They rolled into Tucson and Purdue's small home. Luis looked at Nasser. David shook his head. "Let him sleep."

Leaving the motor running, the two men jimmied the lock on the door to the peach-colored house. Inside was tidy—everything orderly, OCD neat and straight. Several photos rested on an accent table. David picked them up in order. All seemed to be Dillard and his mother. "Notice how the expression on his face changes. His eyes become lifeless. That's when he was first molested."

Luis opened a drawer. "Oh, shit."

"What?"

Luis handed David a folder with Polaroid shots—young blond boys all dressed in blue button-down shirts.

"They look healthy here, even cared for," Luis muttered.

"Dillard. Somewhere in the process, Phillip takes over, molests, abuses, and kills them. Corbin is in trouble. He's such a great kid. Put these back. We'll tell Pickering, and he can get a warrant. Phillip must have another place—somewhere."

Luis put the pictures back and they left the house. David muttered, "God! We have to stakeout the whole damned plantation. He'll bring Corbin back there to kill him."

"We need to go find out what new discovery they made."

While David worked to stop a trafficker of young girls, and sometimes boys, into sex slavery, Sunrise, Mississippi, experienced round after round of severe weather. Flooding in the low-lying areas uncovered a door on Purdue Plantation that previously had been hidden.

At first light after the last storm, Special Agent Ed Pickering and Sheriff Ulmer descended on the heavy wooden double doors held closed by a padlock.

Dr. Daiwa joined law enforcement and Penny looked up to see Tanner wedging his way through with Laura Beth clutching his arm. Penny placed her uninjured hand on his chest. "I have to be here!" he yelled. "Just in case Corbin's in there."

Penny pointed toward the cadaver dogs. "They didn't pick up a fresh body. This could turn out to be nothing more than an old storm cellar."

"It's a damned long way from the house." He arced his hand in a half circle. "Mid-level of the bluffs on the river. Not very practical for a storm cellar."

"Just stand back." Penny looked at Laura Beth. "Keep your hands on him." She gave a nod to her deputy once Laura Beth latched onto Tanner's arm.

The deputy used bolt cutters to snip the old lock.

Flashlights shining, Penny and Pickering, followed by Daiwa, descended a low set of stairs. The odor of mold and old decay weighed heavily in the air.

"Oh, shit!" Penny declared. "Get me some bright light in here!"

A couple of hours later, spotlights run by generators illuminated the hole in the ground. The back wall was lined with shelves on which the remains of a dozen bodies lay. Another wall held an assortment of canes and whips. The last wall, to the left of the entrance contained a small shelf with various sex toys and a ring attached to the wall from which leather shackles hung. Below the ring on the floor were a series of small protruding loops, and a number of metallic rods lay against the wall. Daiwa poked them with his cane. "Pull your jaw in, Sheriff. This is either a torture chamber or a den of sexual exploration."

He pointed to a leather padded bench and a chair dead center of the room with frayed leather straps on the arms and legs. One strap had snapped. "All items used in BDSM."

Penny pointed to the human remains. "I'd say they were tortured and had no desire to participate in warped sex games. How old are they?"

Daiwa picked up an article of clothing. "Looking at this, I would venture to say these young men were killed in the late 1940s to early 1950s.

"My God!" Tanner exclaimed from the entrance. "Doug Blanchard dreamed about boys his age being tortured and killed."

Penny nodded. "Old Orin Purdue. Guys and gals, we have three generations of perverted killers." She looked at the remains again.

Pickering spoke up. "Leave 'em be."

Penny jerked her head around.

"For now," Pickering finished. "Let's leave this place undisturbed. I think he'll come back here. Let's let him believe we don't know about it, but we'll be watching." He walked to Tanner. "We'll get your son back—alive."

When David and crew got back, Penny showed them the macabre find. She explained the plan and replaced the lock with a duplicate that looked exactly like the one that had been on the door and one that would use the same key as the previous one. The went to great lengths the make the new lock look old.

Then, they waited.

31
My Daddy Taught Me Well

Corbin McGill showered and changed into his karate gi. Looking in his gym bag, he realized he had left his homework in his locker. "Coach," he called.

"Yeah, C?"

"Is the school still unlocked? I must have left my English book, but I could have sworn I put it in my bag."

"Should be open, C. Take your things so I can lock up here. I'll stay here 'til your dad comes and send him to the back entrance."

"Okay. I'll hurry."

As he rushed up the long set of steps to the back entrance, a man with platinum blond hair stepped from an alcove where benches sat, and students often congregated before and after school. Holding up a grammar book, the man said, "Looking for this?"

"How'd you get my book?" Corbin began to back up and was suddenly hit with fifty thousand volts from a stun gun that had been hidden behind the textbook.

The man scooped up the stunned boy and flew down the stairs to a dark gray Chevy Silverado where he bound his hands, ankles, and mouth with duct tape and slid him under a tarp over the truck bed.

Millicent Shapiro and Laura Beth Copeland pulled up in front of the field house. "I don't see anyone still practicing," Laura Beth said. "I'm stepping inside."

As she got to the door of the field house, she saw the coach through the glass doors. Cracking the door, she called, "Coach Daly!"

Having stepped into his office, he stuck his head out. "Mrs. Copeland."

"Tanner has a police emergency. I'm here to pick up Corbin."

"He ran back to the school. Said he forgot a book." He walked her to the door after locking his office. He pointed across the drive that circled the school. "Back entrance. Janitors usually lock that one last—about seven. A few teachers stay late."

"Thanks." She went back to the car and directed Millicent where to drive. As they looped through where the busses loaded and unloaded each day, neither woman saw Corbin. Millicent parked. "You think he's inside?"

"Maybe. Let's wait a second." Then, Laura Beth's eyes glimpsed the end of a gold and green gym bag—school colors. "No!" she shouted and bounded from the car.

Millicent dogged her steps. At the top of the stairs, Laura Beth screamed, "Corbin!"

She pulled open the door and yelled down the hallway.

Hearing her shrill cries all the way down the hill at the field house, Coach Daly raced to her. "What's wrong?" he hollered as he rounded the corner.

Almost hysterical, Laura Beth chanted, "He's gone; he's gone." She called Tanner with shaking hands. The call went to voicemail. She dialed Marge Montoya who left immediately.

Again and again and again, Laura Beth called Tanner.

Marge jumped from her car, leaving the door open. "Laura Beth, talk to me!"

Laura Beth and Daly spoke at once while Millicent paced.

Within ten minutes, Marge had issued an Amber Alert and had everyone still in the school corralled in the cafeteria. She called every available patrolman to the scene. They combed the grounds and the building and helped interview the half dozen people on the premises.

Coach Daly was nearly as upset as Laura Beth. "I should have walked with him," he lamented.

"Stop!" Marge barked. "You had no way to know, but think—anything you saw or heard."

"It took me about fifteen minutes to get the field house squared away. Then Mrs. Copeland came in." He dropped his face into his hands. "A gray truck. I saw the bed of a gray truck sort of sticking out."

"Make? Model? Driver?"

"I didn't pay attention. I just went back inside when Corbin ran off."

"It's something."

"I noticed a gray truck drive by while Laura Beth was in the field house," Millicent said. "But I didn't think to even look at the driver since I was watching the door of the field house for Laura Beth." She scrunched up her face. "But I don't think there was but one person in the cab." She plopped onto the chair beside Daly. "I'm sorry."

Tanner McGill arrived at the martial arts school after getting Penny Ulmer to the ER when she was shot. Almost losing one of his closest friends could only be eclipsed by the news that his son was missing—delivered with a right hook from Laura Beth.

Weeks later, finding a torture chamber where authorities felt certain Corbin would end up sent Tanner into an emotional plummet, prompting him to take a leave of absence.

Laura Beth dragged him and his daughter, Roslyn, home with her. She refused to let the man she was falling in love with give in to despair.

Somewhere in Louisiana, Corbin McGill woke from the shock to his system. He felt the rhythmic rotation of tires and heard the constant swish of cars passing. His eyes adjusted to the gloom.

He made out headlights through a narrow gap. *Where am I?* A moment's disorientation gave way to sheer panic as the events of the day flooded his mind. *The same truck was at the grocery store last year. The dead kid.*

Squirming sent a sharp pain up his arms. He jerked his bound wrists behind his back to no avail against duct tape. Mumbling incoherently behind the strip across his mouth, tears sprang to his eyes and bile crept up his esophagus. He swallowed it back, fully aware he would only asphyxiate if he allowed himself to give way to nausea. *Don't panic, Corbin. What did Dad teach me?*

The truck veered a slight right. Another half hour of turns, and it came to a stop. The door opened and closed with a creak. When the tarp curled back, Corbin wiggled away from the blond man.

"I thought you might be awake. You can sit up front if you behave. We'll be to our destination soon. What'll it be? Cab or bed?"

Corbin rolled his eyes toward the cab. *Stay calm. Look for an escape.* He looked around. Except for the lights of the truck, the night was pitch black—not even a sliver of a moon.

The man pulled Corbin by his feet to the tailgate and let it down. Taking a sharp blade from his shirt pocket, he slit the tape on the boy's feet. "Get out and stand up."

Corbin edged his way to the end of the tailgate. When his feet hit the ground, tingling and numbness together caused him to fall to the ground, landing on his knees right in front of his captor.

The man put a hand on Corbin's head. "Soon enough. Stand up now. You've dirtied that nice white get-up you're wearing."

Lifting Corbin by the elbow, the man helped him stand. Corbin mumbled around the tape.

The man took an edge of the tape with his thumb and index finger and jerked. Corbin yelped as the tape tore tiny facial hairs with its removal.

"Sh."

"Where are we?" Corbin managed to say.

"Caddo Lake. I rented all the cabins, so nobody will bother us."

The man led Corbin around the truck to the passenger door. The boy took in his surroundings. The lights of the truck illuminated a sign. Corbin shook his head, doubting what he read—The Church of Uncertain.

"Seriously?" He mumbled.

"I've never been certain. Are you?"

"Yeah. I know Jesus died for me, and when I die, I'm *certain* I'll go to Heaven. Are you going to kill me?"

"I might just keep you." He opened the door and lifted his captive inside, taking hold of the seatbelt.

"My hands?"

"Nope."

"My arms hurt."

With a scowl on his face, the man opened the glove box and took out the stun gun and the roll of duct tape. "If you pull anything, I'll zap you. Got it?"

Corbin nodded.

The man cut the tape around the boy's wrists. Corbin let out a soft groan as the pressure on his shoulder relaxed.

"Take off the gi top," the man said in a voice devoid of feeling.

"Why?"

The man held up the stun gun.

Corbin untied his black belt and slipped off the top of his karate uniform. "If you know this is called a gi, you know I have a black belt."

"I also know your daddy taught you to stay alive. Sit with your back flush against the seat and lift your arms."

"I need to pee."

"Soon. At the cabin."

With a huff, Corbin lifted his arms.

"My, my. You're almost too old." The man tugged one of Corbin's few underarm hairs.

"Almost thirteen. You could just leave me here if I'm too old."

"I said, 'Almost.'" He proceeded to loop tape around Corbin's torso and the bucket seat. He slipped the gi over the boy's arms and tucked it behind his back. "Hands down and clasp them in front of you."

Corbin did as he was told. The man wrapped the tape around his wrists three times. "That should hold you." He returned the tape and the stun gun to the glove box, closed the door, and got back behind the steering wheel. He made a noose with the belt and slipped it over the boy's head. "Don't make me tighten it." Making a U-turn, he drove a short way, taking numerous turns.

Corbin realized he was hopelessly lost, but come morning, he would follow the sun and head east.

As they turned down a road not much bigger than a goat path, Corbin noted the ancient bald cypress trees standing in murky swamp water and bit lighter in color than the sky. The trees loomed like jagged gray pikes against an inky background. The yellowish foliage on the trees cast a ghostly silhouette on the obsidian sky. A little lighter grayish-green Spanish moss draped eerily over the pallid limbs. A brisk breeze caused the moss to sway back and forth like long dangling curls.

They rounded a bend. A number of rustic cabins greeted them.

The man pulled to the farthest one from a small diner.

Diner equals food and cooks and servers, ran through Corbin's mind. *Even if he rented all the cabins, these folks will come to work.*

Lightning danced between clouds.

"What's your name?" Corbin asked.

"Phil."

"Are you going to kill me?"

"Not today."

I have time. Corbin visibly relaxed.

32
Stayin' Alive

Phil guided his prisoner up a short set of stairs, looped his right arm through Corbin's bound ones, and opened the cabin door.

The boy took in the layout—*One door. Right—couch and chair with TV. Left—recessed bed, no lockable door. Bathroom. Kitchenette with table and four chairs. Must be another bed on the other side of the bathroom.*

They walked directly to the bathroom. "You can pee now," Phil said.

Corbin glared at his captor. "A little privacy?"

"Afraid not."

After a huff, Corbin relieved his bladder with hands still bound as Phil leaned against the door jamb, loosely holding his makeshift leash.

"Sit at the table," Phil instructed. "You must be starved."

Corbin sat down.

First, Phil knelt by him and examined the burn mark on the child's rib cage. "You'll heal." He slipped the knotted noose from around the boy's neck.

"What do you want with me? Did you kill all those boys?"

"I only killed the monster."

"Pre-teen boys are monsters?"

"You have no clue." Phil stood, turned on the oven, and took out frozen corndogs from the freezer. "It's not a huge meal, but you need food and rest."

"Why, if you just plan to kill me?"

Phil placed the food in the oven and turned back to Corbin. He stroked the child's hair. "Oh, pretty boy, we're gonna have some fun. And I might just keep you."

"Your voice sounds different."

"Hush now." He let his fingers walk down the boy's chest and into the gi bottoms. Corbin tensed all over. "Relax," Phil murmured. "I'm not gonna hurt you—yet."

Tears flowed freely down the child's face. "Stop crying!" Phil snapped. "Or I'll give you a reason to cry."

Corbin caught his breath in gulps. *He's crazy—truly crazy.*

Phill went on, "You can treat me after you've had your supper."

"I-I-I'm not hungry."

A few minutes later, Phil slammed two corndogs in front of the boy. "You will eat," he snarled. "Mustard, ketchup, or both?"

Stay alive, Corbin. Play along. He hasn't hurt you yet—just humiliated you. And your little 'tool,' as Grammy calls it, went along for the ride.

"Both," he muttered.

The boy choked down the food. When he was done, Phil washed the dishes. He turned back to Corbin and grinned. "My turn." He dropped his jeans.

Corbin looked up with big blue eyes. *Stay alive; stay alive; stay alive* he chanted in his head as he reached out his still bound hands.

Corbin awoke to the sound of two voices arguing. He lay flat on his back, both hands secured to the headboard of the bed farthest from the door. Nude and uncovered, he shivered in the early morning chill.

"What are you doing?" an unfamiliar voice demanded. "You promised no more."

Phil's voice chimed in, "Relax, bro. I might just keep this one."

"That's what you said last time, and the time before. I won't let you do it again."

Cotton-mouthed, Corbin croaked, "Help me! He has me duct taped to the bed."

The sound of scuffling ended with the door opening and closing with a bang.

Stark naked, Phil appeared in the open area where the bed Corbin was on faced the kitchenette. He held his jaw. "Don't ever do that again if you don't want to be punished."

"Where's your brother? He might go to the cops."

Phil's laugh rang with hollow bitterness. "He doesn't have the balls. He wouldn't want the monster to know he's gay."

"Help!" Corbin struggled against his bonds.

Phil marched to the bed and jerked Corbin by the hair. "I told you not to do that." He found the roll of duct tape and wrenched off the tape around the boy's left arm.

Corbin shrieked as the hair on his arm ripped free.

Phil bound Corbin's hands together before he cut the tape from the other side of the headboard. "Time for a shower," he growled.

"I won't pick up the soap." Corbin could not keep the sarcasm from his voice. *Stay alive; stay alive; stay alive.*

"Yes, you will."

A week...ten days...two weeks. Corbin lost count of how long. He heard rain, caught glimpses of lightning, watched the edges of sunrises, noticed the treetops changing color.

Hands always bound together and to the headboard each night, Phil had rotated placing Corbin on his back, alternated sides, and his stomach. Corbin dreaded the nights on his stomach. He knew sodomy always came the next morning,

237

often with Phil pulling his head back with the knotted gi around his neck.

Curled on his left side, loud booming thunder jarred him awake. "Stay alive," he whispered to himself, as he did every morning. With each passing day, his mantra sounded less sure.

His captor fed him bare sustenance. The boy could not keep his tears in check this morning.

Phil appeared at the foot of the bed. He cut the tape that connected to the wood. "Don't try to run." He removed the tape from the boy's arms and tossed his karate gi to him. "Get dressed fast."

This can't be good. Trembling, Corbin dressed.

Before he could tie the belt, Phil snatched it and wrapped and knotted it around his wrists. "You're too slow." With a shove, he said, "In the bathroom."

"I'm dressed."

"Tornado."

"I hope to God it blows you away." Then his spirit prayed a silent plea for help and guidance.

In Sunrise, Laura Beth stroked Tanner's brow. "Coffee, darling."

"Any news?"

"No. I'm just doing my best to keep you alive—for Corbin—for Roslyn—for me." She let her tears fall. "I love you, Tanner. It's killing me to see you like this."

"I can't help it. I failed my son."

"No, you did not. You taught him well. I feel certain he'll come home to us. You have to believe it. If you don't pull yourself together, you *will* fail Roslyn. She cries all the time. She needs her daddy."

"You're right, Sugar." He sat up. "Has it really been three months?" He released a long, loud sigh. "Do you think David will call Purdue again today?"

"He calls every day." She put a light kiss on his lips. "A year ago, I wanted Diego Marin dead. Today, I'm glad he became David Black." Her dream of Marin saving Corbin floated back to her.

Tanner laughed sadly. "And Enrique de la Vega."

33
A Kink and a Chink

Phil looked at his phone. "Seems the bad stuff has passed."

"Your phone rings every day, but you never answer it. Is it your brother?"

"No. Someone who means something to my brother."

"Don't you have anybody that means something to you?"

"My brother, but the monster killed him." He led Corbin to the dining chair. "Sit down. I'll make us some breakfast." He laid his phone on the table and got out eggs from the refrigerator.

"How long did you rent this place?" Corbin asked.

"Christmas."

"Of course." He laid his head on the table just as Phil's phone rang. Corbin's eyes caught the caller I.D.—Enrique de la Vega.

He lifted his head. *David Black! Dad doesn't realize I heard him and Laura Beth talking. Phil? Is he Dillard Purdue? They're still looking for me.* "You should answer it," he said aloud.

Phil clamped a hand on Corbin's mouth from behind the boy. He answered the phone. "You should stop calling, Mr. de la Vega. My brother has gone away."

"Do not play games with me, Dillard Purdue. Have you not heard you are being sought by the FBI? I went to Tucson. Your home was torn apart. Your rig has been impounded. The supplies and merchandise you dealt in have been arrested, killed, or confiscated. You should come to the plantation. Let me get you to my villa in Argentina."

"Now, who's playing games? If the FBI is looking for Dill, they'll be all over that place."

Suddenly, Phil yelped as Corbin bit the hand over his mouth. Phil jerked his hand away.

"Caddo Lake! Caddo Lake!" Corbin yelled.

Phil threw the phone across the room, shattering it to pieces.

"You little shit!" He slapped Corbin hard enough to knock him off the chair.

"Stop it!" A different voice came from Phil's mouth. "Don't hurt him."

Phil grabbed is head and screamed, "I told you to stay away! Why must you always throw a kink into my plans?"

Corbin stared in horror as the two sides of Purdue waged war. He took in the blond hair with black roots. "You are crazy!" the boy yelled.

"Shut up!" Phil shrieked. He jerked Corbin up. "We're outa here."

The rain still fell in torrents as he dragged the boy to the truck and shoved him in. He backhanded Corbin and grabbed duct tape from the glove box, slapped a piece over the boy's mouth, and took the karate belt noose, looping it over Corbin's head. "Cooperate, or I'll choke the life out of you."

"That was Corbin!" Tanner yelled when the phone line went dead.

David had used his speaker phone. A number of people congregated each morning in the sheriff's dining room for David to make his daily call. Finally, there had been an answer.

Luis sat nearby with a triangulating program running. "Not enough time to get an exact fix, but I have something. Sending coordinates to Pickering."

"Caddo Lake!" David said, jumping to his feet. "I know the place."

"Big place to search. Let Pickering work." Luis pointed.

Tanner and David turned to see Pickering talking on his phone. The FBI agent said, "Louisiana State Police on their way, and Texas Rangers are on their way from their side. I gave them Luis's data." The older man nodded with approval toward the young man who had been his dead son's best friend.

Laura Beth clutched Tanner's hand. "He's alive. And still fighting."

"Yeah. David, I don't know how to thank you." Tanner released a held breath.

David shrugged. "Be my friend."

With a nod, Tanner said, "Done deal." The two men clasped hands and ended with a bro-hug.

Penny rubbed her husband's arm when he stepped back. "You just showed all of us the chink in your armor." She smiled.

"I love kids." David put his arm around her.

"That's not a chink," Laura Beth said. "That's a jewel in your crown." She looked around. "Do you think he'll come back here? He sounded like he's on to the watch."

"He'll come back," Pickering said with an assuring nod.

Louisiana and Texas authorities descended on the camp where Purdue had rented the slot of cabins. They broke down doors. "Here!" A Ranger yelled. "They left in a hurry."

A woman from the diner across the way came out. "What's going on?"

The Ranger pointed. "The occupants. Tell me about them."

"A man and his son. He rented the whole line of cabins—a family reunion, but nobody else ever came."

"That didn't strike you as odd?" He scowled at the woman "How long?"

"Until Christmas."

Arching an eyebrow, the Ranger went on, "And that wasn't strange to you either?"

"I never saw them. They caused no trouble and paid the rental price. Never saw the kid until a couple of hours ago."

"And?"

"We had that tornado threat. Soon after, the man dragged the kid out. The kid looked tied up. If you check records, I called 9-1-1."

The Ranger waved over a Louisiana trooper. "Technically this is your side of the lake, but we need to work together here. Get a description. License plate?"

"Yes," the woman said and went back to the diner, followed by the officer.

Purdue pulled into a rest stop on I-20. He took off his car tag and replaced it with a different license plate.

"Stop this!" the other voice said.

"Shut up!"

"Okay. Home. Take us home, and I'll shut up. Just don't hurt the kid. Please?"

"Home? You hate that place."

"Phil, it has to stop."

"Yes, Dill. One more monster to kill."

34
They always Come Home

Pickering contacted all personnel watching Purdue Plantation. He let them know the most recent developments and cautioned them to be extra-vigilant.

His ringing phone caused the assembled worried friends and family of Corbin McGill to jump. Pickering answered.

"Steve Journey here," the voice on the other end of the line said. "I can't get back there to help with this case, but I've been following your progress since I left. Just had the urge to call with encouragement."

"Thanks. Putting you on speaker."

"Fine."

Pickering hit his speaker button. "So, encourage."

"You should expect your killer to come home—they always do. Serial killers tend to revisit the scene of the crime."

"We have the place staked out."

"He should be there soon if he sticks to his pattern. Wish you all the best."

The call ended.

"We already knew that," Tanner said.

Nodding, Pickering added, "Yeah, but to get a profiler like Steve to confirm our suspicions is almost as good as having it written in stone."

Phil drove without speaking, eyes glued to the road.

Removing the tape from his own mouth, Corbin stole a glance at him. "Can I turn on the radio?" he asked with tremulous voice. "I'm sorry."

Phil gave a curt nod. Corbin pushed the ON button. "Christmas music? What day is it?"

After a quick glance right, Phil mumbled, "December sixteenth."

"I missed the whole semester. I was seventh-grade quarterback. I had three girlfriends." He brushed unwanted tears from his cheeks. "Where are we going?"

"Home."

"Are you going to kill me now?"

"I have to kill the monster." ·

"I'm not a monster." He leaned his head against the cool glass and watched the rain spatter the window for a while. Then he said, "Neither was that boy I saw in the parking lot at the grocery store. I'm Corbin McGill. I missed my thirteenth birthday."

"I made you a cake."

"I hate spice cake."

"It was gingerbread."

"Same difference."

"What kind of cake do you like?" Phil glanced toward his passenger.

"Lemon."

"Next time, I'll make lemon."

"But you're going to kill me."

"I have to kill the monster."

"I'm not a monster."

Just on the Louisiana side of the Mississippi River, Phil stopped at a cheap motel. He checked in and paid the cashier for two nights, leaving Corbin duct taped to the truck seat.

The boy stared straight ahead and watched the raindrops roll down the windshield. *I must look just like that boy I saw. He knew he was going to die.* He released a loud groan. "I refuse to die," he said when Phil got back in the truck.

"Our room is on the opposite side. We need to rest."

"What? No sex?"

"Too tired." He put his hand on the boy's head. "I'd like to keep you. I promise we'll have more play time."

"You are a sick bastard. You know, Phil, you're the real monster."

"Hush now. Don't make me mad." He pulled the knotted belt around Corbin's throat a little tighter.

"Okay," Corbin croaked, clawing at the makeshift noose. "Sleep sounds good. How about a burger and a Coke?"

"Yeah. I'm hungry." He let go of the belt.

Corbin closed his eyes. *Stay alive.*

Left untouched for two days, Corbin began to feel half-normal. He knew his battle was far from over, but he also found renewed determination to stay alive.

When check-out time came, Phil presented Corbin with a pair of new blue jeans and a blue button-down shirt. Corbin eyed him with wariness. "I wondered where you went when you left me alone."

"Get dressed." He held up the stun gun. "No shenanigans."

Corbin folded his grungy gi and took the new clothes. He went in the bathroom and came out dressed. "The pants are a little big."

Phil grunted and placed his hand on a chair. "Sit here."

Corbin sat down. Phil pulled a Polaroid camera from a bag and took a picture. "You are such a pretty boy. I never want to forget you."

"I don't know how you could forget any of the boys you've killed."

"Hush now." He handed Corbin a shoebox with a new pair of Converse sneakers. "Put them on. We need to go."

Once the boy was fully dressed, Phil bound his wrists again. "It's nippy out. Get in the truck fast."

In the truck, Phil pulled Corbin's shirt from its tucked state and again wrapped tape around the boy and the seat.

Corbin grunted. "No wonder that boy I saw was so still. He couldn't move. He'd already given up." *The body wore new jeans and a blue oxford shirt, just like these. That shoe Freckles found was Converse. He must dress all his <u>monsters</u> alike.*

Phil got behind the steering wheel without comment and headed east. Corbin stole glances at his captor. Phil's jaw clenched and unclenched. He appeared deep in thought.

Across the Mississippi River, Phil turned north and followed the state highway parallel to the river toward Sunrise.

"Home," Corbin muttered. "They always come home. I saw that on *Criminal Minds*."

The ride continued in silence. Corbin kept his head against the glass of the window, praying that God would give him a way to escape. When he recognized the turn-off toward Sunrise, he sat up straight.

Phil bypassed the turn.

"Where are we going?" Corbin asked.

"Home."

Various law enforcement agencies sat in vigilance around Purdue Plantation keeping watch, especially on the hidden storm cellar door. Radios crackled from time to time with status reports.

One of Penny's deputies reported, "Nothing. After the kid alerted authorities, I expected them by now."

Pickering's agent at his post responded, "Dead here too. Don't fall asleep."

A Sunrise officer weighed in. "Whizzing in the bushes. Give me two." A short moment later he came back. "Starting to rain. Feels like sleet."

"Just great," the deputy chimed in.

The agent added, "I'm from Maine. This is mild."

Chatter stopped and the authorities waited as they had for weeks.

Phil turned the Silverado onto a back, gravel road that wound down the bluffs to a trail where off-road vehicles traveled close to the river. The tires splashed through standing water.

"We must have had a lot of rain," Corbin said.

"Just a challenge to overcome," Phil grunted. "I'm pretty sure the front entrance is being watched." He glared at his passenger. "Thanks to your little outburst. This could have been so much easier."

Corbin let out a bitter laugh. "If I die, I'll go down fighting. I will be your little monster."

With a guttural growl, Phil slammed the truck into park. Like a viper strike, he punched the boy in the mouth. Blood poured from Corbin's lip. Phil looped the noose he had created from the child's karate belt back over Corbin's head and pulled. Reaching into his pocket he pulled out a box cutter and slit the duct tape around the boy's torso, and then unbuckled the seatbelt.

"We're home. Come on." He dragged Corbin across seats, out the driver's door.

Corbin groped with his bound hands at the tightness around his throat. He fell with a splat into the frigid mud.

"Get up! You're getting dirty!" Phil screamed. He kicked the fallen boy.

Scrambling to his feet, Corbin let out an agonizing bellow.

35
Nightmare on Elm Street

Laura Beth stared with red-rimmed eyes at her naked Christmas tree. She looked over her shoulder at Tanner and her three children with his daughter. None of them had the heart to hang an ornament with Corbin still missing.

Seventeen-month-old Riker Copeland picked up a delicate crystal angel and toddled to his mother. She picked him up and helped him hang the ornament. Placing a kiss on his cheek she whispered, "Innocence. No more decorations until Corbin comes home." She ran an index finger across the adornment. "Corbin's guardian angel. Bring him home. Please, God?"

All of a sudden, Freckles jumped from his dog bed by the fireplace and charged the front door, snarling and growling.

Tanner groaned, "Sorry, Sugar. I still haven't installed the pet door."

"Freckles, go place!" Laura Beth commanded. The Pitbull whined but went back to his bed. Laura Beth followed and rubbed his head. "What's wrong with you? The weather is just too nasty to walk." She thought, *you've gotten so big, and we didn't have a first doggie birthday. Sorry, boy. We'll celebrate when Corbin comes home.*

She turned to Tanner. "We're gonna need an extra-large door."

David dialed Dillard Purdue's number again. "Something is really wrong, Penny."

"Not even voicemail?"

"Nothing." He buried his face in his hands. "I let Corbin down."

Penny laid her hand on his head. "No, you didn't. Both you and Tanner have taught him to survive."

Their three children and two Great Danes came away from the huge bay window in the kitchen. Abel leaned on David's shoulder. "No snow, Papa."

Penny laughed. "If it snows this early in Mississippi, it's a miracle. We often go years without eve a flake. I've worn shorts and flip-flops on Christmas Day."

Without warning, the two dogs raced to the back door and barked in frenzy. Penny shook her head. "No!"

Leather and Lace barked more.

"No!" Penny said again.

Emma said, "They already went out before it started raining so hard."

"That's sleet," said Aaron.

Abel took his siblings' hands. "Let's go play *Mario Party*."

The deputy on watch hit his radio. "Did anyone hear a scream?"

"Negative," replied the Sunrise officer.

"No," the FBI echoed.

The state trooper weighed in, "All I hear is the ice pelting my car. There is no movement near the main house."

"Not on the drive in either," reaffirmed the Sunrise officer.

"I could have sworn I heard something," the deputy said.

"Keep listening," said the agent. "If you hear anything else, we'll converge."

"Roger that."

Phil dragged Corbin up an incline to a rust-colored door camouflaged against the Yazoo clay cliffs. He gripped the noose tighter and fumbled in his pocket for a key. Corbin struggled against his bindings. Phil jerked the noose. "Stop!" He hissed.

The lock clicked and the door creaked open. Phil reached into a crevice and pulled out a flashlight. He yanked Corbin inside and closed the door.

Like a dog on a leash, Phil led Corbin down a short flight of steps. The light danced along, casting creepy shadows on the walls, highlighting crystalline lime deposits from frequent floods.

At what appeared to be a wall, Phil wrapped the belt around his arm multiple times, dug his finger into a groove, and pushed the wall forward.

He grabbed Corbin by the shoulders and pushed him into a room. After he himself stepped through, he pushed the wall back in place.

"Aah!" Corbin shrieked when he saw shelves with skeletons on them.

Phil reached on the top shelf and grabbed ever-present duct tape. He slapped a piece over Corbin's mouth and forced the boy onto the chair in the center of the room. He secured one of the boy's arms and then cut the tape holding Corbin's wrists together.

With his hand momentarily free, Corbin took the opportunity to hit his captor upside the head. Then, he kicked Phil in the shin.

Phil slapped Corbin with great force, twisted the boy's arm, and taped it firmly to the other arm of the chair.

"Damn you!" he roared as Corbin continued to kick.

Pressing his whole body's weight against the boy, Phil unsnapped the child's jeans and stepped back to flick off Corbin's shoes and jerk the jeans off.

Corbin kept up his fight, rocking the chair.

Phil managed to secure one of Corbin's ankles to a leg and then the other. He stepped back, winded. "Damn! You put up a fight. But look at you—trussed up like a Thanksgiving turkey." He took his box cutter and sliced off the boy's briefs. "Ah. Exposed."

He walked to a side wall where an assortment of canes and whips hung. "I have to get you under control." He chose a beaded flogger and walked back to the boy.

Touching Corbin in his private parts, Phil ran his hand up the boy's stomach and unbuttoned his shirt. He pinched the boy's nipples. "Hmm." He gave his prisoner a whack with the flogger along his lower abdomen.

Corbin flinched and shook his head.

Phil laughed. He walked to the other wall and picked up a set of clamps. Bringing them back, he attached them to Corbin's nipples and pulled, hard.

The boy sobbed behind his gag.

"Oh, did that hurt?" He pulled again, and then struck with the flogger hard enough to bring a welt just above the pubic bone. Again, he flogged the boy. And again, he yanked the nipple clamps.

"Oh!" Phil moaned as his erection strained against denim.

"I have something special for you." He got another set of larger clamps and knelt in front of the half-naked boy.

Corbin thrashed.

"Wait!" The voice belonged to Dillard Purdue. "At least give him one dose of morphine."

"I left it in the truck."

"Get it. He's not going anywhere."

"Oh, hell."

"This is the last monster—remember? Do it right. Slow."

"Fine."

Phil stood and gathered the flashlight.

"Leave the light," Dillard's voice said. "There's another on the shelf."

Phil leaned over Corbin and clutched his budding manhood. "I'll be right back. Don't bother trying to yell behind the tape. Nobody can hear you underground and with sleet falling."

Nobody? What about *something?* Corbin had a fleeting hope.

36
The Karate Kid

Corbin heard the body-filled wall slide open. *Hurry.* His thoughts flew as he surveyed the room. *Dillard is giving me time.*

Rocking his body back and forth, Corbin gave one hard lean right and toppled the chair on its side. He felt the old wood give. He jerked his right arm forward. The whole armrest pulled loose.

Though still connected to the wood, Corbin could move his arm. He reached across and tore the duct tape off his left arm, and then back he went to his right.

Not caring if hair came out with the tape, he ripped his ankles free and last his mouth.

Springing to his feet, Corbin took in the broken chair. He picked up the arm with the dowel connected. *It looks like a tonfa. David said broken chair legs could make usable tonfa.* He stomped the other armrest loose in the same manner as the one he held— oblivious to splinters in his feet from the jagged edges.

Finally feeling the sting of the nipple clamps, he removed them and looked down at the larger clamps. He snatched them up and raced to the wall with shelves of items he had never seen.

He spotted two large quasi-diamond shaped rubbery items with a base. He picked them up. *Not very heavy, but it might work. Nearly the same size and weight.*

Corbin swung his improvised tonfa. *Not bad.* He looked at the rubbery objects and the metal clamps. Then, he looped the chain around each base with a clamp, but the objects did not stay connected when swung hard. *Duct tape. Just call me*

MacGyver. Corbin  picked up the pieces of duct tape and secured the clamps to the bases of the objects. He swung his homemade meteor hammer. *Nice flow.*

Hearing shuffling in the corridor, Corbin stood to the side of the secret opening and waited.

Phil stepped into the old storm cellar turned dungeon, and his mouth fell open when he saw the shattered chair.

"What the hell?" he bellowed.

Phil turned just as Corbin swung his meteor hammer and delivered a loud, "Ki ai!" The weight caught Phil against his head. It did not inflict a great deal of pain, but the blow took him by surprise.

Corbin pulled back and used the makeshift balls and chain to entangle Phil's feet, causing him to land hard on the packed dirt. The boy darted forward with the constructed tonfa and delivered blow after blow—each accompanied with the loud and long signature, "Ki ai!"

Blood began to run from Phil's nose and mouth.

"Run, boy! Run!" Dillard's voice rang out.

Tonfa still in hand, Corbin dashed out the opening in the wall.

"I heard something, damn it all!" the deputy said into his walkie-talkie. "Get down here!"

37

Canine Justice

Freckles growled and charged the door. "Good God!" Tanner yelled. "Let the dog out."

Laura Beth barely opened the door before the Pitbull bolted out and streaked toward Purdue Plantation.

Tanner came to the door and watched brindled fur disappear into the woods. He slapped the door jamb. "Sugar, he heard something. Corbin!" No jacket in fast falling sleet, he took off after the dog.

"Tanner! Take the car!" Laura Beth hollered after him. "Shit!"

"Mommy! You cussed!" Stacey said.

"Sorry. Roslyn, you're in charge. Lock the door until I get back." She grabbed Tanner's coat, her coat, the dog's leash, her handbag, and her keys and jumped in her Jaguar.

Reaching in her jean pocket, she pulled out her cell and dialed Penny.

"What's up?" the sheriff answered.

"Are your dogs acting strange?"

"Yes."

"Let them out. If they head toward Purdue Plantation, get over there."

Penny opened her back door, and her two Great Danes tore across the field toward her new chain-link fence. "Good Lord! The way they're galloping, they'll jump the fence. Something's up, David. Let's go. Kids, stay here. Lock the doors."

She dialed Pickering on the fly.

Law enforcers scouring the undergrowth near the locked entrance to the storm cellar were bowled over as three massive canines raced past them. Two men landed in mud and two hugged trees to stay on their feet.

"They're headed down the bluffs!" the deputy yelled.

"Down?" Tanner asked catching his breath as he followed Freckles. "Come on!"

Corbin barreled down the dark passageway. A brownish, snarling, bear-like shadow bumped into him, stopping long enough to deliver a lick. Two more enormous creatures surged past him. He kept running. Agonizing wails followed him as he burst out the hidden door.

Five men slipped and slid down the muddy clay bluffs.

"Dad!" Corbin hollered when he saw who one of them was.

Right behind the men, came Laura Beth, Penny, and David, having seen which way the others had gone.

Tanner reached his son and engulfed him. The other four men continued into the tunnel.

Laura Beth got to Tanner and Corbin. She hastily threw Tanner's coat over the mostly naked child.

Corbin's next words shut every adults' mouths. "Miss Laura Beth! They'll kill him. Make the dogs stop."

"Who cares?" Tanner yelled.

"Please?" the boy sobbed. "Dillard saved me. He wants to die, at least kill Phil. But if Phil dies, so does Dillard. The dogs will kill him."

Without a second thought, Laura Beth raced inside, yet another entrance to the Purdue tomb. None of the four officers were having any luck getting the dogs off the man and suffered a few bites of their own. "Break, Freckles!" Laura Beth shouted. The Pitbull let go and moved away.

"Leather! Lace!" Penny's voice rang out. Both Danes sat.

Dillard Purdue moaned, blood flowing freely from a myriad of bites.

The front entrance opened, and Pickering stepped in. "Well, shit! I guess I need two ambulances."

The deputy lifted a hand that dripped its own blood. "Maybe more than that."

Pickering pointed to his agent. "Can you drive your colleagues to the hospital?"

Sucking on his thumb, the agent answered, "Yeah. Mine's not much more than a scratch."

"Then, go." He took a second to ask with great sarcasm, "Ladies, have they had their shots?"

The two women chorused, "Yes."

As he spoke, a siren screamed closer. Penny pointed. "Get him to the hospital before he bleeds to death." She got close to Purdue. "You're under arrest."

"Thank God," Dillard said.

"Little monster," Phil's voice said.

"Why can't you die?" Dillard said.

3.8
In His Father's Arms

Tanner held fast to Corbin. "I can't believe you care whether that bastard lives or dies. You have your mother's heart."

"He's crazy, Dad, truly crazy."

Laura Beth and Penny came out of the tunnel with dogs on their heels.

David approached Corbin. "Thank God, you're alive! I'm sorry I didn't get to him first."

Corbin said, "You helped me." He pointed, still holding the constructed tonfa. "You should go inside and see what I made." A proud smile crossed the boy's face. "My own tonfa and meteor hammer."

David tapped the wood. "I see. I'm proud of you." He turned. "I'm going in." Pointing at Corbin, he continued, "Take him to the ER."

"Right now," Tanner said.

Laura Beth said, "My car is up the slope."

Penny called a deputy. "Take these dogs home. The Danes are mine. Freckles belongs to Mrs. Copeland. All of them are up to date on shots. We'll call our kids and tell them you're coming."

"Yes, Sheriff."

"Go!" both women commanded the animals.

The canines followed the deputy, and the mothers called home.

Roslyn squealed when she heard her brother was safe and begged to go to the hospital. "I'll get you there," Laura Beth told her. "Let me call Miss Madeleine. Call your grandmother."

She made the call quick and gave her friends the bare bones. Then, she put an arm around Corbin and hugged him close. "Hospital to get checked out." She kissed him on the head. "I was so scared. I love you, darling." She glanced up at Tanner. "And you."

A huge breath escaped Tanner's lungs. "You drive us, Sugar. I think I'll sit in the back with my son."

"You got it, Cream."

"Cream Puff."

The three headed off toward the cars.

Penny jerked her head toward the tunnel as she and David heard the wail of the siren. "The dogs almost killed him," she whispered.

They went into the room. The coroner had arrived to take the old remains and try to identify them. Dr. Daiwa stood by. "Sheriff"—He dipped his head toward Penny—"I think the nightmare on Elm Street is over."

"I hope so."

David knelt and picked up the pieces of broken chair. "Corbin is a smart boy."

Penny pointed to black objects duct taped to the large clamps. "Look at that."

David picked up Corbin's improvised meteor hammer. He roared with laughter.

"What is so damned funny?" asked Pickering.

David held up the make-do weapon. "He used nipple clamps and butt plugs."

"Oh, my God!" Penny gasped and examined the device closer. "Those *are* butt plugs." She pointed. "From over there."

Pickering chuckled. "Well, once all this *stuff* is carted away, what will Mr. de la Vega do with this room?"

"I'll ask him," David said with a smug grin.

"Yeah." Pickering shoved his hands into his pockets. "You do that."

At the hospital Dillard Purdue received over a hundred stitches before he was placed in a private room, handcuffed to the bed and a guard at the door. His pretty face now resembled the work of Dr. Frankenstein.

Tanner held his son close to his side as they entered the ER at the same time Purdue was being wheeled to the elevator. He stepped between the gurney and the child.

"Good work, pretty boy," Purdue murmured when he saw Corbin. "I tried to make him stop. Sorry."

"Sorry!" Tanner roared and took a step toward the man.

"Dad!" Corbin grabbed his father's right arm.

Laura Beth snagged his left. "Stop. He poked the wrong pig."

Tanner shook with rage. "Let me finish what Freckles started."

Purdue mumbled, "Phil is gone—I hope."

"You think you're gonna get an insanity plea?" Tanner huffed in agitation.

"He's nuts, Dad," Corbin said again.

"Get him out of my sight," Tanner growled. He then demanded immediate care for Corbin.

Doctors examined the child thoroughly and drew blood to test for STDs, including HIV, but other than several deep contusions, some deep abrasions, and a cut along his eyebrow that required five stiches, the doctors found no reason to admit him. He had no broken bones and no concussion. He would have a black eye and be sore for a while.

"We're going to my house," Laura Beth declared. "We have a Christmas tree waiting just for you."

"That's fine." Corbin yawned. "Maybe tomorrow? I'm so tired."

Tanner nodded. "Tomorrow. You have some clothes at Laura Beth's."

They prepared to leave at the very moment Doug Blanchard arrived with Roslyn. The little girl ran to her brother. "You're naked," she squeaked.

Tanner wrapped his large coat more securely around Corbin who reached up like a little boy to be picked up. His father gathered him in his arms.

Laura Beth put her arm around Roslyn's shoulders. "You can sit up front with me on the way home if Dad promises not to arrest me since you're not twelve yet."

"I'll turn a blind eye, Sugar," Tanner said.

Doug Blanchard cleared his throat. "I'll be back shortly." He headed toward the information desk.

The tall, distinguished gentleman with aristocratic high cheekbones and snow-white hair approached the guard at the door of Purdue's room just as Enrique de la Vega came from the other direction with Millicent Shapiro in tow. Doug Blanchard raised an eyebrow in question as they met.

"Open the door," Shapiro said. "Counsel for Mr. Purdue."

"All of you?" the guard asked.

"Yes."

He shook his head. "He's gonna need a team." After frisking the three, he allowed them passage.

Purdue lifted heavy eyelids as his visitors came in. Sluggishly, he mumbled, "My lawyer—Okay. Plead guilty by reason of mental defect. I'll go quietly to the loony bin. I swear I had no control when Phil took over."

"I can do that," Millicent said.

"I'm still gay." He reached a hand toward Enrique. "I guess this is good-bye."

"Sí, but I had to see you one last time."

Purdue tried to laugh. "I think you are not what you pretend, but I do appreciate you coming."

He turned toward Doug Blanchard. "Who are you?"

Both others looked at the older man. Doug took a deep breath. "I'm pretty sure I'm your father. I was intimate with your mother at the right time, and you look a lot like me. Just know she never told me about you."

"Ah. I know. I saw you a long time ago, but she never told me your name."

"Doug Blanchard."

"So, why are you here now?"

"You need support. If I had known, I would have taken you."

"I wish you had. Maybe then, Phil never would have shown his ugly face."

"Is it too late?"

"If Millicent can get me committed, I'll be glad to know you. I'm smart enough to know I can never be free—just in case."

"I'll start some paperwork," Millicent said. "What Corbin McGill says will be of utmost importance."

Enrique muttered, "He will ask for clemency."

"How do you know?" asked Doug.

De la Vega gave a tight-lipped smile. "Señor Blanchard, we must talk before I go back to Argentina. Now, Dill"—He took the man's hand and squeezed—"I must leave. Vaya con dios."

"Dad?" Purdue mumbled.

"Doug, until tests come back."

"Even after, it will be best." He drifted off.

39

Give the Dog a Bone

Corbin awoke with something warm and wet on his toes. His half-asleep whimper was met by a whine.

The boy slowly opened his eyes. After months of being bound to a headboard, it took several long seconds for him to realize he was in the guest bedroom at Laura Beth's house. He glanced at his feet to see brown, speckled fur and the head of a huge dog licking his feet.

"Ooh, Freckles! Toe jam."

The dog gave a yip.

Sore all over, Corbin groaned when he moved. He patted his chest. "Here, boy."

The massive Pitbull belly crawled up the bed and stretched full out beside the boy. Corbin laughed. "You're longer than I am tall." He rubbed the dog's head. "Thanks for coming. He said nobody would hear me, but I knew *you* would. And you brought reinforcements." He chuckled. "I guess Leather and Lace heard me too."

The door, barely cracked, creaked a little further open. "May we come in?" Laura Beth asked. "We brought breakfast."

"Sure." He sat up with effort and grunts. "Just not scrambled eggs. I might never eat them again."

"How about French toast and sausage?" Tanner asked, pushing the door wide open.

"Orange juice?"

"Absolutely," Laura Beth assured.

Corbin's eyes widened, and he grinned. "And chocolate milk! Yeah!" He turned toward his father as his sister and Laura Beth's two girls crept in behind the adults. "You didn't put my face on a bulletin board, did you?"

Tanner ruffled his son's hair. "It was close. Agent Pickering did plaster it all over television and social media, though."

Laura Beth shooed the dog to the floor and set the tray across Corbin's legs.

Roslyn sat beside her brother and laid her head on his shoulder. She sniffled, "I won't ever fight with you again."

"Sure, you will." He bumped his head against hers. "Ow. Let's not do that right now."

The girl giggled.

Corbin went on, "That's what brothers and sisters do— argue. Doesn't mean we don't love each other."

Stacey and Tonya Copeland went to the other side of the bed and gave Corbin hugs. He grunted since he was sore all over. Corbin winked at his father. "Two more little sisters and a little brother?"

Laura Beth felt a burn in her face. Tanner crossed his arms across his chest. "We'll see."

Corbin picked up a sausage link and took a bite. Freckles whined. Corbin gave the dog the rest of the meat.

"Corbin!" Tanner scolded, half-heartedly.

"He deserves a treat. He came to my rescue." The boy downed the chocolate milk without a breath.

"We'll get him some really good dog treats," Laura Beth said with a laugh.

Jabbering across the hall got her attention. She pointed. "That possible little brother is demanding breakfast."

"Can't have mine." Corbin grinned and tore into the French toast.

Corbin rested the whole day but insisted he wanted to get up the next day. In the afternoon, Tanner's phone rang. He took the call in private.Coming back into the family area, he let out a loud breath. "Good news or bad news?"

"Bad first," Laura Beth said with a scowl.

"I got interrupted on one call and ended up having two. The prosecutor is willing to have Purdue sent to the Mississippi State Mental Hospital for the Criminally Insane, if Corbin agrees." Tanner ground his teeth at the thought. "He swears Purdue'll never get out since no psychiatrist can predict if this other personality will show itself again. I want the bastard dead. I'm sure other parents do too."

"Dad," Corbin said with wisdom beyond his years. "He was abused and molested. Dillard is innocent. Phil, well, I guess he thought he was protecting Dill. He kept saying he had to kill the monster. I get that the blond hair and blue eyes reminded him of his father, and he couldn't separate the two. Yeah, I'll say send him to the nuthouse."

He brushed tears from his face. Laura Beth sat beside him and put her arms around him.

Corbin went on, "I think I'll become a psychiatrist and help people like him."

Tanner put his hand over his mouth and turned away. *"Lord, my son does have Your Spirit. I can't bring myself to that point yet. Thank You for giving him back to me. Help me be the father he deserves."* After steadying himself, he turned back. "Okay. If that's what you want."

"Yes, sir. What about other states?"

"Too smart." Tanner shook his head. "A federal prosecutor is handling this case, and he will recommend Dillard stay in Mississippi in the mental facility for the rest of his life."

"What's the good news?" Laura Beth asked.

Tanner nodded. "Two things. First, the doctor called. All Corbin's tests were negative."

"Thank God!" Laura Beth gushed out.

"You said two," Corbin prompted.

"Yes. Well, it seems one family member and two of our neighbors are receiving commendations."

"*Our* neighbors? *Family* member?" Corbin closed one eye and pursed his lips. "What happened while I was away?"

Tilting his head to the side, Tanner said, "Topic for later."

"Humph!" Corbin bit his lip. "Okay. So, I take it Freckles, Leather, and Lace are being honored." Corbin stretched his eyes wide, gingerly touched his cheek at the discomfort the action caused, and drummed the fingers of his right hand on his left arm.

Tanner knew there was a lot to discuss. He nodded. "Yep. Tomorrow on the steps of city hall. The mayor has requested your presence on the steps."

"Sounds like fun. Can we go to Gus's after?"

Laura Beth laughed. "Anywhere you want."

Bright blue skies and brisk temperatures greeted the honorees, spectators, and media on this December morning just before Christmas.

Corbin still had a bruise on his face but looked good otherwise. The doctor had used light colored sutures, so they blended with the boy's eyebrow. He dressed in a heavy black turtle-neck sweater and khakis, just like his father. Laura Beth wore dark green slacks with a peach and green striped sweater. The girls wore jeans and sweaters of their choice.

The McGills and Copelands met Penny, David, and family a few minutes before the ceremony. David chuckled and whispered to Tanner, "You taking over my black?"

"Nope."

David wore a royal-blue sweater and charcoal trousers. Penny had on her uniform with a jacket. Their children looked much like the other group. Emma reached out to hold Riker when the mayor came onto the steps behind the podium and the mic that were set up. Local news crews aimed cameras and zoomed in when necessary.

Greg Mims, mayor, waved everyone forward and indicated where they should stand.

"Welcome to this unusual gathering," he said before the microphone gave loud feedback.

Luis Montoya shook his head and jumped up the steps to adjust the device. He nuzzled Marge's ear when he stepped back down.

"If you weren't awake before, you should be now," joked Mims.

"I won't keep you long. Our town has just come through a torturous time. We are so relieved and blessed to have Corbin McGill back with us." He nodded toward the boy and the crowd applauded.

Corbin gave a shy wave, not really enjoying the attention.

The mayor continued, "The sick individual responsible for terrible acts has been apprehended and will never see freedom again."

The throng clapped again.

"This person's capture was due in large part to three unlikely heroes." He looked at Leather and Lace on one side of the podium and Freckles on the other. "Because of their acts of valor, it gives this old man pleasure to give the dogs a bone."

A ripple of laughter made all three canines perk up their ears.

Mims picked up three bone-shaped bronze medals. "For acts of valor and service to Sunrise, Mississippi, I hereby award Freckles a Bronze Bone." He bent down and hooked the three-inch-long medal to the dog's collar. Freckles lifted his paw, and the mayor shook it with a hearty laugh. Then he repeated the same phrase and action for Leather and Lace.

"Ladies and gentlemen, I would that all humans showed this loyalty and love. Maybe we should learn a lesson from these brave dogs. Let's give them one more bone."

The steps of city hall were suddenly littered with Milk Bones, which the canines unceremoniously gobbled up to roars of laughter and applause.

40
They Need a Mother

As the spectators began to disperse with handshaking and backslapping, Marge Montoya hit the concrete in a dead faint. Luis, her husband, knelt beside her and gently patted her cheeks.

Within seconds Tanner was beside them. "What's wrong? Do we need an ambulance?"

"No," Luis said. "I don't think this is the way she wanted to tell you."

"Ah, shit. She's pregnant."

"Yeah. Due June seventh."

"Well, congrats. Will she be leaving me?"

"No. Just maternity leave. She'll be back. She loves her job and her boss." Luis grinned. "Should I be jealous?"

Tanner laughed. "Think she can help me make Laura Beth jealous?"

"I heard y'all," Marge mumbled. "I don't wanna take on that little tigress. She shot David in the ass."

"Sh," both men said.

"Aha!" She sat up. "I knew it."

Tanner cracked up. "Faker. I taught *you* well." Both he and Luis helped Marge stand.

Laura Beth finally got to them after putting Freckles in the car. "What's wrong?"

"Just having a baby." Marge smiled.

"That's wonderful!"

"Yeah, if I can ever stop being sick and dizzy. Now that my boss is back, a day off would be nice."

"Am I back?" Tanner said with mock shock on his face.

Marge scowled. "You better be."

"I still sort of need help with my kids. My mom has moved to Madison." He glanced at Laura Beth.

She huffed and walked away.

"Smooth move, Ex-lax," Marge muttered. "Don't use your kids to get to her."

"She said she loves me."

"Then play that angle. I'm taking today off."

"Come to Gus's and eat with us."

"Sure. Then, I'm going home. The office is yours."

Corbin dragged his family along with Laura Beth's, the Blacks, the Montoyas, and Ed Pickering to Gus's Goulash in celebration of freedom. Since it was early winter, Gus had closed his patio until New Year's Eve. He allowed the three dogs to stay there while the humans ate.

First with a bowl of goulash, and then Gus's chili-cheeseburger, Corbin stuffed himself.

During the camaraderie, Gus approached Penny. "I'm so glad you're okay. That one day was the pits—you shot, Corbin taken, me robbed." The older man shook his head and looked toward his son, Todd, who had taken a seat by Emma. "At least it was a wakeup call for him."

Penny nodded. "Omar too. Apparently, he got mixed up with cocaine. But Purdue had nothing to do with Omar's problem. Omar confessed to several home thefts. He'd get to Jackson and pawn the stuff to buy a supply. He's gone to juvenile rehab—courtesy of our tax dollars."

"His mother has been by several times." Gus closed his eyes and sighed. "She's done a good job as a single mom. Omar broke her heart."

"But he's getting a second chance. I just hope he doesn't blow it."

David came over. "You flirting with my wife, Gus?"

"Not a chance now that you snagged her, even if my kids do need a mother."

Penny laughed. "You've done a good job as a single parent too, Gus." She pointed toward her daughter and his son. "Might be a good quasi-mother to Todd. He did ask Emma out and I relented with the provision he have her home by eleven."

"Good deal."

The door of the restaurant dinged. Madeleine and Doug Blanchard came in. David excused himself. He greeted the older couple. Madeleine hugged him and moved to Corbin. Doug whispered, "Did you tell them? I know Enrique told you."

"No. It's yours to tell when you're ready."

Doug studied David and smiled. "Thanks. I'll keep your secret too."

"My secret?"

Doug leaned close to David's ear. "Sí, Enrique. That you care about my son—not in an inappropriate way, but you care."

"Does Madeleine know?"

"Your secret identity? Or should I say identities?"

David stepped back.

Doug waved a hand. "Don't sweat it. No, she doesn't. As long as you treat Penny right, she'll love you."

"Good to know." He jerked his head toward the crowd. "Let's celebrate."

After lunch, the families returned home—The McGills to Laura Beth's place.

Tonya ran to boxes stacked in the corner, pulling Corbin by the hand. "Mommy said we couldn't decorate the tree until you got home." She thrust an ornament into his hand. "Here."

"Tonya!" Laura Beth scolded.

Corbin smiled and patted the little girl on the head. He took her hand. "Come on. I'd like to decorate a Christmas tree." He nodded toward Laura Beth. "It's okay. I need normal too."

"Okay then. I'll make some punch and eggnog." She winked at Tanner. "You get the assembly line going."

"Yes, ma'am." He made as if tipping a hat toward her.

Tanner hung a few high decorations and then let the children place lower ones. He stared toward the kitchen where he heard the blender and began to smell cinnamon and nutmeg.

Corbin gave his father's arm a gentle punch. "She's awesome, Dad. I could accept her as my stepmother."

"I do love her, C."

"I can tell." The boy grinned. "Looks like we might have already moved in here."

"Not officially. I admit Ros and I stayed here while you were gone. My heart was breaking." He put his arm around his son's shoulders. "I am so proud of you. I was terrified." Tanner choked up.

"It's okay to cry, Dad. I was scared too." He brushed his own tears from his cheeks. "I just kept telling myself to stay alive and praying God would give me a way to escape."

Laura Beth came in with a tray of drinks. "Snacks are in the kitchen."

The children stormed toward the kitchen. Corbin walked behind the rest, giving his father an encouraging nod.

Laura Beth caught the exchange. Tanner started to speak. She shook her head. "Tomorrow."

Early the next day, David woke and reached for his wife. The bed was empty. "Pretty Penny?" he called.

"Bathroom."

He kicked off the covers and joined her. She sat on the side of the bathtub holding a white tube. "What's wrong?" he asked.

"Nothing." She stared intently at the item in her hand.

David sat beside her. "Is that what I think it is?"

She passed off the stick. "Merry Christmas."

He stared as intently as Penny had. "Positive?"

Nodding, she said, "We're having a baby."

"You told me you wanted one with me."

"I do. I'm happy, but I'm scared." She released a long sigh. "I mean, I'm worried. I'll be forty when this baby gets here. There are a lot of risks with first pregnancies at my age— Down's and other complications."

He pulled her to him. "I love you. If there is a situation, we'll deal with it."

"Ninja Man, I kind of need a mother myself right now. Maybe this is a good time to call your mother."

"If that's what you want."

"Yeah. The house is huge. She can have the whole third floor to herself."

He stood and pulled her with him. "Come on."

Back sitting on the bed, David dialed Marta Marin and put the call on speaker.

"Diego, qué ha pasado?" Marta asked, breathless and in Spanish. ("Diego, what has happened?")

"Madre, English. And remember it's David—Please?"

"Sí. I'm sorry. You scared me. The sun is not even up yet."

"It is here, almost. Everything is good. If I recall, you promised to come here when the girls were settled. I think they've all been returned home. Listen. You're on speaker. Penny is listening."

"Hello, Penny."

"Madre."

"Ooh! I like that."

"Good," David said. "We have news."

"Let me guess—Abuela by blood?"

"Sí." He gave Penny a nod.

"Madre," she said, "I'd like you to come and live with us. I need a mother myself."

"Oh!"

Nobody spoke for a moment. Finally, Marta said, "Yes. Let's start the New Year with me there. Will that be soon enough?"

"Perfect."

"Don't tell the children. Let it be a late Christmas surprise."

"Okay," David and Penny said together. The call ended.

Penny lay back. "I'm glad I'm off today."

A few miles away, Tanner rose up on his elbow and watched Laura Beth sleep.

Sensing the intensity beside her, Laura Beth opened her eyes.

In the predawn light, she focused on Tanner's blue eyes. He leaned down and kissed her. "It's tomorrow, Sugar."

"Tanner," she groaned.

"No 'Cream'? Not a good sign."

She reached up and threaded her fingers through his unruly short blond hair. "I'm not a morning person."

"I can't put this off. I love you. I want this relationship to be permanent. I want to make love to you. I want to wake up beside you every morning and not because one of us is a basket case. It's been a year since our first date. I'm patient, but I want and need more."

She started to speak. He put a finger to her lips. "Let me finish, get it all out."

"Okay."

"Sex? Yeah. I want real sex. But it's more. I want to share my life with you. My kids adore you. I think yours like me pretty well. We're good together."

Laura Beth grabbed his hair with both hands and pulled hard. "Will you shut up? I love you. Make love to me. I've wanted to for months, but with all the stuff, it wasn't a top priority. It is now. I put condoms in the bedside table drawer. For God's sake! Use one or two or..."

His mouth claimed hers.

41
Moving On

Laura Beth moaned, "God! We have to do this again in a place where I don't have to be quiet." She reached over and felt an empty bed and then saw bright red numbers reading 10:00 A.M. on the alarm clock. She grabbed her cell phone from the nightstand to verify the time.

"Tanner!" She bolted from bed, threw on her robe, and raced down the hallway. She had to steady herself in the entrance to the family room from the sudden blood rush to her head. *That was not a dream. God, tell me that was not a dream. When did I go back to sleep?*

Mid-morning sun blazed through windows. All three girls sat in the floor playing with Barbie dolls. Riker stood inside his playpen and jabbered baby talk at them.

"Where's Tanner?" Laura Beth demanded.

Roslyn said without looking back, "Dad said to let you sleep. He took Corbin to meet with a counselor."

"I forgot that was today." She leaned her head against the door jamb and released a relieved sigh.

As she went on to the kitchen, her phone rang. "Hello," she said without checking caller I.D.

"Hey."

"Penny?"

"Yeah. I called to share my news."

"Good, I hope."

"Yeah. I'm pregnant."

"Congrats! You and Marge. I refuse to drink that water."

Penny laughed. "Last I heard, you have to have sex."

Prolonged silence led Penny to exclaim, "You are!"

"I'm moving on."

"Good for you, and about damned time."

Laura Beth made a pot of coffee and chatted with her friend.

Tanner and his son waited for the child psychologist who had made special arrangements to meet them on a Saturday. The man had been highly recommended by the Blacks since both Emma and Aaron were seeing him on a weekly basis, and he volunteered his time at the local schools for children who lacked funds or insurance.

Wearing a Nickelback t-shirt and jeans, Dr. Stellan Geiger, new to the area, opened his office door. "Corbin," he said and extended a hand.

The boy looked the thirty-something man over. Short, gelled, strawberry-blond hair, coppery brown eyes, soul-patch of hair just below his bottom lip, diamond studs in both ears, and the clothes he wore put Corbin at ease. They shook hands.

Geiger turned to Tanner who stood and shook hands. "Detective McGill, will you be joining us or waiting here?"

Tanner looked toward Corbin. "Depends on what my son wants."

"Corbin?" Geiger prompted.

"I'll be okay, Dad. Just be here when I come out."

"You bet." Tanner gave a smile that looked disappointed.

Geiger said, "Detective, if you need time with me too, I'll work you in. As a matter of fact, I'll do family sessions if you want and need them."

"Might be a good idea, Dad," Corbin said. "All of us—Miss Laura Beth and her girls too. We *will* be family."

Tanner puffed out his cheeks as he felt the blood creeping up his face. "I'll ask and get back to you, Doctor." He sat back down and picked up *Sports Illustrated*. "I'll be right here."

Corbin nodded and followed Dr. Geiger.

Inside the inner office, Corbin surveyed the décor. Muted mauve, cream, and brown offered neutrality. Rather than the stereotypical sofa, the room was arranged with a half dozen comfortable leather chairs around a low mahogany table. Geiger's personal desk sat in the back, left corner with the ninety-degree angle behind his chair. The corner was filled with a corner curio that contained a number of toys and games. Against the inside wall was a massive saltwater aquarium. Across from that wall was plate glass overlooking the pristine lawn with circular flowerbeds, now dormant. He looked to his right and left to see bookshelves on both sides of the door.

Lit candles on the table emitted lemon and sandalwood. Indicating with his hand, Geiger said, "Choose a seat."

Corbin sat on the edge of the chair nearest the aquarium. "What's with the candles and toys?"

"Sandalwood and lemon are relaxing aromas. If they bother you, blow them out." He nodded toward the toys. "Younger children sometimes need toys to show what might have happened to them because they lack vocabulary to tell." He sat in the chair next to Corbin.

"Oh. Like little kids show you where someone touched them on dolls?"

"Yes."

"Okay."

The doctor pointed to a recorder. "It's easier for my records so I can just listen and talk without notes."

"Fine."

Geiger pressed the record button. "What do you need to help you tell me what happened?"

"Nothing. You know I'm here because Dillard Purdue's alternate personality kidnapped me. He sexually molested me for over three months. He was going to kill me."

"You say that matter-of-factly. How does it make you feel?"

"Really? Gee, let's see—just hunky-dory."

"Now I sense anger."

"No shit, Sherlock. Yeah, I'm angry. And I'm scared and sad. I feel disgusted with myself because I did the things he asked and wanted so I could stay alive and look for my chance to escape."

"You were brave and mature to think about escape. What's disgusting about that?"

"Oh, I'm real sure my future girlfriends will want to know I had butt sex and gave blow jobs."

"Ah, a positive thought—you want a future girlfriend."

"I'm not gay." He let his back hit the chair. "And even if I were, I shouldn't have to tell my special person I was forced to do things I didn't want to do."

"What's so bad about doing what you had to do to stay alive?"

Corbin bit his bottom lip. "I saw the good side of Purdue. Dillard tried to help me. I felt sorry for him because I realized the man who raised him did the same things to him." He gripped the armrests. "When I did get loose, I created my own tonfa. When I had him down, hitting him"—He brushed tears from his cheeks—"I wanted to kill him. I *could* have. I deliberately never hit him in a fatal spot. Dillard came out and told me to run. I did." He heaved a great sigh. "Now, I've agreed to send him to the looney bin, not trial where he might face the death penalty. My dad isn't happy about that. I think I disappointed him."

Geiger leaned toward the boy. "First, the *U.S. Constitution* prohibits the execution of the insane, if you didn't know. Second, Dillard would never get real psychological help in prison, but he will at an institution for the criminally insane. Third, don't you think your dad should know how you feel? Do you want him in here?"

"Laura Beth understands."

"Your dad's girlfriend?"

Corbin nodded.

"You like her?"

"Yeah. She's good for my dad." He stared at the flickering candles. "I prayed. I kept asking God for my dad to find me. When I ran out of that storm cellar, I saw my dad. He looked so scared. I've never seen my dad scared. He didn't care I was half-naked—didn't even notice my junk exposed to the world. He just held on to me. Laura Beth—she got there and covered me."

Corbin closed his eyes and choked, "I missed my thirteenth birthday."

"Corbin, we can have your birthdate legally changed by a year, and you can go back and celebrate it."

The boy shook his head. "No. The memories wouldn't change. It would just be a lie. I want to move forward—reclaim my life." He licked his lips and rolled them together. "Dad already got with school officials. I'll stay late and catch up with my teachers, hopefully I'll be able to pass seventh grade like that. Coach Daly wants me in spring practice." He put the heels of his hands to his eyes. "I kind of dread facing the kids at school."

"What scares you most about going back to school?"

"I don't want to have to explain what happened to me."

"You know, I come out there every Friday morning. I think I can persuade your principal to have a program to talk about awareness of abuse and sexual assault. What do you think?"

"And not mention me by name?"

"Not at all. Only you can make the call to talk about what we say in here, unless I think you might hurt yourself or someone else. Of course, you *are* a minor and I can discuss things with your dad—especially if I think it would benefit you. Do you want your dad now?"

Corbin nodded.

"Do you want him to know what we talked about?"

The child nodded.

Geiger went to the waiting area and got Tanner.

Tanner knelt in front of his son after listening to the recording. "No. I am *not* disappointed in you. I'm proud of you. I love you. That's why I'm having a hard time not flaying the bastard and having his carcass hung from the town square flagpole. Your compassion astounds me." He put his hand on the side of his son's head. "I think you're right. Let's do some sessions as a family."

"Okay."

Tanner looked up at Geiger. "When can you fit us in?"

"I have Corbin every Saturday morning for the next three months. He can decide if he wants more time after that. Can you guys do Monday right after school or would Sunday afternoon work better?"

"Don't you take a day off?"

"Normally, Saturday. I'm Jewish—not orthodox, obviously."

"We can probably swing one of those but let me call you."

Christmas was rather quiet in Sunrise. Both Tanner and Laura Beth brought their families for a session with Geiger and Corbin the day after Christmas.

The doctor sat down with the younger girls. He handed both of them a yarn doll about three inches long. "I have a daughter who's seven. Her mom left several years ago. Naomi, my daughter, makes these dolls to give to little girls who might hurt here"—He tapped his chest over his heart—"like she did. Recently, somebody the two of you love was hurt. Do you understand what happened?"

Stacey nodded. "A bad man took Corbin and hurt him. Mommy says she wants us to learn karate so we can be brave like Corbin if anybody ever tries to hurt us."

"That's a good idea," Geiger said.

Tonya whispered, "The bad man touched him in private places. Mommy told us to tell her if anybody ever does that to us."

"Your mommy sounds very wise." The doctor looked toward his client. "Does either of you want to say anything to Corbin?"

Both little girls ran to him, hugged him, and said, "I love you."

Stacey sat on Tanner's knee and looked at Dr. Geiger. "Our daddy went away. Mommy says he's in Heaven like Corbin's mom. Mr. Tanner's our new daddy."

Laura Beth coughed and started to scold her daughter. Geiger held up a hand to silence her.

Stacey went on, "Corbin's our brother and Ros is our sister."

Laura Beth glared at Tanner. He shrugged.

"How do you feel about that?" asked Geiger.

"I love Mr. Tanner. C and Ros are the best."

Tonya nodded agreement and still clung to Corbin's arm.

Geiger turned to Roslyn. "What do you think?"

"About Dad and Laura Beth? It's cool. About my brother?" She looked toward Corbin. "I was so scared. I thought I'd never see him again—like my mom. Dad was totally messed up. If it hadn't been for Laura Beth, nobody would've cared how I felt."

Tanner reached for his daughter. "I'm sorry."

Roslyn sat on the arm of the chair by her father. He put his arm around her. "I love you, Ros," he said. "I never meant to make you feel like I didn't."

"I know. You were scared too."

"Yes, I was."

"Corbin?" Geiger prompted. "What's going on in your head right now?"

"I'm feeling kind of happy. This is my family. They love me and never gave up on me. I think it's time we moved on. A new year is coming. I think we should have a party and invite all our friends. Dr. Geiger, you can come and bring your daughter."

Laura Beth laughed. "Corbin, you just want to be awake at midnight." She reached out and took his hand. "It's an excellent suggestion. I'll get to work on it this afternoon."

They left the doctor's office with a plan.

Laura Beth threw together a party for their closest friends, including her boss, Peg Shriver, and oddly she felt compelled to invite Millicent Shapiro.

The Blacks arrived with an extra person. David introduced his mother—Marta. "But anyone under eighteen has my permission to call me Abuela," she said with a smile.

Millicent, always full of questions, asked, "Mr. Black?"

With gracious aplomb, Marta replied, "David's father died when David was eleven."

Socializing continued and Marta whispered to her son, "So? I must be Mrs. Black?"

"It would be most helpful." He smirked.

"Should have mentioned it, Diego."

"Sh. I'll have the paperwork expedited."

"And just what did I do before I moved here?"

"Truth. You were a teacher and child advocate in Texas." He puckered his lips. "That gives me an idea for Purdue Plantation—a sanctuary/school for molested children. They can come there and learn. I'll turn it into an agricultural-skills in addition to normal classroom instruction. I can get teachers and their families to live in the houses. Spouses can be farm workers."

At his elbow, David heard, "Sounds promising."

He turned to see Tanner nodding approval and offering him a beer. He took it, and they continued the discussion.

Tanner watched Laura Beth across the room as she introduced Millicent to Dr. Geiger and his daughter. "Excuse me." He chuckled. "Looks like Enrique can breathe."

Walking to the three, he kissed Laura Beth just below her ear. "You're needed in the kitchen."

She made her excuses and went with Tanner. In the kitchen, she asked, "What's the…"

Tanner stopped her questions with a kiss. "I was hungry," he answered when he broke the lip lock.

"You're silly."

"And you're matchmaking."

She shrugged.

"Why not with Peg?"

"Her divorce isn't final. Too much baggage." She shivered. "You should hear the screaming matches when Leland calls the office. He's taken to using different pre-paid cell numbers. As soon as we block one, he gets another."

"Threats?"

"Some."

"Why hasn't she filed a complaint with the department?"

Laura Beth rolled her eyes. "Still in denial about abuse. Of course, I saw him with a fat lip once. And Penny has witnessed the screaming matches when she stopped by to see me That's just a toxic relationship." She looked toward her boss. "I'll talk to her about a formal complaint when we get back to the office day after tomorrow. I'll also put a bug in Millicent's ear since she's handling the divorce."

Tanner looked at his watch. "Speaking of which. Let's go see if Millie gets a smooch. It's almost midnight."

"About next year…"

"Yes?" He wiggled mischievous eyebrows.

"Maybe you shouldn't renew your lease in April. You could move in here."

He folded his arms across his chest. "Cohabitate? Or more permanent?"

Grinning, she said, "Ask me again in April." She led him back to the party.

I

Laura Beth went to the office January second with her heart light for the first time in a long year and a half. She booted her computer and checked the calendar. *Peg is showing a house on Poplar Drive.* She checked her watch. *Now. It's pretty close to Marge.* She squinted at the name. *Geiger. Okay.* She set about typing a contract just as other agents arrived.

About ten, the office phone rang. Laura Beth answered with a cheerful greeting.

"Mrs. Copeland?" a voice asked.

"Yes."

"Stellan Geiger. Mrs. Shriver was supposed to meet me this morning to see the house on Poplar. She's not here. I mean, her car is, but she isn't. I've called her cell several times. It goes directly to voicemail. Any chance you can run over and show me the house?"

"Her car is there?"

"Yes."

"Is the house open?"

"No."

"Sounds off. Would you mind if I got Tanner to meet us?"

"Not at all."

"I'll call him and see you in about fifteen minutes."

"That'll work. My first client is in an hour."

Laura Beth left Tanner a message to come to the house when his phone went to voicemail.

She pulled behind Geiger's white Acura, noticing Peg's gold Cadillac on the street.

Geiger got out and pulled his jacket collar over his ears. "Hey. Thanks again for the party." He held up his phone. "I just dialed her again. You try."

Laura Beth dialed Peg's number and got voicemail. She jiggled the lock box. "I have a very bad feeling. Tanner needs to hurry."

A few snow flurries fell as she spoke. "Let's go in. I hate to keep you waiting."

Opening the door and stepping inside, the metallic scent of blood overpowered them.

Laura Beth shrieked at what she saw and turned into Geiger's chest.

"That scream is never good! What this time?" Tanner yelled, vaulting through the door.

About the Author

Like many of her characters, Janet is a history buff and loves anything of historical significance from old cars to old cemeteries. Get to know Janet and you'll see why she's been critically acclaimed at the Faulkner Wisdom Competition and why her writing continues to receive 4- and 5-star reviews. Her novel, *Spirits' Desire*, the second book in her *Legend of Draconis* series, won The Critter's, Preditor's and Editor's Award while the third book in *The Raiford Chronicles*, *Broken*, was a short-list finalist (top 20) at the Faulkner Competition. It could be that readers see so much of her in her characters: mother, grandmother, educator, author, editor, a leader in the Mississippi writing community as head of the Middle Mississippi chapter of the Mississippi Writers Guild and board member of the Mississippi Writers' Guild, and a person who has overcome great obstacles and still holds on to her faith in her Lord and Savior, Jesus Christ.

http://www.janettaylorperry.com/

http://janettaylor-perry.blogspot.com/

https://authorcentral.amazon.com/gp/profile

https://www.facebook.com/Author-Janet-Taylor-Perry-299698950061301/

janettaylorperry@gmail.com

https://www.facebook.com/janettaylorperrybooks/

Instagram: @janettaylorperry & @jtaylorperry

X: Janet Taylor-Perry— @mom5kidz421

Goodreads: https://www.goodreads.com/author/show/7376480Janet_Taylor_Perry

Pinterest: https://www.pinterest.com/mumzy25/

YouTube: https://bit.ly/30hJsYg

Amazon Associates ID_myfacebo0822a-20

Janettaylorperry.com—For a reading experience
EXTRAORDINAIRE!

Laura Beth and Tanner will be back in...

Skin Deep

"I find dead people," should be Laura Beth Copeland's catch phrase. She's a magnet for finding murder victims, or at least their body parts.

As a real estate agent, Laura Beth arrives to show a house for sale. Sensing something's off, she calls Detective Tanner McGill to come to the address where her boss's car is parked but deserted.

Unlocking the property's door reveals the first in a succession of flayed women.

Laura Beth and several of her friends are threatened with the same fate. Once again, she must fight to stay alive. But can she succeed against a man who is set on revenge?